# The Uncivil War

## Based on True Events

### DAVID LEE CORLEY

Sign-up for my never-annoying newsletter and receive a bonus epilogue of The Uncivil War. I will also send you new release updates, special offers, and my thoughts on just about everything. Sign-up for my newsletter here:
https://dl.bookfunnel.com/hjcboqld1f

THE UNCIVIL WAR

# DEDICATION

For all the men and women that fought for their country.
History will not forget your sacrifices.

DAVID LEE CORLEY

"He will win who knows when to fight
and when not to fight."

Sun Tzu – The Art of War

# OPERATION VULCAN

## February 14, 1962 - Quang Khe, North Vietnam

Waves lapped against a ship's dark wooden hull. Just past midnight, Nautilus II, a Chinese junk converted into an undercover CIA paramilitary boat, sailed along the coastline near the mouth of the Gianh River about thirty miles north of Dong Hoi. Its target was the Quang Khe naval base, one mile upriver and home to the North Vietnamese coastal defense fleet. The fleet was mostly made up of Chinese-made Swatow gunboats. Each gunboat was eighty-three-feet long and carried three 37mm autocannons, two twin heavy machine guns, and eight depth charges. The Swatows had a top speed of twenty-eight knots and used their surface-search radar to detect incoming boats.

On any wooden ship, there was always the danger of fire, especially at night when torches were often used. The junk's captain was more worried about the attention a fire would draw than roasting alive. To be safe, the crew used paper lanterns with flickering candles to illuminate their way. Orange light reflected off the waves and gave the junk a romantic appearance. Harmless.

Lucien Conein was the master of mayhem. He lived to create chaos and "blow shit up." Which was why he eagerly accepted his current assignment to wreak havoc on the North Vietnamese Navy. As the covert paramilitary team leader, Conein wore the clothes of a Chinese sea trader – not as poor as a fisherman, but not as rich as a merchantman. The difference was that the holes and tears in his trousers and shirt were neatly patched. In the dark, nobody could determine his true nationality – French turned American. He was CIA working for Colonel

Lansdale out of Saigon. The most that could be said of Conein was that he was reliably unpredictable and predictably unconventional, but he usually got the job done and that was all most of his commanders cared about. The soldiers he worked with knew him as a scoundrel that drank too much and gambled away most of his salary. He womanized every chance he got without regard to marital status or nationality. He had learned his trade in sabotage from the Corsican mafia during World War II when they fought against the Nazis in southern France.

Although highly decorated for his military achievements, Conein also had several black marks in his personnel record from some of his past commanders, including a light colonel that had caught Conein in bed with his wife. His current commander, Lansdale, knew what he was getting when he recruited Conein to lead one of his two paramilitary teams based in Saigon. Lansdale didn't care about Conein's personal life as long as it didn't interfere with his professional career as a CIA officer and team leader. Like Conein, Lansdale often thought out-of-the-box when it came to accomplishing his objectives and had no qualms about using morally ambiguous team leaders.

Using binoculars, Conein kept low to prevent revealing his silhouette against the night sky. He didn't want to alert the North Vietnamese patrol boats that someone was taking a close look at them. He needed to ensure that all the chickens were in the coup before ordering his team to execute their mission. Conein was good at planning and even better at thinking on his feet when everything went south which it often did in paramilitary operations. Despite his questionable morals and unethical tactics, Conein was a patriot. He loved his adopted country and would do anything that he believed was necessary to defend it and its citizens. He also hated communists. The fact that the CIA encouraged him to generate anarchy among America's enemies was a bonus. His current occupation was a perfect fit for a soldier like Conein.

Operation Vulcan began five months earlier when the MAAG officers working out of the American embassy became interested in the North Vietnamese navy. It wasn't much of a navy, but it was enough to protect the Chinese freighters that moved in and out of the North Vietnamese ports carrying weapons and ammunition to be sent south on the Ho Chi Minh Trail. In exchange for the weapons, the civilian freighters carried back rice and raw materials to mainland China.

President Kennedy had personally reviewed the operation when the North Vietnamese stepped up their efforts to bolster the Viet Cong and Laotian rebels with more weapons and supplies. The CIA suggested cutting off the supplies before they entered North Vietnam. The problem was the small but effective North Vietnamese navy that defended the ports and sea lanes. If the navy was eliminated, covert South Vietnamese warships could attack and sink the Chinese freighters once they had entered North Vietnamese territory. There were other consequences that needed to be taken into account if South Vietnam choose to attack Chinese ships, but even the viable threat of attack on commercial ships would reduce shipments of weapons and supplies. No civilian captain wanted his ship sunk, especially when he was behind the wheel.

Operation Vulcan was simple enough. The CIA and MAAG planners envisioned that a paramilitary team would travel up the coastline from South Vietnam to North Vietnam using a specially modified Chinese junk. Once they reached the mouth of the Gianh River, the commandos would slip over the side of their boat, steal up the river to the North Vietnamese naval base using scuba gear, and set underwater charges with delayed detonators against the gunboats and other military boats that might be moored at the base. The commandos would make their escape back down the river and out to the junk before the explosions gave away the operation. With the help of a hidden motor, the junk would speed its way back to South Vietnam territory. JFK, a former US Navy officer, liked the plan and even made a couple of suggestions. That was enough to get it approved.

The Americans had sent the submarine – the U.S.S. Catfish, a decommissioned WWII relict commandeered by MAAG, to take a closer look at the North Vietnamese navy base. The operation was code-named "Wise Tiger." For several weeks the diesel-powered submarine held its position in international waters just outside North Vietnamese territory and secretly watched the naval activity in and out of the river. The reconnaissance team counted boats, weapons, and crews. They studied the enemy's operations and noted the routes they took once at sea. They measured each boat's speed and agility. And most importantly, they watched the patrol boats that guarded the mouth of the river and protected the naval base. In addition to the submarine, an unmarked reconnaissance plane passed overhead of the naval base and took aerial photos of the layout.

It was determined that the operation would be best executed by the CIA's paramilitary teams and not MAAG advisors or the Special Operations Group known as SOG. It needed to be a South Vietnamese team in case of capture. The CIA often worked with the South Vietnamese 5th Bureau on counterintelligence operations and the destruction of military targets across the border. They had a strong working relationship, and the South Vietnamese trusted the American team leaders.

Once the reconnaissance part of the mission was completed, all the intelligence collected was turned over to Colonel Lansdale who turned it over to Conein. Both team leaders, Conein and Rene Granier had worked in Vietnam's rivers, but Conein had more experience working in the sea. He was assigned the mission and permitted to select his team. A veteran of several wars, Conein was a stickler for competence and valued field experience in his team members. Surprisingly, he didn't choose from the 5th

Bureau. Instead, he selected soldiers from the South Vietnamese navy that had proficiency with diving equipment. There weren't many. Even when they worked on boats and ships, most Vietnamese were not strong swimmers. They feared what they could not see below the water, especially water dragons and underwater demons. All Vietnamese boats had eyes painted on the bow to ward off crocodiles and water demons.

Training was fast and basic. The divers needed to learn how to navigate underwater at night and they needed to learn how to operate a limpet mine with a delayed fuse in the dark. They practiced at night on obsolete South Vietnamese freighters that were ready for the scrapyard. It took two months of training with blindfolds before Conein felt they were prepared. The way he figured it, the more time they spent in the water at night the better. As he had hoped, their fear of the dark water slipped away. Conein spent another week going over the details of the plan with the demolition team members. He made them repeat the details and the timeline of the mission back to him again and again. When the day to leave finally came, the team was prepared and confident.

The Nautilus II was a Chinese junk that had been retrofitted with hidden compartments that could be used to hide the team and their equipment. The technicians had cut sections of the floorboards in the junk's cargo hold, then made removable floorboards out a mix of old wood and new wood. They stressed the new wood to match the existing floorboards by beating it with rusted chains and scratching it with icepicks so that it looked well-worn. A coat of dirt was thrown on the new wood and then brushed off before stain and lacquer were applied. The deception had to be perfect. The lives of Conein and his men depended on it. The final results were impressive. Conein, who considered himself an expert at forgeries, was embarrassed when he picked the wrong section of floorboards and tried to pry them up with a Ka-Bar.

Chinese trading ships were common along the North Vietnamese coast. It took the Nautilus II several days under sail to reach North Vietnamese waters. The junk traveled far out to sea before venturing back into North Vietnamese waters. Conein wanted to give anyone watching the boat's movements the idea that it was coming in from the sea and not traveling up the coast from the south. The crew did not use the hidden engine that had been installed in the aft of the junk. It was only to be used for an emergency getaway. A Chinese junk rarely had any type of propulsion beyond its sails. To strengthen the deception, several of the crew members were Taiwanese that spoke perfect Mandarin and were indistinguishable from the sailors of mainland Chinese. All other crew members were Vietnamese that understood and spoke basic Mandarin. The demolition team members could move freely below deck while the junk was at sea. Conein was the only team member allowed on deck.

As the junk approached the North Vietnamese shoreline, an enemy patrol boat moved to intercept. Conein and his demolition team scrambled into hidden spaces below the floorboards. Once the removable floorboards were in place, two of junk's crew members placed cargo on top of the boards to further disguise the hidden compartments. While it helped with the concealment, it also trapped Conein and his men. They would not be able to fight if discovered.

The North Vietnamese contacted the junk's crew using a bullhorn and demanded they be allowed to board and inspect the boat. Intentionally unarmed, the junk's crew secured the boat's sails and the boat slowed to a stop. The bow and aft deck guns – twin 20-mm autocannons, pointed toward the junk and its crew. The patrol boat's autocannons could easily tear apart the wooden cabins and kill everyone on board. Pulling alongside, five North Vietnamese sailors armed with rifles boarded the junk and began their search. Three went below deck, while the other two checked the paperwork of the crew. They asked the crew where they came from, where they were going, and what was their cargo. A veteran of deceit, Conein had made the crew rehearse their stories until he was sure they had not only memorized them but could repeat them under duress. It worked. The junk's crew didn't raise any suspension.

Below deck, the North Vietnamese sailors searched the cabins and the cargo hold. A young sailor was sent to inspect the area where Conein and his team lay hidden. The sailor did a cursory inspection and was about to leave when he noticed fresh marking on the floorboards. A nail from a palate of machine parts had dug into the wooden deck and exposed new wood underneath the coating of stain and varnish.

Conein was directly below him and was staring up through a thin space in the floorboards. Conein slowly removed his pistol and placed the end of the gun's muzzle flat against the boards. If the sailor discovered the hidden compartment, Conein would shoot him through the board. He knew it wouldn't matter much and that he and the team would be unable to escape before being riddled with gunfire, but he didn't care. He was going to take the overly curious sailor with them. It seemed only fair.

A voice called out. The corporal in charge of the search party ordered everyone back to the ship. Picking up a piece of dislodged vanish and rolling in his fingers, the young sailor considered whether it was worth reporting. It was almost time for their evening meal, and he was hungry. An expanded inspection would take time, maybe even an hour. Conein could hear the young man's stomach growl at the thought. The young sailor decided against it and joined the other two sailors as they exited the hold.

The junk's crew waited until the patrol boat rounded a bend in the shoreline before moving the cargo and releasing Conein and his team. Everyone was relieved. They had survived and the mission was still a go.

While traveling the rest of the way to their destination,

Conein took the opportunity to review the aerial photos. Studying the images with a magnifying glass he determined that while there were many smaller boats at the naval base, only the gunboats were made of steel. The rest were made of wood. This limited the effectiveness of the limpet mines which were magnetic and could only attach to metal. He used his binoculars to survey the naval port in the distance. From what he could tell, there were only three out of five gunboats at the port. He cursed. Three were less than he had hoped, but it was too late to wait for any of the other two to arrive. He decided to reduce the number of divers that would swim into the river and thereby reduce the odds of anyone being detected. He chose his three best swimmers – Le Van Kinh, Nguyen Van Tam, and Nguyen Huu Thao. A fourth commando, Nguyen Chuyen, would stay in the skiff used to carry the demolition team to the mouth of the river.

It was a moonless night just as Conein had planned it. The Nautilus II joined a dozen freighters and trading ships anchored off the coast near the mouth of the river.

After eating a hearty meal to give them strength for the two-mile swim they were about to undertake, the demolition team checked their gear and made last-minute preparations. Each scuba diver drank his fill of water to avoid dehydration when using their air tanks. The three divers each carried a limpet mine strapped to their chests. They carried no other weapons and no flares or flashlights to help guide them.

Just past midnight, Conein surveyed the area one last time. Satisfied that no patrol boats were near, he ordered the team to go. The demolition team set the delay timers on the limpet mines for two hours. That should have given them plenty of time to sail to the mouth of the river in the skiff, swim to the base, place the mines, and return to the junk before detonation. The crew lowered a skiff over the side of the junk. The four-man team climbed into the skiff. Conein watched as they started the outboard motor on the back of the small boat and sped off into the darkness. Conein wanted to lead the team, but Lansdale had specifically ordered him not to participate in the demolition beyond supervising from the junk. If captured, the North Vietnamese would know the Americans were involved and parade their prisoner in front of the international press. With the Cold War gaining momentum, America needed the international community on its side.

As the skiff moved through the water, the commandos' eyes adjusted to the darkness, and they could see the mouth of the river. They were excited and anxious. They had been entrusted with one of the most important covert missions up to that point in the war. It was the type of operation that made heroes… and careers if completed successfully. The skiff stopped short of entering the river. Chuyen quietly dropped an anchor over the side of the boat. Kinh, Tam, and Thao turned on the air flowing from their scuba tanks, pulled their masks down, and slipped the regulators into their mouths. A quick pull of air to make sure everything was working properly, and they slid over the side of the boat into the black water. Moments later, they disappeared. Chuyen felt very alone sitting in the skiff by himself in the darkness. He hoped his friends were not swallowed by a foul creature or worse… the ghost of someone who drowned in the sea. The only sound he heard was the slap of the waves against the little boat's side. He wondered if it would reveal his position to the North Vietnamese.

Underwater it was pitch black to the point where the divers could barely see each other. They swam together at a moderate speed. They didn't want to overexert themselves. There was no hurry. Stealth was far more important than speed. Every three hundred feet, the team leader would poke his head up and survey the horizon. He had picked a point and determined that they needed to swim just to the left of it to find their target.

It only took them thirty minutes to reach the naval base. The three gunboats were tied to different piers. Kinh used hand signals to assign a gunboat to each of the divers, then gave the hand signal for the team to split up and seek out their targets. They once again submerged and swam in different directions.

Tam reached his gunboat first. He swam to the rear of the boat, removed his mine, and attached it to the hull near the engine compartment. There was a dull thud when the magnet attached to the metal hull. With the mine set, he swam back to the rendezvous point on the far side of the river.

Kinh was next. Swimming underwater to the rear of the gunboat, he placed his mine.

As Kinh was finishing up with his mine and swimming toward the rendezvous point, Tao was about to set his mine when he heard a commotion on the deck of the gunboat. Somebody was yelling. Believing that he had been discovered, Tao panicked. He fumbled his mine and it slipped from his hands. As it fell toward the bottom of the river, Tao reached out and grabbed it. The mine exploded. Tao was killed instantly. Even though the mine was not attached to the hull of the gunboat, it did extensive damage to the rudder and propellors rending the vessel useless. The concussive effect prematurely set off the other two mines attached to the gunboats blowing large holes into their hulls. Both gunboats partially sank until they reached the end of the ropes that tied them to the pier. A few moments later, the mooring bollards gave way ripping the heavy cleats from the docks and allowing the gunboats to continue their journey to the bottom of the river.

Not far off, Kinh was hit in the back of the head from the mines' concussive effect. He was stunned and lost his weight belt. Without the weight belt to hold him down, he floated to the surface and bobbed in the waves.

Already on the other side of the river and far enough away not to feel the full effect of the blasts, Tam saw Kinh struggling and swam to help his teammate. With Tam's help, the two swam on the surface toward the mouth of the river.

Conein knew that they were in trouble when he heard the first blast a full hour before it was supposed to explode. The second and third explosions confirmed his fears. His team had muffed it. Now, he needed to focus and save what he could. He had little doubt the enemy would be coming. He ordered the junk's crew to way anchor and to start the hidden engine.

Beneath the water, the hull of the junk opened toward the rear and a propellor emerged. Moments later, the propellor was spinning churning white water and pushing the junk forward.

Conein told the junk's pilot to steer toward the skiff where he knew the divers, if still alive, would be headed. Conein ordered the junk crew and the rest of his team to prepare for battle. They retrieved their weapons from the hidden storage compartments below the floorboards. They didn't have much. Mostly submachine guns, a light machine gun, and a box of grenades. Certainly not enough to hold off a gunboat.

But the wrecked gunboats were not coming. Instead, the North Vietnamese radioed for help and climbed into the remaining wooden boats tied to the dock. Four small boats filled with soldiers set out toward the mouth of the river. They had a light machine gun which they placed on the bow of the lead boat.

Already tired, Tam and Kihn heard the rough thrum of outboard engines as they swam for the river's mouth. They looked back and saw the North Vietnamese boats were coming. They could see that the boats would easily catch up with them before they reached the safety of the mouth of the river. They had used up most of the air in the scuba tanks but decided to submerge anyway for however long they could last underwater. Without his weight belt, Kihn struggled to stay submerged as the boats passed overhead. Exhausted and dizzy from the explosions, he floated toward the surface. Tam grabbed one of Kinh's fins and tried to pull him down but was unsuccessful. The last boat passed over Kinh and he was hit by the outboard motor. The spinning propellor sliced into his shoulder and blood flowed. Tam could see that Kinh would bleed out unless he was given medical attention quickly. He swam to the surface, grabbed Kinh by his tank's harness, and called out to the enemy soldiers on board the last boat. The last boat turned around and picked up the two divers. The remaining three boats continued toward the mouth of the river.

The Nautilus II approached the skiff. Conein called out to Chuyen to find out if the team had returned. They hadn't. A searchlight from one of the enemy boats illuminated the junk. The North Vietnamese had reached the mouth of the river and were speeding towards the junk and the skiff. Conein ordered Chuyen to climb aboard the junk. Conein searched the water between the mouth of the river and the junk for signs of the divers. Nothing. He searched the shoreline. Still nothing. He hated the idea of abandoning his team members. But he also knew it was likely they had been killed by the explosions or captured. Whatever their fate, there was little he could do for them and he needed to think about the rest of the team and the Junk's crew.

The light machine gun on the bow of the lead enemy boat opened fire ripping into the junk.

Conein ordered his men to return fire. However small it was, the enemy flotilla outmanned and outgunned the junk. Several of Conein's men were hit. Conein could see it was all going to shit. He took one last look for his divers, then ordered the pilot to head back to South Vietnam. Still under fire, the junk turned and sped toward open water. The small enemy boats pursued but at a slower pace. The junk put distance between itself and the enemy. The men on board the junk cheered as the enemy broke off the chase. Conein was in no mood to celebrate. In his mind, not only had his team failed to accomplish their mission, three of his team members were captured or dead. Then things went from bad to worse...

A cannon fired on the horizon lit up the night sky. The shell landed in the water in front and to the port side of the junk. Conein turned to see a North Vietnamese gunboat sailing towards the junk at full speed. It was coming from the open sea which meant it was not one of the three gunboats in the river, but a fourth gunboat returning to port. It had received the North Vietnamese radio distress call and had responded. Its front 37mm cannon fired again with a bright flash as the projectile left the barrel.

The shell hit the back mast of the junk and exploded sending shards of wood into the crew and team members on deck. Conein watched with dismay as the mast cracked in half and the giant sail tipped over falling over the side and into the ocean. The sail's rigging was still attached. Dragging the mast, the junk slowed. Conein acted. He pulled out his Ka-Bar and went to work cutting loose the rigging. The rest of the team followed his example using whatever was available to cut the rigging. A team member with a shotgun fired into the last rope. The rope ripped in half and the mast was free. But the junk was crippled.

Another cannon shot sounded, and the shell crashed into the back of the junk blowing a gaping hole into the wooden deck. Conein could see it was only a matter of time before the enemy blew the junk apart piece by piece. Two thoughts hit him— The first was that his team and the crew would most likely die if they continued to fight. And the second was that it was highly likely he would be captured. Lansdale had given him specific instructions that he was not to be captured even if it meant his death by suicide. Conein didn't like that idea.

As the gunboat drew closer, Conein ordered the crew and his team to surrender. There was no sense in them sacrificing their lives. As the junk slowed and the gunboat pulled alongside, Conein, wearing scuba gear and the laces of his boots tied to one of his trousers' belt loops, slipped over the opposite side. He submerged and swam as far as he could underwater until his air tank emptied. He cast off the air tank, rid himself of his weight belt, and swam for shore as the sun peaked over the horizon. It was going to be a long, hot day…

Saigon, South Vietnam

Several weeks later, after making his way back across the border and hitching a ride on a C-47 to Saigon, Conein was called into Lansdale's office. He wasn't looking forward to the dressing-down he was sure to receive from Lansdale for failing to accomplish his mission. To his surprise, it was just the opposite. Lansdale congratulated him and his team. After reviewing the after-battle aerial reconnaissance photos and seeing the two gunboats on the bottom of the river, the mission had been deemed an overwhelming success but at a high cost. MAAG and the CIA were busy planning the next mission to destroy the North Vietnamese Navy and finally attack the Chinese freighters. Operation Vulcan was just beginning. As a reward, Conein was given a three-day vacation anywhere he wanted to go. He spent it in Saigon drinking, gambling, and visiting his favorite flower boat – a Vietnamese junk used as a brothel.

# A BAD IDEA

March 3, 1962 - Tan Son Nhut Air Base, South Vietnam

Having returned from an early morning mission in the Mekong Delta, Tom Coyle and Rene Granier sat in a bar sipping their beers. The mission was a milk run. Granier was checking in with the villagers that had recently entered the strategic hamlet program. There was nothing to report except a bothersome hog that had been knocking down fences and raiding the hamlet's gardens. Granier negotiated a fair price with the animal's owner, shot it, and left. It wasn't that Granier was onery or hated swine, he just wanted things to run smoothly, and he figured the villagers could use the extra protein. He was a problem solver that preferred the simplest solution whenever possible.

On the stage in front of them, a teenage go-go dancer wearing white boots and a miniskirt pranced around to "Please Mr. Postman," by The Marvelettes. Neither of the two Americans was interested. Both men were staring off into space deep in thought. They were trying to come up with a plan that would save Coyle's girlfriend Bian. Bian was President Diem's personal translator. After becoming involved romantically with Bian, Coyle had discovered that she was also an agent for North Vietnamese intelligence. Her father, an officer in the French Colonial Army, had been captured after the fall of Diem Bien Phu and was being held in a Hanoi prison. Threatening to torture or kill her father, the North Vietnamese blackmailed Bian into becoming a covert operative. As Diem's translator, she worked in the palace with Diem's brother Nhu, the head of South Vietnam's internal security and counterintelligence. It was far from an ideal situation, but Coyle loved Bian and was determined to find a way to save her. He enlisted Granier to help him. Granier saw Bian's situation as an opportunity to create a very important double agent if they could keep her alive. "What if…" said Granier, then fell silent.

"What if what?" said Coyle.

"Nevermind. Bad idea."

"I don't think there are any bad ideas at this point. I got nothing."

"Look, the problem is getting the North Vietnamese to believe Bian is still a viable agent once we break her father out of prison."

"No. The real problem is keeping Brother Nhu from assassinating her when he finds out she's been spying for North Vietnamese intelligence."

"Potayto-potahto."

"Right."

Both men took another pull from their beer cans. The beer wasn't helping them think any better, but it did make them stress a bit less. A young bargirl approached and placed her arm around Coyle's waist. "No," said Coyle in a low menacing tone.

Without missing a beat, she moved to Granier and placed her hands on his shoulders to give him a massage. "No," said Granier in the same tone.

She called them something vulgar in Vietnamese and moved off to find a new customer. "The problem is that the North Vietnamese are going to know that it was the CIA that broke her father out of prison," said Coyle.

"How are they gonna know that?" said Granier.

"Two white guys with guns?"

"Yeah, well, there's that."

"What if we used a 5th Bureau team to help us?"

"No go. Nhu will find out for sure."

"Right. No 5th Bureau. What about gangsters?"

"They'd most likely whack us on the heads and turn us over to the North Vietnamese for a reward."

"Yeah, not exactly a trustworthy bunch."

"Although, the idea has merit…"

"What do you mean?"

"Using someone else to boost the dad from prison. Someone that would divert attention away from Bian."

"Who would want to break the father out of prison besides his daughter and her crazy boyfriend?"

"I don't know. The South Vietnamese military I suppose."

"No. I don't think they give two shits about a Vietnamese captain that fought for the French. They just as soon let him rot in prison."

"True."

"So, who else?"

"How about the French? He was their officer when he

was captured."

"I don't think the French military has any interest in getting involved in Vietnam again."

"Maybe not. But we only need one recognizable face to give the deception credibility."

It suddenly dawned on Coyle what Granier was suggesting, "You can't be serious?"

"Why not? Colonel Bigeard is famous and recognizable."

"He's also batshit crazy."

"Right. So, nobody could say this is not a stunt he might try to pull off."

"Yeah, but... Bruno? Why would he do it?"

"I don't know... notoriety? French pride?"

"He is quite full of himself. And he does owe me for stealing my fiancé," said Coyle thinking back.

"There you go. It's only fair."

"The best way to recruit Bruno is to make him think it was his idea."

"Manipulation. That's the spirit."

They finished their beers and ordered two more. The more they drank, the better the plan seemed. "I'll need to fly to Paris and do this in person if it is going to work," said Coyle.

"I agree. Deceit is best face-to-face," said Granier.

"Any chance of getting some recon on the prison before I go? It would help convince Bruno if we were sure the father was there."

"We still have a few operatives in the North. I'll see what I can do. I might be able to get my hands on some aerial photographs too."

"This is crazy, you know?"

"The best plans often are. The North Vietnamese will never see it coming."

Saigon, South Vietnam

The smell of charred wood and gasoline permeated the air around the scorched Presidential Palace. President Diem, his brother Nhu, and sister-in-law Madame Nhu with her broken arm in a sling stood on the back patio. They watched as work crews used canvas tarps to hide the extensive damage to the structure. The dust had invaded Diem's nasal passages and lungs causing a runny nose and occasional coughing attack. Most of the residential wing had been destroyed by the aerial bombing and the fire that followed. All three seemed annoyed by the site and the harsh memories it evoked of that terrible morning.

Flying American-made Douglas A-1 Skyraiders, the two South Vietnamese pilots that had attempted to assassinate Diem and his family used napalm canisters in addition to conventional bombs and rockets. They believed that nobody could escape the inferno they had created. They were wrong. Whether it was by sheer luck or God's divine providence as Diem claimed, the President of South Vietnam had survived the aerial bombardment with barely a scratch. Only Madame Nhu had suffered a serious wound when a bomb exploded in her bedroom and the ceiling caved in breaking her arm. It was Diem's brother Nhu's quick reaction and leadership at a time of crisis that saved everyone as they held up in the palace basement until the danger had passed. Believing it another coup, Nhu had expected a ground force to attack the palace, but none came. The two pilots had acted on their own, hoping their actions might bring about a change in government once Diem and his family were dead. The change never transpired. "I cannot watch this. The memory is too painful," said Madame Nhu.

"You should go inside and lie down, my dear," said Nhu.

"Yes, I insist," said Diem. "There is no sense in dwelling on it."

"Perhaps you are right," said Madame Nhu as she retreated into the palace.

"I think you should seriously consider building the new

palace you have wanted," said Nhu.

"You think now is the time?" said Diem surprised.

"As long as this building stands, it will remind the people of the assassination attempt. It makes you look weak."

"I see. Then you would have me demolish it?"

"Yes, as soon as practical."

"Where shall we stay while the new palace is being constructed?"

"I've looked into some of the luxury hotels in Saigon. None suit your security needs. Even with the damage, this palace is still a compound with a high wall surrounding it. It's the safest location at the moment."

"You are suggesting we stay here? But doesn't that go against what you just said about reminding the people of the assassination attempt?"

"It's not ideal, but it is the best solution we have available. The sooner you can announce plans for a new palace, the better. It's important that you look like you are moving forward into the future and not dwelling on the past."

"I agree. I shall instruct my staff to find a suitable architect."

"Good. There is one more thing we should discuss. The more I think about what happened, the more I am convinced that the American's may have been involved. It is too much of a coincidence that the CIA pilot Coyle had taken control of the palace air defenses right when the aerial attack happened."

"Do you think Colonel Lansdale was involved?"

"No. While I don't always agree with Lansdale, I have little doubt he is loyal to you. But that doesn't mean that there were no other members in the CIA or American embassy involved. It's hard to believe the two pilots acted on their own."

"What do you suggest we do?"

"Nothing at the moment. We still need America's financial and military support. But we should all be aware that your ally may be waning in its support of you and your government."

"To the point where they would have me assassinated?"

"It's possible."

"God will not let that happen."

The unintended consequence of the bombing was that Diem became more paranoid than ever and withdrew even more from public life and his people. He gave Brother Nhu and his security forces a free hand to find the assassins and bringing their accomplices to justice. Nhu used the roundup of suspects as an excuse to jail Diem's political opponents and competitors against the businesses Nhu owned. Madame Nhu insisted that Diem was far too important to the country to expose himself to more danger. As Diem withdrew, Nhu and his wife stepped forward and became the face of government. In Diem's public absence, the Nhu's ruled with iron fists which only enraged the people further.

While they waited for plans to be drawn up for the new palace, Diem and his family had relocated to the opposite wing in the damaged palace. Nhu brought in an abundance of anti-aircraft guns to prevent any further aerial attacks and stepped up the number of palace guards. Security was his responsibility and he had let the family down. Even though the assassination attempt had failed, Nhu was determined not to allow anything like it to happen again.

Coyle's girlfriend, Bian had gone back to work several days after the bombing of the palace. She felt on edge knowing that Coyle and Granier knew she was working for North Vietnamese intelligence. She trusted Coyle, but she had just met Granier. The only thing she knew about him was that he was CIA and was somewhat ambivalent about whether she lived or died. It was Coyle that had stopped Granier from killing her, but she wasn't sure for how long Coyle could hold him back. Killing seemed to come naturally to

Granier.

The only thing she cared about was saving her father even if it meant her life was forfeited. She felt depressed but knew that might be a giveaway that something was amiss if others saw her in such a state. She put on a smile as best she could and forced herself to chat with her co-workers when required. Everything seemed so trivial compared to her situation.

Bian did not want to raise any suspensions about her self-inflicted wound from her failed suicide attempt. She wrapped her wrist bandage in white fabric, then let out the sleeves of her ao dai a bit so the fabric was covered. It was to no avail. After a few days, Bian was waiting for a meeting between the new architects that had been selected to design the new palace and the Diem family. It was then that Madame Nhu noticed the white dressing and said, "Bian, did you hurt yourself?"

"Yes, Madame. During the air raid, I was running toward the palace to ensure the president and his family were safe. A shop window shattered, and I was cut by the falling glass," said Bian.

"Did you need stitches?"

"Yes, but the doctor said it would heal fine in a few weeks."

"You should have the palace doctor look at it. He is a surgeon."

"Thank you, Madame. But I think it will be fine if I just keep it covered with the bandage."

"Bian, you are far too valuable to my brother-in-law to lose. Have the doctor check the wound."

"Yes, Madame. I will."

Later in the day, Bian was visited by the palace doctor in the presidential study. He removed the wrappings and the bandage to examine the wound. "It is a strange angle for a wound from falling glass," said the doctor.

"Yes. The doctor at the hospital said the same thing,"

said Bian.

"Really? Which hospital?"

"Saigon Adventist on the Phú Nhuận crossroads."

"I know it well. My son is doing his internship there. What was the name of the doctor?"

"Dr. Nyugen, I think."

"Which one? There are so many."

"I'm not sure. He didn't give me his first name."

"Ah, just as well. They are very busy over there. I will give you some ointment that will help the wound heal faster and leave less of a scar."

"Thank you, Doctor."

He put on some ointment over the injury and rewrapped the wound with a new dressing. Bian had lied about the hospital and the name of the doctor. She was worried she might get caught if the doctor checked further and that he might inform Madame Nhu... or worse her husband, Brother Nhu. If Nhu found out she was a spy, he would surely kill her, but not before torturing her to find out the information she had given to the North Vietnamese. She didn't fear death, but torture was another matter. She had heard the rumors of what Nhu's secret police did to people before they disappeared. But even torture she would be willing to endure if it saved her father. But she knew it wouldn't. Once the North Vietnamese found out Bian had been compromised, her father was a dead man.

When the doctor left the study, he was informed that Madame Nhu wished to see him on the back veranda. The doctor had learned it was not wise to keep the dragon lady waiting. He moved quickly to the back doors.

Sitting at a white iron table, Madame Nhu was nursing a cup of coffee and said, "Thank you for coming, doctor. How is our patient?"

"I gave her some ointment. The wound should heal just fine," said the doctor.

"Nothing strange to report?"

"No. whoever sutured her wound did an excellent job. Although, I must admit…"

"Yes?"

"The angle of the wound was peculiar for the situation she described."

"In what way?"

"The wound was vertical, straight down from the elbow to the wrist. If a shard of glass had fallen from a window, I would have expected more of an angle."

"Do you think the wound was self-inflicted?"

"I suppose it's possible, but we both know Bian. She doesn't seem depressed and has everything to live for. I don't know why she would do something like that."

"Everyone has a reason for what they do, doctor. It's just a matter of finding out what it is."

To avoid further suspension, Bian stuck to her normal routine which included visiting the park and checking the base of the lamppost for the signal that a message from her handler had been left. She was lucky the first two weeks. No message. Then she saw the X on the base of the lamppost. She walked to through the park until she spotted a bench with a crumpled paper bag stuffed in the ironwork. She sat and after a few minutes carefully retrieved the piece of paper holding the message from the bottom of the bench seat. She placed the paper in a book, rose, and walked away.

When she returned home, Coyle was waiting outside. He gently kissed her on the cheek. "How was work?" he said.

"Uneventful," she said.

"That's good."

They went inside and she prepared dinner. Bian was torn on whether to show Coyle the message she had picked up. She knew he was a good man and meant well, but she was unsure he would be able to free her father. If the North Vietnamese found out she had betrayed them and had been turned into a double agent, they were sure to kill her father and her. She decided to wait until she had decoded the message and found out what information was being requested.

When they went to bed, Bian made love to Coyle for the first time since her suicide attempt. Afterward, he slept soundly. She rose from the bed and retrieved the message from her book. She pulled a common French novel – The Count of Monte Cristo from a shelf and used it as a key to translate the coded message. It was a request for the name of the construction firm that had been selected to build the new palace. North Vietnamese intelligence wanted to plant workers in the firm in hopes of installing listening devices in the walls of the palace. They also needed an early copy of the blueprints to determine the best locations to hide the microphones.

She climbed back into bed and looked over at Coyle. She had betrayed this man and yet he was about to risk his life to free her father. She remembered the moments she treasured with him – their first dinner, their walk through the zoo, the first time they made love. She had strong feelings for him, maybe even love. She also thought of her father, especially when she was little. He had seemed so big and handsome in his uniform. She was overwhelmed with feelings and tears rolled down her cheeks. She was unsure of what to do and slept little that night.

The next morning, she made Coyle breakfast before heading off to work. When she sat down with him, she said, "I received a coded message from North Vietnamese intelligence."

"You did? When?" said Coyle.

"Yesterday before I came home from work."

"Why didn't you tell me?"

"It needed to be decoded… and if you will remember… we were busy last night."

"Oh, right. So, what did it say?"

Bian considered for a moment, then lied, "They want to

know about the increased security at the palace. How many new guards? What types of weapon upgrades, especially anti-aircraft?"

"Huh. I wonder why they want to know that? Do you think they are considering an attack on the palace?"

"I don't know. They don't tell me that sort of thing."

"Of course not. There's no need for you to know. Anyway, it shouldn't be too much trouble to come up with some made-up information that they will believe."

"But what if they find out I've been lying?"

"By the time they find anything, your father will be free and you'll be off the hook permanently."

"And Brother Nhu?"

"I admit. He's a different problem. We are going to have to convince him that you are still valuable as a double agent. But don't worry. Granier and I are working on that. I think it's gonna be okay."

"Why are you doing this?"

"What do you mean why? I love you, Bian."

Bian teared up and said, "That's the first time you've said it."

"I should have said it sooner. But it's true just the same."

"And I love you," she said unsure if it was the truth or just another lie.

Bian made a reconnaissance visit to the architect's office — a modern four-story building that accommodated just under 100 employees, most of which were draftsmen. Breaking into the building would be simple once everyone had left for the day but finding the blueprints for the new palace would be far more difficult. She had no idea where to look. She imagined something like that might be kept in a safe. She dared not go in and scout the location during the day for fear of being recognized. If her presence at the architect's office was revealed to Nhu, he would question her about the visit and possibly trip up her story. Nhu was known for his ability to find the truth.

The architects had made several visits to the palace to discuss the design with Diem, Nhu, and Madame Nhu. Bian had been there and listened in. She was not considered an advisor, but Diem valued her opinion as an educated citizen. When asked by Diem about the design sketches, Bian responded, "I think a modern design will project a forward-looking government."

"That is what I thought," said Diem.

"I think it should have a European design. French perhaps," said Madame Nhu.

"Piss on the French. We have enough French-style buildings to create another Paris. We don't need another. Especially not my palace," said Diem.

"Perhaps more American. Like the buildings in New York or Chicago," said Brother Nhu.

"Interesting. The Americans would like that," said Diem shifting his attention to the architects. "You should consider that approach in your design."

"As you wish," said the lead architect. "Is there any particular building you like?"

"Something modern that projects power, I think," said Diem.

"The United Nations office building projects power," said Madame Nhu.

"Yes, the United Nations building is a good example," said Diem.

"You had originally mentioned a horizontal layout. The UN office building is a skyscraper," said the architect.

"Right. Of course. I am not a designer. You are. But you get the idea."

"Yes. Something like the UN building."

"Maybe you could ask the opinion of that American architect Frank Lloyd Wright," said Madame Nhu.

"That would be difficult. He passed away three years ago," said the architect.

"That's too bad. I heard he was quite creative."

"Yes. He was."

Bian watched when the architect slipped the designs into his portfolio and exited with his associates.

Bain waited until the architects finished their sketches and had them approved by Diem and his family. By the time she was ready to break into their offices, the architects were well underway with the process of creating the initial blueprints. If she was able to photograph a set, they wouldn't be the final design of the palace, but she thought it would be enough to satisfy North Vietnamese intelligence.

She waited until the weekend when there were fewer employees in the building. When she arrived just after dark on Sunday, there were still lights on in the building. She waited until the lights went out and the last employee had locked the front door and left.

She carried a lock pick set that the North Vietnamese had taught her to use. She unlocked the front door, then relocked it once she was inside. It was a big building and she dared not turn on the lights. She made her way to the elevator. The door was open, and the inside of the elevator car was dark. She concluded that the last employee must have locked it preventing it from operating. She entered the stairwell and climbed up to the fourth floor. She guessed the lead architect's office was probably a good place to start. His door was locked. She picked the lock and went inside.

The shadows in his office were long from a full moon beaming through the floor-to-ceiling windows. Once her eyes adjusted, she could see well enough. The furniture was modern as was the art on the walls and the sculpted artworks on the bookshelves, side tables, and credenza. She had a small flashlight that she could cup her hand around to keep the light from being seen from the outside. She went through his desk drawers and the credenza behind the desk. She found nothing of interest. Next, she moved to the file cabinets and searched each draw. There were lots of drawings and sketches but not the ones she was searching for. She looked around the rest of the office. There was no place where blueprints might be stored. She was about to move on to another office when she spotted what she thought was a coat closet. She opened the door and found a large safe. It looked like it was newly installed with wallboard dust next to the door jam. It was Nhu's doing. She was sure of it. He would want to keep the plans for the palace secret, especially after the assassination attempt on Diem and the family. The blueprints would be inside the lead architect's safe and he would be responsible for ensuring they were secure.

A Chinese intelligence advisor had taught her and several other operatives how to crack a small rudimentary safe, but this thing was a beast and modern. She studied the dual dials for a moment and quickly realized it was way over her abilities. The office light came on. Bian turned to see a cleaning man standing in the doorway. "What are you doing here?" said the cleaning man surprised.

"I work here as a secretary," said Bian. "I must have fallen asleep."

"In the director's office?"

"Yes, and if you mention it, he will be angry. He does not want his associates knowing his extracurricular activities."

"What does extracurricular mean?"

"It means you keep your nose of out his business. Do you have keys to let me out?"

"Yes."

"Do so. Now," said Bian in her most commanding tone.

The cleaning man walked her out of the building and locked the door behind her. She had failed at securing a copy of the blueprints, but she had not been revealed. There was still a chance. She moved off into the darkness, her mind grasping for a new plan.

March 16, 1962 – Near Guam, USA

A Lockheed L-1049 Super Constellation flew over the

Pacific Ocean 300 miles west of Guam. It was a sunny day with only a few clouds in the sky. Good flying weather. The four-engine aircraft carried the insignia of the Flying Tiger Line, a remnant of World War II when the American freelance pilots flew for the Chinese against the invading Japanese military.

The crew of eleven was transporting ninety-three American Ranger-trained communications specialists and three South Vietnamese soldiers from Travis Air Force Base, California to Tan Son Nhut Air Base, South Vietnam. The Vietnamese sat together enjoying the Cokes and tuna sandwiches the stewardess had brought them. The fact that they were free made them more enjoyable. The American soldiers read books, talked of their girlfriends and wives, played bridge with the Flying Tiger logo on the back of the cards, and slept.

One of the Vietnamese soldiers removed a satchel from under the seat in front of him and rose. He walked toward the front of the plane. His two comrades called after him reminding him that there was a toilet in the rear of the aircraft. He continued to walk forward until he reached a draped doorway. He pushed his way through disappearing behind the curtain. Thirty seconds later, the aircraft started to descend. The angle was steeper than usual but not out of the question of normal operation.

The soldiers exchanged confused looks with each other. They were still hundreds of miles before landfall. Just as several of the soldiers rose to check to see what was happening, the aircraft leveled out. Through the windows, the soldiers could see the white caps of the waves below. They were less than a thousand feet off the surface. They heard five muffled pops of what sounded like a Colt 45 pistol firing. Alarmed, several Rangers jumped up and ran toward the cockpit. But before they could reach the cockpit door, the aircraft dove once again at a near-vertical decline, and soldiers fell on top of each other on the cockpit wall and door.

The plane with its engines at full power plunged into the ocean and disappeared beneath the surface.

In the days that followed, four branches of the US military carried one of the largest air and sea searches in history for signs of the plane, its crew, and passengers. In the 200,000 square miles and over eight days of searching, no debris or bodies were found. Although there were many theories, there was no plausible explanation of what happened to Flying Tiger Line Flight 739.

# THE JOURNALIST & THE WARRIOR

## March 21, 1962 – Saigon, South Vietnam

A journalist for UPI, Neil Sheehan had been anxious to get to Vietnam before he missed all the action. Three years before becoming a foreign correspondent, he had served in the U.S. military in Korea and Japan. He was searching for the big story that would make him famous and suspected that Vietnam was the place to find it.

Although competitive with the other journalists assigned to Saigon, Sheehan was likable and got along well with the press corps. His military experience served him well when he volunteered to cover ARVN airmobile operations with U.S. helicopter crews and military advisors. The commanders in charge of the operations could see that he knew his way around a battlefield and that they didn't need to worry about him. That made him welcome even on dangerous missions. He loved flying in the helicopters that carried the ARVN troops into battle. It was exciting. Even more so when he was shot at from the ground. Like most journalists in South Vietnam, he carried a camera but preferred to have a Vietnamese photojournalist assigned to his story, so he could use them as a translator if required. That wasn't always possible when he went on helicopter operations. Not all the photojournalists were excited about flying and none liked to get shot at. When no photojournalist was available, he snapped the photos that would accompany his stories. He wasn't bad at photography, but his attention was more focused on getting the story correct. The photos sometimes suffered, and he knew it. He didn't have the patience or the skill of a veteran photojournalist.

Sheehan believed in America's Cold War strategy and that communist expansionism needed to be stopped, especially in Southeast Asia where the governments were unusually fragile, and the people were easily swayed by the communist dogma. He considered himself an American patriot and wanted what was best for his country.

To get to Saigon, Sheehan had flown on a commercial airliner to Guam, then hitched a ride on a military plane to Saigon. He could have flown commercial to Saigon like the other journalists, but Sheehan wasn't like other journalists. He knew that long military flights were a good way to strike up conversations with officers and hopefully form friendships that would serve him later while in-country.

On that flight, he sat next to thirty-seven-year-old Lieutenant Colonel John Paul Vann who had taken leave in Hawaii before reporting to his current assignment as a senior military adviser to Colonel Huỳnh Văn Cao, commander of the ARVN IV Corps. Vann was small for an American at five-foot-seven and one-hundred-and-fifty pounds. But what Vann lacked in size, he more than made up for in pure tenacity and aggression. "So, you believe in the war?" said Sheehan.

"Believe in it? It's a reality. The Viet Cong are not just going to disappear on their own, not while the North Vietnamese and China are sending them weapons and supplies," said Vann.

"Okay. It's a reality. But do you think it can be won?"

"Of course, it can be won. The Viet Cong are guerilla fighters. They still can't field anything bigger than a battalion. They've got no Air Force and most of their artillery consists of light mortars and recoilless rifles."

"Then why do the ARVN keep losing territory?"

"Training mostly. You gotta remember, South Vietnam has only been in existence for seven years. It's a very young country with an inexperienced military. It was the French that fought the Viet Minh, not the ARVN. And it was the French that shirked their responsibility to train a South Vietnamese Army to replace them before they left. Hell, the ARVN were using World War II hand-me-downs and fighting street gangs in Saigon before the American military stepped up to take over training and military aid. You can't fight a war with police officers. It was sheer luck and a bit of stupidity that kept the Viet Minh from overrunning the country. The North Vietnamese should have backed the Viet Minh while the ARVN were still weak and disorganized. You snooze, you lose. Now, things are different."

"In what way?"

"Well, I'm here for one," said Vann with a grin.

"You think you can make a difference?"

"Sure. As long as the South Vietnamese want to fight, we can train them. We got the experience and the know-how. It's just a matter of time and enough American advisors."

"I've heard there are problems with ARVN leadership."

"Come on… there are always problems with leadership. The ARVN don't have the market cornered on bad leaders. It's just a matter of sorting out the bad apples and promoting those that deserve it."

"I've heard that's the problem. The government riding roughshod over military promotions."

"And you don't think that happens in the U.S. military?"

"I guess I never thought about it."

"Why do you think there are so many American military dynasties?"

"So, you're okay with the government leaders interfering with promotions?"

"Hell, no. It's a reckless strategy that demoralizes the rank and file. But like I said, it's a young country. These things take time to work themselves out."

"So, one foot in front of the other?"

"Something like that. Four or five years from now this is gonna be an entirely different army and an entirely different war."

"You believe that?"

"I wouldn't say it if I didn't. War is unpredictable, but you watch… come hell or high water, we're gonna win this thing."

"I hope you're right, Colonel."

"Bet on it."

Sheehan got what he wanted – a friend in Lt. Colonel Vann. Vann was one of the most aggressive military advisors in South Vietnam. He taught the officers he instructed to lead from the front and attack whenever possible. "Sitting on your ass and waiting for the enemy to attack will get you and your men killed. You are giving up your momentum and it's momentum that wins battles. When you attack, you put the enemy off balance. They can't attack you if they're busy defending their position. Attack, attack, attack… that's the way you win," said Vann. "But don't be stupid about it. Never attack where the enemy knows you must. Find another way. Hit 'em in the flank. Hit 'em in the rear. Or better yet, both at the same time. When your enemy is scrambling to defend all sides of its position, you have the advantage. Seize the moment and attack with everything you got." Sheehan filled his notepads with quotes from Vann. The lieutenant colonel's confidence was inspiring and spilled out of him naturally like a waterfall. It made Sheehan and the others around him want to win and believe that they could.

Sheehan was allowed to accompany Vann whenever he wished. Vann knew the soldier turned journalist knew the risks of battle and could take care of himself if things went badly. But they rarely did with Vann. He knew American weapons and how to use technology to his advantage. He was especially enthralled with helicopters and their ability to carry his troops into battle. They were the embodiment of momentum. He won battle after battle against the Viet Cong. His ARVN counterpart Colonel Cao learned to trust his American advisor and ensured that the officers under his command listened and learned from Vann. Victory won their hearts and minds.

Vann was stationed at Colonel Cao's headquarters in My Tho in the Mekong Delta forty miles south of Saigon. Cao's ARVN forces consisted of three infantry divisions, two mobile, and six border ranger groups. Even with substantial forces under his command, it was a precarious situation. While the northern half of the Delta was contested with running battles between the ARVN and the Viet Cong, the southern half was clearly under the control of the VC.

The Mekong Delta was South Vietnam's rice bowl and provided two-thirds of the nation's rice production. During the monsoon season, alluvial waters raised the level of the Mekong River and most of the swampy land called "The Plain of Reeds" was inundated which made it perfect for growing rice. Over the centuries, the Mekong River and its main tributary, the Bassac River had formed the Delta's plains creating rich soil that made multi-yearly rice harvests possible. Most of the land was less than ten feet above sea level. The terrain consisted of mangrove swamps and rice fields irrigated by an interlocking system of canals. The Delta had sixteen provinces which contained two-thirds of the nation's population making it a prime location for Viet Cong recruitment.

Vann knew that such a large area so near to Saigon could not be left to the VC. Not only would it allow the VC to recruit from the surrounding villages and accumulate supplies, but the VC could also use it as a staging area for a major attack on the capital. Vann wanted it back and convinced Cao that he could retake the enemy territory with the help of the American fighter planes and helicopters. Vann was like that… convincing and confident.

Having commanded a Ranger company in Korea, Vann knew that airmobile forces worked best in flat open areas like the Mekong Delta. Jungles and forests forced the helicopter pilots to land in clearings that were more likely to be known by the enemy and were prone to ambush. In the Mekong Delta, the pilots could land their choppers wherever they pleased. In planning his missions, Vann knew that surprise was important, but confusing the enemy was even more important. He usually suggested multiple landing zones to his South Vietnamese counterpart – one in front to pin the enemy and one or two on the enemy's flank or rear. Nothing frightened and confused the Viet Cong more than being attacked from multiple points. The VC depended on a quick retreat when overwhelmed. They often identified multiple escape routes from the battlefield into a nearby forest or jungle where their movements would be unseen. When those retreat routes were cut off, they were demoralized and unnerved.

Vann always chose to attack where the enemy least expected it. Helicopters helped the ARVN do just that with speed and flexibility. It was the ARVN that could be landed behind enemy lines, execute a surprise attack, then pull out quickly if the enemy forces were too strong. Whenever the enemy was forced to defend its flanks or rear, soldiers were pulled from the front line which weakened their defense against the main attacking force. It was a dangerous situation for the VC. Even the thrumming of the approaching helicopters' rotors put fear into the hearts of the VC. They hated the helicopters.

Sheehan loved helicopters. He readily accepted front-line assignments that put him in harm's way if it meant riding in a helicopter. He was delighted whenever he was allowed to ride by an open door or window. He would look out at the rice paddies and fields sweeping below. He didn't seem overly worried when a helicopter approached a landing zone and the pace of enemy gunfire picked up. He wasn't stupid and he didn't have a death wish, but he prized the excitement and adrenaline that only battle could produce. He considered himself a serious person but couldn't help grinning whenever he rode a helicopter into battle. The soldiers that rode with him were reassured by the American journalist's confidence and enthusiasm but thought he was a bit touched in the head. All except Vann. Vann understood the sensation Sheehan was feeling. He felt it himself. He loved to fight and win. Vann and Sheehan were a pair of adrenaline junkies that refused to believe they could be killed in battle. The naturally generated drug helped them do their jobs without fear. They understood each other and didn't judge too deeply. This strange bond allowed Vann to accept Sheehan as an equal and trust him.

Sheehan and Vann had been on multiple missions together and Sheehan had written several stories on the gutsy lieutenant colonel. It didn't matter much to Vann to see his name in print, but he knew his wife and family would be proud. Sheehan was making Vann famous whether he liked it or not.

While hanging around Vann's office hoping to find a story, Sheehan overheard a radio call between Vann and Cao. They were preparing for another mission. Sheehan felt a bit hurt that Vann had not invited him along and wondered if he had done something to upset the American advisor. When the call was over, Sheehan approached Vann and said, "Are you heading out?"

"Yeah. The VC have been sniping at fishing boats on a tributary of the Mekong. Seems like there are trying to lure us into battle. We've decided to oblige them," said Vann.

"Sounds like it could be a good story."

"Maybe… but this little outing isn't gonna be like the

others."

"How's that?"

"We're pretty sure it's an ambush."

"But you're going anyway?"

"Yeah. We think we can turn the tables on them."

"I see. And you don't want me to tag along?"

"Not on this one."

"Colonel, this is the kind of story I have been searching for."

"I know. And if I thought it was safe, I'd extend an invitation. But it ain't."

"Now, you're just pissing me off."

Vann laughed, "I wouldn't want to do that."

"I can take care of myself. You know that."

"You can. I admit that. But this is just one mission. There will be others. I just don't have a good feeling about you going."

"It's my job, Colonel. It should be my call, not yours."

"But it is my call. And I say 'no' this time, Neil. Sorry."

Sheehan walked out in a huff. Vann shrugged it off.

Two days later, an ARVN battalion was on the airfield apron waiting for their ride into battle. Vann, Cao, and the battalion commander were going over last-minute intelligence as to the enemy's expected location. Sheehan, his rucksack over his shoulder, approached. "You don't take 'no' for an answer too well, do ya, Neil?" said Vann.

"I doubt I'd be much of a reporter if I did, would I?" said Sheehan.

Vann considered for a moment, then shrugged, "It's your life."

Vann turned to Cao and said, "You got any objections to him going?"

Cao shook his head. "You'll ride with me," said Vann to Sheehan.

Sheehan grinned and moved off. "He's gonna make you famous or die trying," said Cao.

"I suppose any aspirations I had about being a spy are off the table," said Vann.

"Good thing. You're not subtle enough to be a good spy. You'd get yourself hung."

"Maybe," said Vann turning to see the helicopters on approach.

Inside the cockpit of the lead H-21C Shawnee helicopter, Lieutenant Scott Dickson sat in the co-pilot's chair. He had control of the aircraft. Sitting in the pilot's chair, his commander knew that the young lieutenant needed as much practice as possible, and he let him take the controls whenever they were not flying with passengers. Eventually, Scott would take full control of the aircraft and fly in every situation, but he needed more hours in the air. Scott was confident that he was a good pilot, but he also understood that nothing replaces experience in the cockpit.

Scott set the helicopter down fifty feet from Vann and his team. He kept the blades churning. He didn't expect to stay on the ground long.

Vann was the first to climb into the aircraft when the crew chief opened the door. Sheehan followed. Vann entered the cockpit. "Morning, gentlemen. You ready to hunt VC?" said Vann.

"Damned right," said the pilot.

"You know where we're headed?"

"Affirmative."

"Outstanding."

Forty minutes later, the helicopters were approaching the designated landing zones in the Mekong Delta. Vann didn't like what he saw as his helicopter did a recon pass over the suspected enemy location. No VC. No gunfire. He scanned the horizon and detected a large group of mangroves near the site. "There," he said pointing.

The pilot flew over the mangroves. It was impossible to see through the thick canopy. "They're here," said Vann. "I'm sure of it."

"Why aren't they shooting at us?" said Scott.

"They're waiting for bigger fish. I'm going down for a look."

"Where do you want me to land?" said the pilot.

"I don't. Do you have a cable to sling cargo under this thing?"

"Yeah. It's in the back. The crew chief knows where."

"Alright. See if you can find a clearing in the canopy somewhere in the center of the grove. I'll use the cable to climb down."

"You're gonna what?!"

"Trust me. It'll work."

"Nobody's ever done that before," said Scott.

"Well, I guess I'll never learn any younger then," said Vann.

"I can't let you do that. It's not safe," said the pilot.

"I wasn't asking. Now, find me a clearing."

"This my ship. I am in command, Colonel."

"Look, I'm not arguing that. But this is the safest way to get behind the enemy. It's never been done before, so they won't expect it. It's my ass if it goes wrong."

"Alright. We'll hold it as steady as possible."

"I appreciate it."

Vann moved back into the cargo area and sent the crew chief in search of the cable. The crew chief brought him the cable and the cargo net. "Just the cable. Tie one end to cargo hooks on the deck. I'll throw the other end out the door once we find a clearing," said Vann. As the crew chief secured the cable, Vann turned to the twenty ARVN soldiers seated in the aircraft hold and said, "Who has mountaineer training?"

Five soldiers raised their hands. "You five are with me. Leave your packs and fill your pockets with grenades and all the ammunition you can carry from the others," said Vann as he pulled a AN/PRC-6 walkie-talkie from his rucksack. He checked to ensure the batteries still had juice and that it was functioning properly. He could feel the helicopter hovering. He moved back into the cockpit, showed the pilot his radio, and said, "This thing probably ain't gonna have much of a range down in those trees. So, I'm gonna need you guys to hover around until I find the enemy's position and radio it back up to you. You then radio the position to the battalion commander. Got it?"

"Got it," said the pilot. "Good luck, Colonel."

Vann moved off again and looked out of the open doorway. He could see a small clearing in the jungle canopy. He lowered the cable through the hole. He could see that it was short of the ground. He said to the crew chief, "Have 'em take it down another ten feet."

The helicopter lowered ten more feet and the end of the cable scrapped along the ground.

Vann turned to the five soldiers going with him and said, "If you fall, it probably won't kill you. But it ain't gonna feel too good, so don't do that. Once you get down, form a defensive perimeter and wait for the others. I'll go first."

Vann ripped two strips of cloth off a rag, then looked over at Sheehan and said, "Are you coming?"

Sheehan's first reaction was a "Who me?" look on his face. "This is crazy. You know that?" said Sheehan.

"I prefer unorthodox."

"It's never even been tried before."

"That's what makes it brilliant. The VC will never expect it."

"Because they're not crazy."

"Look. That's where the story is," said Vann nodding toward the clearing. "It's go time. Are you coming or not?"

"Yeah, I'm coming," said Sheehan.

"Atta boy!" said Vann with a grin. "You follow the others. Okay?"

Sheehan gave him a weak nod. Vann tucked the radio into his shirt and slung his rifle over his back. Almost without hesitation he was out the doorway and climbing down the cable using the strips of cloth as makeshift gloves. He let his weight do the work and let the cable slip through his hands and legs. Five seconds later he was on the ground. He unslung his rifle and knelt beside a thick tree trunk. The rest of the soldiers followed. Not surprisingly, nobody fell. Sheehan, unsure, was the last one out the doorway. When he made it to the ground, the crew chief signaled the pilot and watched to ensure the cable didn't get snagged in the tree canopy as the helicopter rose. The crew chief waited until the cable had cleared the top of the canopy before pulling the cable inside. The helicopter flew in a circle around the top of the trees so as not to give away Vann's team position.

Beneath the trees, it was dark and the air was thick. The ground was soggy and slippery. Thin shafts of daylight pierced the leafy canopy giving the jungle a mystic ambiance. Vann did a quick radio check and was relieved to hear the pilot respond. The AN/PRC-6 used vacuum tubes which were easily broken, and Vann didn't have any spares. On Vann's hand motions, the team fanned out and searched for the enemy.

The team advanced quietly through the mangrove forest, their boots stepping between the tangle of roots. The ground was covered with puddles of brown water. It was difficult not to slosh. Sheehan was surprised the enemy had not closed on their position as they roped down from the chopper. Vann had been right. The VC never suspected soldiers descending from a hovering helicopter. They assumed the helicopter above them was trying to draw their fire and reveal their location. They knew better. The ARVN had always exited the aircraft on landing in a field or rice paddy and the VC could see them. This was something different. The VC were preoccupied with the helicopters that had landed at a distance. That is where they expected their enemy would advance from, not behind them.

It didn't take long for Vann's team to find the enemy. It was a small grove when compared to the massive tree swamps in the south. The VC were clumped together at the edge of the grove and looking in the opposite direction.

Vann didn't want to make contact. It was a recon mission. If he could avoid a fight he would. Even though his team would have the advantage of surprise, they would be vastly outnumbered and outgunned. They crouched down behind a giant root as Vann counted the VC. Twelve that he could see. He was sure there were plenty more he couldn't see. As usual, the VC were lightly armed with antiquated rifles and grenades. A few had knee mortars hanging off their belts. There was a VC gunner with a BREN - a British-made light machine gun. Vann wondered where they had found the WWII relic and imagined it was captured during the Indochina War from a foreign legionnaire. Vann could see the line of VC disappearing into a thicker line of trees to the south. He wanted to get a better idea of the size of force the ARVN would be facing.

He ordered his team and Sheehan to stay put while he moved through the trees to determine the size of the enemy's front line. Sheehan was happy to stay put this close to the enemy. He knew Vann could take care of himself and if things went south that Vann would stand a better chance of making a run for it without him. It wasn't that Sheehan thought himself inept as much as Vann was a solider of uncanny ability. He stayed put and watched Vann disappear among the mangroves.

A few minutes later, there were gunshots. The VC in front of the team were alert and turned their attention to the south where Vann had gone. Moments later, Vann appeared through the trees at a dead run across the soggy soil trying desperately not to trip on the roots sprawled across the jungle floor. Several VC on the front line were surprised to see an American running behind them. They hesitated, but only a moment. They opened fire at Vann.

The ARVN team returned fire giving Vann cover as he ran. Vann leapt over the giant root where the team was located and didn't slow down. "Move," he shouted without looking back. Sheehan and the team took off after him. Bullets whizzed around them. It was a miracle nobody was hit. Vann disappeared behind a thick tree trunk, then reappeared with his rifle laying down covering fire as Sheehan and the team passed him, then formed a defensive position another ten yards into the trees. Hearing his team open fire, Vann ceased firing and made a run for another tree trunk next to their position. He pulled out the radio and called the helicopter to relay the enemy's position and strength. Vann pulled out a map and called out several sets of coordinates. Sheehan looked puzzled but kept his head down as he listened. Vann was remarkably calm considering a superior enemy force was closing in on their position. He gave very specific instructions on where he wanted the ARVN forces. Once he finished his broadcast, he ordered the team and Sheehan to fall back to the opposite edge of the forest. Nobody had any idea of its direction. Vann pointed the direction, reloaded his rifle, and laid down covering fire as the team and Sheehan sprinted from their positions deeper into the forest.

An entire company of VC was hot on their tail as they raced through the woods. Sheehan tripped on a root and fell hard smashing his chin against a rock. Blood flowed. Sheehan was stunned. Vann ran past him, reached down, and grabbed him by his shirt collar. With Vann's help, Sheehan stumbled to his feet. Continuing to support Sheehan, Vann slung his empty rifle, pulled his semi-automatic pistol from his belt, chambered a round using his hip instead of a hand, and fired three rounds toward the VC in pursuit. He didn't expect to hit anything but didn't want to give them a free pass either. He was amazed when the lead VC grabbed his chest and fell. Seeing their comrade mortally wounded, the rest of the VC took cover. Vann didn't give it a second thought and kept running. "I'm okay. Let go," said Sheehan.

Vann released Sheehan who quickly picked up speed and ran ahead of Vann. Vann pivoted and fired two more rounds. He had to conserve ammunition. He only had two more pistol clips with him and no rifle ammunition. He knew his team would be running low on ammunition too. More bullets whizzed around him as he ran. The VC were catching up and mad as hornets. There were a lot of them now and they weren't afraid of their prey's counterfire. Numbers gave them courage.

A bullet hit one of the team members in the thigh. He went down dropping his rifle. Sheehan stopped to help the soldier as Vann fired at the enemy to slow their advance and buy Sheehan time. As Sheehan helped the wounded soldier to his feet, he glanced over at the rifle on the ground. He knew that if he left the rifle the VC would capture it and probably use it against ARVN forces. But he also knew that if he picked up the rifle he could be seen as a combatant. Since he was an American, he doubted the VC would treat him any differently whether he was armed or unarmed. He picked the rifle up and slung it over his back. Sheehan supported the wounded soldier as they continued their run through the forest. Vann followed protecting their rear.

They reached the opposite end of the forest. Sheehan stopped for a moment and looked out at the rice paddies in front of them. Open ground. "Keep going," said Vann turning to fire a few more rounds at the enemy still in the forest. Sheehan and the wounded soldier continued to run across the first rice paddy, splashing up water, their boots sinking in the mud, trampling the young rice plants. They slowed. Sheehan knew they were an easy target. He was pissed at Vann for leading them out of the forest and into a field with little cover. He was going to die and it was Vann's fault. As they approached the berm on the opposite side of the field, the VC broke through the mangroves and entered the rice paddy. The enemy fire grew to a cacophony as bullets splashed around them and whizzed by their heads. "Down," shouted Vann.

Vann, Sheehan, and the team dove face-first into the muddy water. It would only be a matter of moments before the VC were on them. There was little doubt they would be killed or captured. Exhausted, Sheehan wanted neither, but he had no more energy to run. He looked up from the water and saw an entire company of ARVN soldiers rise from behind the berm in front of him. They opened fire on the VC that were now in the middle of the rice paddy without cover. It was a turkey shoot. A two-way highway of bullets zinged overhead. Sheehan kept as low as he could without drowning in what he was sure was water fertilized with human waste.

The ARVN had superior weapons, plenty of ammunition, and a protected firing position as they lay prone on the opposite side of the dirt berm. Twelve VC were killed in the first minute. Their comrades grabbed their corpses and fell back continuing to fire their rifles.

Just as the VC reached the back of the rice paddy, a second company of ARVN opened fire from the berm on the southern side of the rice paddy. The VC were flanked. They panicked leaving the corpses and scattering in every direction away from the enemy. Some ran for the forest, while others ran into adjacent fields. The ARVN kept up their rate of fire, reloading three and four times until there were no VC left standing. Few had escaped. Dozens were wounded. The ARVN soldiers cheered. It was a great victory with few losses.

The gunfire gone, Sheehan and Vann rose from the muddy water. "That was the stupidest thing I've ever seen in my life. They could have killed us," said Sheehan.

"Yep. That was a close one," said Vann. "You should have that chin looked at by the medic. I think you're gonna need a couple of stitches."

"I don't give a damn about my chin. What made you think for a moment that we could outrun them?"

"We did, didn't we?"

"It was sheer luck and you know it."

"Yeah. I suppose your right. It's like my dad always said, 'A faint heart never filled a flush.'"

"That's fool's courage."

"You wanna talk about fool's courage… What the hell

were you thinking following me down that cable into the forest? I never thought you'd actually do it."

"You said that's where the story was."

"I wasn't wrong. It's gonna make a Helluva story."

"Yeah. I guess it will."

"Isn't that why you came?"

"Yeah, but next time don't shame me into it. I decide when to risk my life, not you."

"Of course. I wouldn't have it any other way."

"Dammit. I think I may have shit myself."

"How can you tell?" said Vann looking at his soiled shirt and pants drenched in paddy water.


Saigon, South Vietnam


Walking cautiously with her eyes surveying the surrounding area, Bian approached an abandoned warehouse. It was early morning and the sun had just risen. Except for a stray dog nosing through a pile of garbage, nothing moved. She was alone. A risky situation for a young woman, it was what Bian had hoped for. She did not want anyone to see her.

She entered the warehouse. Orange shafts of light shone through the broken windows and were defined by the dust in the air. Broken pallets and empty sacks of rice were strewn across the floor. A bag moved and a rat scurried out. Bian was not frightened. She had other things on her mind. She heard the crack of a window's shard being broken on the floor. She turned to see Zhou Youyong standing in the former warehouse manager's office. He had purposely broken the glass to grab her attention. A veteran intelligence officer, everything Youyong did had a purpose.

Bian walked over and bowed politely to acknowledge that Youyong was her master and deserved her respect. Youyong got right to the matter at hand, "You have not delivered what was requested."

"No, but I will. I broke into the architect's office and found a safe I could not open," said Bian. "I believe the plans for the palace are kept inside."

"Why did you not contact me for help?"

"I was going to but then I came up with a better plan to get the blueprints."

"And what is that?"

"The architect brings the latest blueprints and drawings to the palace for Diem and his family's inspection. I believe I can gain access to the blueprints while he is there."

"I see. Very well, but you should always contact me when plans change. You know that."

"I am sorry. It was an oversight. It will not happen again."

"Good. When will you have photographs of the blueprints?"

"Tuesday if everything goes well."

"See that it does, Bian. The North grows impatient."

"Yes. I will do my best."

"How are things progressing with the CIA pilot?"

"I believe he loves me."

"Good. He will be very useful. You must start acquiring useful information from him at the earliest moment possible."

"I understand and I will. He is almost ready. My father… is he well?"

"Of course. As long as you comply with our requests, he will be well looked after. No harm will come to him."

"Will you give him a letter from me?" said Bian pulling an envelope from her pocket.

"Yes. But I cannot promise when he will read it. Brother Nhu's counterintelligence team has been very active since the assassination attempt. We must be careful."

"I understand. Maybe when I have photographs of the blueprints?"

"Perhaps. I will do my best," said Youyong taking the envelope from her.

# CALCULATING VICTORY

May 5, 1962 - Saigon, South Vietnam

Secretary of Defense Robert McNamara made his first visit to South Vietnam where he was besieged by foreign journalists as he stepped off the plane. The biggest question was if America was going to commit ground troops to Vietnam. McNamara artfully dodged the question by simply saying that America would do whatever was necessary to defend its allies, including South Vietnam, against communist aggression. McNamara went on to explain that every quantitative measurement showed that South Vietnam with America's help was winning the war. But as reporters like Halberstam and Sheehan dug deeper into McNamara's methods they questioned the use of number-crunching computers and statistics to calculate victory. "What about the human factor? What about the morale of the ARVN troops? What about the attitude of the populace and the support of the government?" asked the reporters.

"An attitude doesn't kill communists," said McNamara.

"Neither will a statistic," said Sheehan in response.

It wasn't that McNamara refused to recognize the flaws in his calculations, it was more that he didn't know what to do about it. The more he thought about it, the more he realized that the journalists were right. There was a lot more to calculate the outcome of a war than the quantity of enemy killed, the number of trained battalions, or the occupation of strategic hamlets. But public opinion and troop morale were hard to quantify and didn't fit neatly into McNamara's computer punch cards. His solution was more data that he and his analysts could use to devise a formula that would determine the outcome of the war. Data was always the solution for McNamara.

The one positive outcome of McNamara's visit was that he asked a lot of questions of the generals and advisors, many of which they couldn't answer. It got people thinking deeply about how to win the war. Was it winnable and what would be required? Could the South Vietnamese stand on their own one day and defend their nation against the Viet Cong and the North Vietnamese? What about the Chinese and the Soviets? McNamara was not afraid to ask questions even if he didn't like the answers. All data was welcome. All data filled in the puzzle he was building.

McNamara spent time visiting and consulting with President Diem and his family. He didn't like them much, but he was cordial and listened to their complaints about American interference and lack of funding. He listened to Madame Nhu's veiled slights and Brother Nhu's probing questions as to America's intentions. He was not there to pass judgment, not yet. He needed more information, and he wasn't going to get it sitting around a broken palace sipping tea. His time in-country was short.

As soon as he was able and escorted by a convoy of military vehicles, McNamara headed for the countryside. He was anxious to talk with the village chiefs and hear their thoughts on what was going right and what was going wrong with the war. He wanted to hear from more American advisors in the field and listen to their opinions, many of which were only too happy to give them. He would talk with American pilots to help determine the effectiveness of airpower and the effectiveness of the newly developed napalm canisters. He wanted to hear from the South Vietnamese soldiers and measure their current training level, fighting spirit, and esprit de corps. He wanted data. More and more data. Data that he could take back and analyze. He filled notebooks with observations, questions and answers, and data points to be included in the next version of his computer program. If he asked the right questions and got accurate answers, he was certain he could run the war efficiently and bring it to a victorious conclusion at some point in the future.

When he returned to the United States, it only took him a few days to develop the forms that would give him the data he needed from the field. People always grumbled about filling out forms, especially in the military. But McNamara didn't care about their complaints if his forms were filled out correctly, the data collated at unit headquarters in the field, and the results sent to Washington in the form of reports.

The more data that was generated, the bigger and faster the computers that were required to process it. Everything had to be translated into ones and zeros. The Americans were becoming experts at crunching numbers. IBM was the defense department's best friend.

But the data used to develop life and death decisions required by the military were only as good as the sources that provided the answers. It was a South Vietnamese general that answered a journalist's question by saying, "Ah, les statistiques! Your secretary of defense loves statistics. We Vietnamese can give him all he wants. If he wants them to go up, they will go up. If he wants them to go down, they will go down. It is all the same to us. Just give us the weapons and money we need to win." There was more truth in the general's answer than anyone in the White House or the Pentagon cared to admit.

McNamara loved explaining his numbers and charts to President Kennedy who listened to his presentations intently. Kennedy never admitted that he didn't always understand what McNamara was explaining or why.

McNamara was so sure of his calculations that he ordered the Pentagon to prepare plans to withdraw all American military advisors by 1964 because the war would be won by then.

The chiefs of staff were not so confident but drew up the plans anyway. There was nothing to be gained by arguing against McNamara's conclusions. He could easily bury anyone with statistics and charts that demonstrated he was right. After all, McNamara was the Secretary of Defense, and it wasn't smart to piss him off.

## Saigon, South Vietnam

A few weeks after McNamara's visit, President Diem's lead architect came to the palace for approval of several design changes on the new palace. Diem and his family were gathered in the study looking over the drawings and commenting on them. Bian was with them. She could see that the drawings were nearing completion. Her window was closing. She decided it was now or never. She watched as the architect finished his second cup of tea and motioned for a third to the footman. As the footman replenished the biscuits on the desk and retrieved the architect's cup, Bian moved to the serving table and dripped liquid from a hidden vial into the spout of the teapot and moved away. The footman walked to the serving table and poured the architect's tea adding two lumps of sugar.

As the footman served the architect his tea, Bian moved back to the table and knocked off the teapot splashing tea on her white ao dai. She apologized for her clumsiness and excused herself to clean the tea stain from her dress.

After fifteen minutes the architect complained of stomach problems and asked to reschedule the meeting. The meeting adjourned, the architect placed the blueprints in his portfolio case and left the room looking for the closest toilet. "Where is Bian?" said Diem.

"Clumsy girl probably went to clean her ao dai. Tea is a difficult stain, especially against white," said Madame Nhu. "I will check on her."

Madame Nhu left the study.

The architect entered the toilet, set his portfolio case on a table inside the toilet's foyer, and entered one of the stalls. His gastric distress was unleased with loud reverberations off the toilet walls. Hidden in the farthest stall, Bian exited quietly and moved into the foyer. She had already removed most of the tea stain and had a large wet spot on the front of her ao dai. She placed a chair against the door, opened the portfolio, and withdrew the blueprints. She used a micro camera the North Vietnamese had given her and took two photos of each page of the blueprints. Two minutes later, she placed the blueprints back in the case and set it back on the table. The chair against the door moved. Someone was trying to get in. Bian thought about hiding again but knew there would be no explanation for the chair against the door and whoever was trying to get in might search the toilet. She removed the chair and opened the door. Madame Nhu was standing on the other side. "Bian, why was the door locked?" said Madame Nhu.

"I don't know, Madame. Perhaps the architect did not want to be disturbed. I don't think he is feeling well," said Bian motioning toward the stalls.

Releasing another loud volley of gastric distress, the architect moaned. "I see," said Madame Nhu. "Perhaps we should leave him alone."

"I think that would be wise, Madame."

As Bian closed the door, Madame Nhu caught a glance of the architect's portfolio laying on the table. Bian could see her interest and the wheels in her clever mind beginning to turn. "I wasn't able to get the stain entirely out. I hope my ao dai is not ruined," said Bian.

"I wouldn't fret too much. You must have others. It seems that is all you ever wear," said Madame Nhu.

"Yes, Madame. I have others. I am just so embarrassed by my clumsiness."

"I am sure you will do better in the future, my dear."

Bian excused herself and went in search of Diem. Madame Nhu entered the toilet, opened the architect's case, and examined the blueprints. Everything seemed in order. The toilet flushed several times as the architect prepared to leave the stall. Madame Nhu closed the portfolio and left the toilet avoiding an awkward encounter.

# OPERATION ANADYR

## May 12, 1962 - Moscow, Russia

Summers in Moscow were far from balmy with an average temperature of seventy-five degrees Fahrenheit, but even that was a pleasant relief from the bone-cold Russian winters. Rain was expected in the late afternoon. The Russian tourists in Red Square seemed more worried about their viewfinder fitting St. Basil's Cathedral into their Industar cameras than summer showers. Just over the red brick wall that enclosed the government compound, sat the Kremlin – the nation's seat of power.

Inside, the tone was far more serious and not nearly as pleasant. After bragging that the Soviet Union was "making missiles like sausages," Khrushchev met with his military advisors to discuss the ever-widening missile gap between the United States and the Soviet Union. While showing confidence to the press, Khrushchev and his advisors knew that the USSR nuclear weapon program was being crushed by the United States and its allies. The USSR only had twenty operational ICBMs capable of striking the United States. On the other hand, the Americans had over 170 ICBMs and eight nuclear submarines each armed with sixteen Polaris missiles sitting on the Soviet's doorstep ready to launch at a moment's notice. The only shining light for the Soviets was a two to one advantage in tanks and land forces combined with a stockpile of 700 intermediate-range nuclear missiles designated for use against NATO in Europe, but incapable of reaching the contiguous United States. To make matters worse, the Americans had deployed more than 100 intermediate-range nuclear missiles in Italy and Turkey. The NATO missiles could hit the Soviet capital before its military had time to respond.

Khrushchev needed something to counter the new threat and rebalance his first strike capability. Another issue was that currently deployed Soviet missiles were unreliable and inaccurate. Newly designed missiles with better guidance systems and ignition systems would not be ready until 1965. It was a grim picture for the Soviets.

After the Bay of Pigs fiasco, Khrushchev and his advisors believed that President Kennedy was too young and intellectual for making decisions in crisis situations. They believed the young president was weak and would back down when faced with a strong military response from the Soviet Union. But Khrushchev was still worried that the Soviets were losing the nuclear arms race. He knew that even a slight misinterpretation in diplomatic or military communications could trigger a nuclear war, and in its current state, the Soviets would lose such a war.

Convinced that the Americans were just days away from once again invading Cuba to overthrow his government, Fidel Castro had requested Soviet nuclear missiles be deployed on Cuban soil. Although Castro's offer was intriguing Khrushchev was concerned with giving nuclear weapons to a revolutionary like Castro. He was unpredictable and might use the weapons in an imprudent manner against neighboring countries, especially the United States. Khrushchev needed to avoid conflict with the US at all costs until the Soviet Union could rebalance the nuclear arms race.

It was his military advisors that convinced Khrushchev that the benefits of the Cuban missile deployment outweighed the risks. While the USSR had only twenty ICBMs that could reach the United States, it had over 700 intermediate-range missiles that could strike the US on short notice if some were stationed in Cuba which was only ninety miles away from Florida. Washington DC would be within easy reach as was the entire east coast. The Soviets would have had the ability to hit the United States first even if the Americans fired their missiles first. The Cuban missiles would act as a huge deterrent against an American first strike on the Soviet Union.

The advisors also assured Khrushchev that it would be Soviet commanders stationed in Cuba that would have control of the nuclear weapons and not Castro. This was a double-edged sword. Any attack on America or its allies that originated from Cuba would have been seen as an attack from the Soviet Union. It was only his belief that Kennedy was weak and would fail to act that gave Khrushchev the confidence to agree to the deployment in Cuba. Khrushchev believed he could dance with Kennedy long enough for the missile to become operational and once that happened, Kennedy would see it as fait du accompli and do nothing. A lover of chess, Khrushchev knew it was a risky move, but the Soviets did not have many pieces left to play. The mission to deploy Soviet nuclear weapons in Cuba was code-named "Operation Anadyr."

There was another reason Khrushchev agreed to the deployment. He saw the Cuban missiles as a bargaining chip. Although Cuba was important, Khrushchev saw Berlin as the key to securing the western front of the Soviet bloc. If America's resistance to the missiles was greater than Khrushchev and his advisors expected, Khrushchev could negotiate the removal of the missiles in exchange for West Berlin and the removal of missiles from Turkey and Italy. Khrushchev knew it was a big ask to include everything that he wanted in exchange for the Cuban missiles, but he also knew that the Americans would see the missiles so close to their homeland as a titanic threat.

Khrushchev believed he could bully the young Kennedy into overtrading to keep America safe. The key to increasing the value of the missiles as a bargaining chip was to make them operational. While under construction, the missile sites were subject to aerial bombardment by the Americans. After they became operational, they became much more of a current threat and would deter any bombing by the Americans. The bigger the threat to America, the bigger the value for removing the missiles. West Berlin and the enemy missiles in Italy and Turkey were more strategically important to the Soviets than Cuba. Khrushchev would trade away the missiles if necessary.

One month later, Khrushchev and Castro reached an agreement on the deployment of the Soviet missiles on Cuban soil. Both knew it was a risky move that would raise American ire which could trigger an invasion of Cuba or worse… start World War III.

Shortly thereafter, a team of Soviet engineers landed in Havana and were escorted to the proposed missile sites. Plans were drawn and construction began. As part of Khrushchev's plan, anti-aircraft batteries and ground-to-air missiles were installed in a defensive ring around the new missile sites. Those batteries would become operational before the first intermediate-range missile was placed on its launch pad to prevent the Americans from destroying the sites and missiles with aerial assaults. Once the launch site was completed and the nuclear missiles arrived by truck, it would take the Soviet team less than a day to make the nuclear missiles operational. Caught off-guard by the swiftness of the Soviets, the Americans would be faced with a nuclear attack on the US mainland if they attempted to destroy the sites.

Bien Hoa Air Base, South Vietnam

Coyle was doing a preflight check before a supply mission to the Central Highlands. Walking across the tarmac, Granier approached. "What are you doing all the way out here?" said Coyle.

"I just got word from our operative in Hanoi. Bian's father is alive and being held Hoa Lo Prison," said Granier.

"How sure was he?"

"Very. He found a former prisoner that had been released recently. He knew Captain Hoang well and talked with him many times while they were incarcerated together. There are also five other officers that fought for the French being held at the prison."

"That's good news. I'll get my plane ticket for Paris and

go see Bruno right away."

## Buon Ma Thuot, South Vietnam

Hanson's Disease or Leprosy as it was more commonly known as a contagious and deadly disorder if left untreated. Like many indigenous tribes in southeast Asia, the Montagnard cast out those that came down with the disease. It wasn't to be cruel or because they were superstitious. It was the only way they knew to stop the illness from spreading among their people. Medicine was still primitive in most areas of the Central Highlands where the Montagnard lived. Hospitals and clinics were almost nonexistent. With nowhere to go for treatment, the lepers formed colonies that were supported by the surrounding tribes with food and supplies.

Buon Ma Thuot had one of the largest leper colonies in the Central Highlands. And it was there that the Christian and Missionary Alliance had decided to dedicate its resources. Twelve doctors, nurses, and missionaries were assigned to the Buon Ma Thuot Leper Hospital. The hospital was a converted longhouse built on pylons to allow air to flow beneath the building and cool down the interior. It also kept the hospital from flooding during the monsoon season. Dr. Eleanor Ardel Vietti was placed in charge of the facility and was assisted by Dr. Archie Mitchell and Dr. Daniel Gerber. The remaining nurses and missionaries helped with the chores and tended to the patients of which there were hundreds.

When the hospital first opened, the facility was flooded with patients seeking medical attention. Some could be helped and some were already too far gone. Amputation was a common event that dealt with the symptoms in what seemed a cruel and barbaric manner. It was however effective and saved many lives of those that had wasted away for years.

Morning coffee was the highlight of Vietti's day. She loved it, especially when combined with fresh milk from the colony's water buffalo. As the director of the hospital and the only female doctor, the village elders, also stricken with the disease, had given her a hut to call her own. The owners of the nearby coffee plantations donated a large bag of coffee every month to the American team. Every morning, the village women ground the coffee beans by whacking them with sticks on rocks, their primitive version of a mortar and pestle, until the beans were pulverized into a dark brown powder.

Having been cultivated by the French, Vietnamese coffee from the Central Highlands was on par with the world's best coffee. Vietti treasured the few moments she stole before work to sit on a stool in front of her hut and watch the villagers prepare their family's breakfast. She smelled the morning fires and the starch from the boiling rice mixed with the heavenly aroma rising from her coffee mug, her only possession from America beyond her stethoscope and medical bag. The coffee mug was crude in appearance with a light grey glaze covering the inside and a sky-blue glaze outside. She had made it during a college pottery class and carried it with her wherever she was stationed. A few hairline cracks had formed over the years, but it didn't leak and that was all she carried about.

She was born in Texas and had a twin sister and younger brother. She graduated from medical school at the University of Texas. Each year she flew back to America to visit her family and receive more training. During her last visit a month ago, she learned how to repair cleft palates. Cleft palates were not related to leprosy, but there were several untreated cases of cleft palates among the Montagnard. In her mind, the more she knew, the more she could help. At thirty-four years old, she had been in South Vietnam for more than five years far beyond the time she had signed up for originally. She missed her family and her home in Texas, but she couldn't just leave. There were too many that needed her, and she loved to be needed more than anything. It gave her life meaning and purpose. She had grown to love the hill tribesmen she served and while she saw their methods as cruel sometimes, she tried not to judge them too harshly. They were innocent savages after all. Like Jesus, she loved them despite their shortcomings.

Life was simple in the colony. There was nowhere else to go. Because they treated lepers, she and the other Americans were not welcome in the other villages. People kept their distance, even the family members of the victims. Even though the American doctors assured them they could prevent the illness from spreading, the Montagnard didn't understand the disease beyond its physical manifestations which were often disfiguring, turning people into monsters. It was better to be safe and keep those inflicted and those that treated them away. Out of sight. Out of mind.

Several weeks earlier, a wounded Viet Cong soldier had stumbled into the village. The elders wanted to kill him, but Vietti talked them out of it and made them promise not to alert the ARVN outpost nearby. It was a bullet wound that had barely missed the soldier's liver. She removed the bullet and stitched up the wound. She gave him antibiotics to fight the infection that she was sure would form.

The next morning, he was gone. She was relieved in a way. The ARVN could be very vengeful when they found any villagers helping the Viet Cong. She wasn't worried for herself but knew that others could be in danger, including the other Americans on her team. While she prayed he would fully recover, it was good that the wounded soldier had left. She had done what she could for him, but he was safer in the jungle… and so was her team.

When her coffee was finished, she made her way to the longhouse and had breakfast with the other team members while discussing the progress of patients and any items that needed to be dealt with such as a shopping trip to the city. There were plenty of volunteers. The team was young and a shopping trip to a city usually allowed time for dinner at a restaurant and maybe even a movie. It wasn't much, but it was better than staying in the colony. Vietti never volunteered to go. She figured a meal at a restaurant and a movie would just remind her of what she was missing and only make her more homesick. In her mind, it was better to avoid civilization whenever possible. It kept her mind on her work and the people that needed her.

Late that afternoon, Vietti was being assisted by Dr. Gerber and Dr. Mitchell as they operated on a young girl with a cleft palate. Her mother had brought her to the hospital and then left, not wanting to be exposed to leprosy. Vietti wondered if the mother would return but decided to operate anyway. The little girl deserved the best life she could live no matter how her parents felt. It was a successful operation that give the girl a more natural-looking face with a small scar below her nose. Certainly, nothing to prevent her from having a normal life. As they were finishing up, they heard yelling outside the hospital. The nurses took over care of the patient. Vietti, Mitchell, and Gerber headed outside to see about the commotion.

Fear struck the American doctors as they looked out the front door and saw a platoon-sized unit of Viet Cong entering the colony. They were armed and not in the mood for any resistance from the colonists. Afraid of leprosy, they threatened to shoot anyone that came close to them. They continued to advance until they arrived at the foot of the steps leading up to the hospital entrance. Vietti saw the wounded soldier she had helped next to the unit commander. The soldier pointed at Vietti and said, "That's her."

"You will come with us," said the commander pointing to Vietti and the other two doctors.

Vietti's Vietnamese was basic, but she understood and could communicate. "What do you want with us?" said Vietti.

"You come, now."

"No. We have work to do here. Our patients need us."

The commander pulled out his pistol and aimed it at Vietti. "You come or I kill you," he said.

Vietti was fairly sure she understood what had happened. The wounded soldier had survived and now the Viet Cong wanted the American doctors for themselves. "I don't think you will kill me. If you have wounded men, you can bring them here and we will treat them. But come at night, so the ARVN will not see you."

The commander ordered six of his men to fetch Vietti and the two other doctors. They marched up the stairs and grabbed them by the arms. She struggled and kicked at them. Gerber tried to free his arm from a soldiers' grasp. The soldier pushed him away, then hit him in the face with the butt of his gun. Gerber fell to the floor, his nose broken and bleeding.

There was more shouting at the far end of the village. The elders had gathered the young men and were advancing on the rear of the Viet Cong. There was roughly an even number of combatants on both sides, but the Viet Cong were better armed with rifles and pistols. The villagers only had their hunting bows, spears, and a couple of pre-WWI muskets. The villagers would lose if a battle broke out. Vietti could see it plain as day. She didn't want the people she had grown to love to suffer. The two sides faced off and the commander leveled his pistol at the lead elder. "We'll go," she said. "It's our choice. We'll go."

"You come?" said the commander.

"Yes. We need to get our medical bags and some medicine. Is that okay?"

The commander nodded and signaled the soldiers that had grabbed them to follow the doctors inside. A nurse was tending to Gerber as Vietti and Mitchell gathered their bags with as much medicine and supplies as she could carry. "Dr. Gerber, are you okay?" said Vietti.

"I'll live," said Gerber.

"Good. Can you walk?"

"Yeah, but I'm not so sure this is a good idea."

"Do you have a better one that doesn't involve our patients being shot to bits?"

"No."

"Neither do I," she said then turned to the head nurse. "Martha, you are now in charge. Tell the church council what has happened. We will be back as soon as we can. Do you understand?"

"Yes. May God watch over you."

"I'm sure he will. Our work doesn't stop even if it's the enemy we're aiding. We are all God's children."

And those were her last words to her team as she headed out the front door to the hospital with the other two doctors in tow. They said brief goodbyes to the villagers and elders, then joined the Viet Cong. Vietti stopped next to her hut and asked to go inside for a moment. The Viet Cong commander nodded his approval. She went into her hut and came out with her coffee mug wrapped in a shirt and her Bible. She tucked both into her medical bag and joined the other doctors. Moments later, they disappeared into the jungle. The other nine missionaries and nurses were left behind unharmed and continued their work as best they could.

Dr. Archie Mitchell and Dr. Daniel Gerber were never heard of again and presumed dead. Although there were reports in the early 70s of a white woman living with the Viet Cong and preaching Christianity to them, Dr. Eleanor Ardel Vietti was the only American woman unaccounted for when the Vietnam War ended.

June 6, 1962 – West Point, New York, USA

A sea of graduates wearing white caps, grey tunics, and white trousers with burgundy belts listened as President Kennedy addressed the crowd at West Point. He was their commander in chief and they hung on his every word. He was the one that would determine the wars they would fight during their military careers. He, more than anyone, would determine if they lived or died.

Kennedy had thought long and hard about what he wanted to say to these young officers to start them off on the right foot like the cadence that had controlled their marches during their time at the academy. He decided to instill in them his emphasis on counterinsurgency and said, "This is another type of war, new in its intensity, ancient in its origin — war by guerrillas, subversives, insurgents, assassins, war by ambush instead of by combat; by infiltration, instead of aggression, seeking victory by eroding and exhausting the enemy instead of engaging him. It requires a whole new kind of strategy, a wholly different kind of force, and therefore a new and wholly different kind of military training."

Kennedy believed that the modern wars they would fight would require a rethinking of the battlefield and the enemy. They would no longer stand toe-to-toe with the enemy. They could no longer depend on superior firepower and airpower to carry them to victory. It would take more than that. It would mean going after the enemy in his territory, his jungle, his swamps, and his mountains. It would require uncommon bravery and dedication. To put themselves in harm's way and to fight until they had won, never giving an inch, never giving up.

Kennedy didn't want to send these young men into Southeast Asia or anywhere else where they could be wounded or killed so far from home. They were the best America had to offer. He had been one of them. He knew the sacrifices they would face. And yet, sending them was his highest duty… to protect America and democracy from the expansion of communism. The price would be blood and many of these young men would be asked to pay that price. He shuttered at the thought but would not back away from what was required of him. He, like them, would stand his ground and face the oncoming threat head-on. He would keep his promise to his fellow citizens. He would use these young men to keep America safe. He was proud of them and somewhat ashamed that he could find no other way to defeat the enemy. Vietnam would be his Waterloo. By the end of his presidency, he would commit sixteen thousand soldiers as advisors to the fight in Vietnam, many of which stood before him at that moment… listening to his every word.

## Ben Hai, North Vietnam

A five-truck North Vietnamese convoy escorted by an armored car and a jeep headed toward the city of Ben Hai near the demilitarized zone. It was a rainy night making it hard to see the road through the jeep's foggy windshield. The driver struggled to keep the vehicle's wheels out of the roadside ditch that was filled with muddy rainwater making it almost indistinguishable from the level ground around it. In the distance, the driver could barely make out the silhouette of a bridge. Two men stood in front of a barrier preventing vehicles from crossing to the opposite side. They were turning vehicles around as if there was a problem with the bridge or road. Turning to the dozing lieutenant in the jeep's passenger seat, the driver said, "Lieutenant, I think you need to see this."

"See what?" said the groggy lieutenant.

"I think they've closed down the bridge because of the rain. The river must be flooding. We gonna have to turn around and find another way across the river."

"We didn't have any reports about a detour when we left the base."

"That was three hours ago. It wasn't raining."

"Shit. I am gonna catch hell from the captain."

"What do you want me to do?"

"Stop for starters. I'll go see what is going on."

The jeep stopped and the convoy came to a halt. The lieutenant stepped out in the pouring rain and walked toward the two men. He couldn't see their faces under their hats. "What's the problem?" he said.

"Water level is too high. It's not safe to cross," said one of the two men.

The lieutenant walked over to the edge of the bridge and looked down the embankment. "What are you talking about? The water level isn't even close to the bottom of the bridge," said the lieutenant.

"We have our orders."

"And I have mine. Get out of the way. We're crossing."

"We can't let you do that," said the second man in English.

The lieutenant squinted his eyes straining to see in the dark. The second man tilted his head up so the lieutenant could see his European face. It was Conein grinning. The French American pulled a pistol from its holster and fired two shots into the lieutenant's chest. The officer fell dead in the mud.

Hidden along the roadside, Conein's paramilitary team opened fire with their machine guns killing the drivers and passengers in the convoy. A bazooka took out the armored car with a direct hit on its gun turret. It was over in less than twenty seconds. Completely surprised by the ambush, the North Vietnamese soldiers never fired a shot.

Conein moved to the back of the first truck, opened the tailgate, and climbed in. He used a flashlight to examine the cargo. It was filled with crates of ammunition. He examined the labels and found what he wanted. He used a crowbar to open three of the crates. Bullets were packed inside two cases, and mortar shells inside the third. He ordered his men to remove the contents and load them into three empty crates they had brought with them. "I don't understand why we don't just take the crates that the ammo and shells are in?" said one of the American soldiers.

"You don't need to understand. You're not in charge. You just need to do what you are ordered," said Conein.

"Yes, commander."

Conein realized he was being an asshole. The guy was

just curious. "Look, we don't want the PAVN to know we took their ammo and the shells. If they see three crates missing, they're gonna know."

"Okay, but won't they know when they see the crates are empty?"

"That depends on how well we do our jobs."

Conein opened his pack, handed out grenades to his team, and said, "Two for each vehicle. Make sure you put them next to the mortar crates. If you ain't sure. Open the crate and check. We go on my signal."

Once the grenades were in place and the crates of ammo and mortar shells were a safe distance away, Conein gave the order and pulled the safety rings on his two grenades. He tossed the grenades into the open mortar shell crate, jumped out of the back of the truck, and ran for cover along with the rest of his team. All seven vehicles blew up within seconds of each other. The secondary explosions in the back of the trucks shook the ground and lit up the rain clouds above. It was an impressive light show.

Conein checked his team to ensure nobody was missing or wounded. He gave the order to move out across the countryside. The light from the burning vehicles and the continuous explosions lit their way as they disappeared into a grove of trees.

Hue, South Vietnam

It took two days for Conein and his team to slip back across the border with the ammunition cases in tow. Once across, a waiting H-21 helicopter took them to Hue Citadel Airfield. Conein had secured an empty hangar to house the team during the next phase of the operation known as "Project Eldest Son." Several ARVN munitions' technicians were brought in to handle the mortar shells. Conein didn't like bringing in outsiders. He trusted his team. But the mortar shells required special handling and he figured it wasn't worth the risk of blowing everyone up.

The technicians removed the delay fuses from the 82mm mortar shells and sabotaged the fuses so that they would go off the moment they were fired while still in the mortar tube. The explosion would shatter the tube sending shrapnel into the enemy mortar team that fired it.

Conein's team worked on the bullets. The Viet Cong used a wide variety of rifles and machine guns. Some Chinese-made. Some Soviet-made. A large number of weapons had been captured from the French and South Vietnamese. Captured weapons were usually American-made or French-made. The problem was what type of ammunition should the team sabotage. Conein settled on two types of bullets – 7.62×54mm for the rifles and 7.5×54mm for the most common French-made machine guns. It wasn't a perfect plan, but it didn't need to be.

The team removed each bullet from its shell casing, poured out the smokeless powder, and replaced it with high-explosive powder five times more powerful than the factory powder. When a sabotaged bullet was fired, it resulted in the chamber exploding which sent the bolt back into the eye of the soldier firing the weapon killing him instantly. It was a quick but gruesome death.

Conein had been surprised when he originally heard Lansdale's plan. Lansdale was not out to demoralize or kill Viet Cong soldiers, although that was a side benefit to the operation. He wanted to undermine the Soviets and the Chinese by convincing the Viet Cong that the ammunition they had been sent was defective. The Soviets and Chinese took great pride in their munitions manufacturers and when the quality of their products was questioned by the Vietnamese, they took it as an insult. Lansdale hoped to create discord and thereby shatter the communist alliance. It was wishful thinking. It did, however, have a great demoralizing effect on the Viet Cong and North Vietnamese troops. Watching a friend's head explode from a bolt launched backwards had a chilling effect. The more of their comrades that were killed by the sabotaged ammunition, the more timid the Viet Cong became about firing their weapons.

When the sabotaged munitions were complete, Conein turned the operation over to SOG. It was the SOG operatives' job to uncover enemy weapons caches. Instead, of blowing up the weapons and ammunition, the SOG operatives would replace just one bullet or one mortar shell in the center of each case of ammunition. The theory was that the rebels would see one faulty bullet or shell in a case as poor quality control, whereas two bullets or shells meant sabotage.

Before the operation was ended, SOG operatives replaced 11,565 rifle cartridges, 556 machine gun bullets, and 1,968 mortar shells in Viet Cong ammunition caches. Many saw it as a great success while others saw it as a missed opportunity to destroy the weapons and ammunition that were killing South Vietnamese and American troops. In the end, with little evidence to show the results of the sabotaged munitions, the skeptics won the argument, and the program was shut down.

# A MOMENT OF CONSEQUENCE

## Da Nang, South Vietnam

It was just past midnight when Lieutenant Commander Dale Pierce walked down the gangplank of the USS Comorant, a Bluebird-class coastal minesweeper. The ship would take on supplies and fuel before returning to station off the coast of South Vietnam. Pierce was not a normal commander and the Comorant was more than just a minesweeper. He was an officer in Naval Intelligence and the Comorant had been remodeled and outfitted as a covert intelligence vessel spying on the North Vietnamese Navy and coastal facilities. He didn't have a lot of time and needed to report to his superiors. It was the kind of conversation best done in person.

Things were heating up between the US Navy and the North Vietnamese Navy. As part of Operation 34A, the Comorant had been tasked with finding evidence that the USSR and China were supplying weapons and supplies to the North Vietnamese, who were, in turn, sending the weapons and supplies to the Viet Cong via the Ho Chi Minh trail.

Minesweepers operating in coastal waters were routine and innocuous. Outfitted with sophisticated electronic surveillance equipment, the vessels were perfect for intelligence gathering. But somehow, the North Vietnamese had caught on to the American scheme and were becoming more aggressive against intrusions into their territorial waters. They didn't want to start a war with the US, but they couldn't just let the spying continue either. Their solution was intimidation.

Whenever the minesweepers approached North Vietnamese territory, DRVN gunboats would charge the essentially defenseless American vessels at high speed, then veer off at the last minute hoping to drive the US vessels off. It was a highly volatile situation.

Pierce walked to a dark warehouse on the pier and entered. Several CIA officers and Naval Intelligence officers were waiting in the cavernous room. Everyone was drinking coffee to stay alert. Pierce poured himself a cup and sat down. "Three more aggressive maneuvers in the past week," said Pierce. "One gunboat was less than three hundred feet off our bow. I thought for sure we'd ram him."

"Good thing you didn't," said a CIA officer. "We don't need the attention."

"Really?"

"We know it's a tough assignment, but the intel you are collecting is beyond value," said a Navy Intelligence officer.

"Beyond value? The lives of my men should be beyond value."

"And they are... but we have to keep things in

perspective. The US Navy cannot be seen as antagonizing the North Vietnamese Navy. We're not here to pick a fight… at least not yet."

"We should be allowed to defend ourselves in international waters."

"You are… as long as they fire first."

"And if they miscalculate and we ram them by mistake?"

"Your vessel is a lot bigger. I imagine they'll sink."

"Then what?"

"Out of sight. Out of mind. Just be careful of what you put in your report. This is a covert operation and needs to stay that way."

"Are you giving me permission to ram their vessels?"

"Of course, not. But bad things happen at sea. We just don't want to hear about it officially if they do. Do I make myself clear?"

"No. But I understand."

"Good. That's all that is required."

Pierce and the other minesweeper commanders knew it was only a matter of time until somebody made a mistake and hostilities broke out between the two navies. Pierce wasn't sure if that was what his American commanders secretly wanted. Eventually, it would be Operation 34A that would evolve into the Gulf of Tonkin Incident and the American Admirals and Generals would finally get their war.


Saigon, South Vietnam


Journalists in South Vietnam had uniforms. When in a city like Saigon, they dressed in white shirts with dark-colored ties and some even wore sport coats. Shirt sleeves were either short or rolled up with the shirt's top button open and the tie loose. Slacks were worn with a leather belt and dress shoes. In the countryside, foreign correspondents looked more like the soldiers they were reporting on with olive drab shirts and pants. A name tag was sewn above the shirt pocket. They didn't want to stand out in the countryside. They didn't want to become a sniper's target.

Twenty-eight-year-old David Halberstam sat in the Saigon New York Times office which wasn't much more than a few desks with phones and typewriters. No artwork on the walls beyond a few of the photographers' favorite black and white photos and a color photo of JFK in a frame. The telex that allowed him and other journalists to send their stories to the main office was set up in a separate room with reams of paper stacked against the wall. Messages from the main office and stories from other newspapers could be received on the dedicated machine that constantly clacked away chewing up paper like a hungry beaver. It was far from elegant, but it was efficient.

Halberstam had arrived in Vietnam earlier in the month with a simple plan – talk directly with the American military advisors to get the straight scoop on what was happening in the war. It was a great plan except that none of the advisors wanted to talk with him or any other reporter. According to their American commanders what they were doing in Vietnam was considered covert and not for public consumption. It was a cover up and revealing cover ups was the crème de le crème to journalists. But it wasn't easy in a country like South Vietnam where the president and his family had a dislike of foreign journalists. While they weren't seen as the enemy, they were close. Diem didn't understand the concept of free press and thought it was anti-productive to coddle the reporters. Better to just throw them out of the country if they created too much chaos. The foreign press corps was always walking a fine line while occasionally tickling the tiger when they thought a story was worth it.

Halberstam did not believe that confrontation was the best approach for correspondents to get their job done. Having been a foreign war correspondent in the Congo, Halberstam believed in legwork and research to uncover the facts. When he asked a question, it was usually backed with the specifics that he had already discovered and was therefore irrefutable. He wasn't afraid to mix it up with someone he knew was out-and-out lying to him, but he was also willing to give most of the people he interviewed the benefit of the doubt until he was sure of his details.

But on that day, he felt he was being stonewalled and it made him mad. He had asked for permission to board a helicopter and fly south to where he knew a large battle was unfolding. American advisors were with the ARVN troops and putting their lives at risk. It was Halberstam's job to report it, but the battle was in the middle of the Delta and there were few roads to the part of the country. Even if he could find a path to the battlefield, it was very risky to travel by road in the Delta where the Viet Cong controlled much of the territory. The only real way in was by helicopter flown by American pilots who were under the command of the American generals of MACV.

The phone rang and he answered. It was the embassy. He had requested to talk with the ambassador in hopes of making some progress. Instead, he got a secretary that informed him the ambassador was in meetings all day and unavailable. More stonewalling. He changed his tactics and stated what he was about to submit in a story to the New York Times. In fact, he didn't know what he was going to report, but he made it sound like a real story some of which would be considered derogatory to the American military effort. The secretary asked Halberstam to hold the line. A few moments later, Ambassador Frederick Nolting got on the phone and said, "Why do you journalists always look for the hole in the donut? When did you start hating your country so much you lost sight of the truth? I don't know what you think you're doing reporting crap like that, but I am sure your publishers will reject it once received."

"You might be right. But without additional facts about what is happening in the south, I have no choice but to stand by my story," said Halberstam.

"Who are your sources for such drivel?"

"You know I can't reveal that."

"Bullshit. You tell me or I'll cut you off at the knees. You will be banished from the US Embassy and all MACV missions."

"Look, Mr. Ambassador, I'm just trying to find the truth behind what is happening. If you think my information is wrong, then help me correct it."

The was a long silence on the phone. Halberstam knew he had overplayed his cards and was likely to be fired by his publishers. Ambassadors were powerful and not to be trifled with. "Alright. I'll arrange for you to get on a chopper. But if you report one falsehood, I will see you roast."

"I agree, Mr. Ambassador. That's only fair."

"Expect a call within the hour."

The line went dead. Halberstam sat in silence wondering what just happened. He felt bad that he had misled the ambassador. And he felt worse that it had worked to get him what he wanted. It occurred to him that the story he just made up might be true. He would follow up on the details as soon as possible.

Halberstam was part of the new generation of correspondents that would go against their own government in search of the truth that they believed needed to be revealed to the American public. His patriotism would be called into question repeatedly and those in power, including President Kennedy, would try to stop him from revealing what he knew to be true. The days of journalism supporting an American war no matter what was gone. Halberstam and other correspondents like him would hold American leaders to account no matter the consequences. Many would be thrown out of Vietnam by the Diem family unhappy with their stories. Right or wrong, it was a new era for American media. It was the first war to be televised on the nightly news.

July 1962 – Beijing, China

Known to be frugal, the Chinese pulled out all the stops and sent a Tupolev Tu-104 airliner borrowed from the Russians to fetch Ho Chi Minh and the North Vietnamese delegation that included Nguyen Chi Thanh. The Chinese wanted to ensure that the North Vietnamese understood their importance in the communist sphere. North Vietnam was a political beachhead and key to the expansion of communism into Southeast Asia. It was an impressive move, especially since China's aviation industry was fledgling at best and had no jet airliners of its own. Although the Tu-104 could hold over fifty passengers, the North Vietnamese delegation was small which allowed everyone to stretch out. For this Ho Chi Minh was grateful.

Ho had just turned seventy-two, far beyond the years of the average life expectancy of a Vietnamese. Age was quickly catching up with him. He could feel it in his bones and his organs. Everything ached. He refused to use opium to soothe his pain as many of his associates had secretly suggested. He wanted his mind as sharp as possible for whatever time he had left on earth.

More than anything before he died, Ho wanted to see Vietnam reunited and independent from foreign invaders. It was Vietnam's independence that concerned him as he headed for China once again. The Chinese had heavily supported Ho Chi Minh and the Viet Minh in their seven-year struggle against the French in the Indochina War. Chinese assistance never was given without strings attached. That was their way. Reciprocation was expected. The problem was what the Chinese thought was the fair value of the debt owed. It changed according to what the Chinese needed at the moment. The Chinese sent political advisors to reshape Vietnamese philosophies, so they conformed more to Chinese communism. China did not want another Russia, which it often disagreed with, on its southern border.

Ho knew the Chinese. He had first met Mao and many of the Chinese communist leaders in Paris where he was living as an exile many years ago. He had been found guilty of protesting against the emperor Bao Dai. Somewhat naïve and bursting with revolutionary enthusiasm, both Mao and Ho had yet to be confronted with the realities of running a country and successfully maneuvering the international political environment. With communism fervor in common, they became friends and greeted each other warmly over the years as each rose to power.

Up until now, China had given Vietnam substantial military and financial aid, preferring to let the Vietnamese fight the French and Americans. In the last seven years, China had provided 320 million yuan, 270,000 guns, 200 million bullets, 10,000 artillery pieces, two million artillery shells, 5,000 radio transmitters, 1,000 trucks, twenty-eight naval vessels, fifteen planes, and 1.18 million uniforms. Although they had no direct presence in Vietnam, the financial and military aid showed a substantial commitment from the Chinese who saw Vietnam as their little brother in arms.

When his plane touched down in Beijing, Ho was tired. He could not sleep on planes. He didn't trust them and hated air turbulence. The food that was served was a poor imitation of Vietnamese delicacies which he found unpalatable. Ho had been losing too much weight in the last few years. He was noticeably thin, and his skin was more translucent than usual. He didn't look healthy, and he wasn't. Only his smile and sense of humor put those around him at ease. He was still Ho even if he was fading away. Nobody looked forward to Ho's eventual death but there was no way to avoid it. They did their best to keep him healthy and constantly reminded him to slow down and take it easy. He didn't listen. Instead, he chided them that he wasn't dead yet and that he still had something to offer the revolution – his spirit. Even those who on occasion disagreed with Ho's policies respected him for all that he had done for Vietnam and the communist movement.

The plane taxied to the passenger terminal where there was a crowd of over 2,000 Chinese waving signs written in Vietnamese and waving Vietnamese flags. Ho looked out the window at them and smiled. He was sure the Chinese leaders had organized the welcoming committee. The mix of adults to babies and toddlers was the same formula his propaganda team used for foreign dignitaries when visiting Hanoi. It made good film for the newsreels played in theatres for the masses. It was a game nations played and he knew it well. Still, it was good that the Chinese leaders felt the need to try and impress the North Vietnamese delegation. Ho and his comrades were here to ask for much-needed help in fighting the war against the South. Ho would do whatever was required to secure what North Vietnam needed. Those were his roles now – diplomat and beggar.

The ramp rolled up and the door opened. Ho stepped out first. It was what the people expected, and he wasn't going to let them down. The crowd roared. Ho smiled and waved, then made his way down the stairs to meet the dignitaries sent to greet him and the rest of the delegation.

Mao was not there, nor did Ho expect him to be. Mao was far too busy running the world's most populace nation to greet Ho personally. Instead, he sent his best general, party leaders, and diplomats many of which Ho knew personally. But there was also an underlying reason for Mao's absence. As much as he loved his friend Ho, Vietnam was a small nation when compared to China. Mao could not lose face going to Ho. Ho must come to him.

After shaking hands and taking photos for thirty minutes, Ho and his delegation were escorted through the terminal to waiting limousines. They sped off with the crowd cheering even louder. Ho found it charming and hoped they didn't strain their voices too much. He appreciated their effort even if it was contrived.

The farther the limousines traveled the more Ho realized that the crowds standing and cheering along the boulevards went on for miles. He began to wonder if they were real.

That they were there to see him. He was a hero in his own country and often garnered cheers from crowds whenever he appeared. But why did the Chinese care about an old Vietnamese revolutionary? The only thing he could think of was that he and his Viet Minh had defeated a western power – the French and were now fighting the Americans. No Asian military had defeated a western power, not even the Chinese. The struggle in Korea had ended in a stalemate, not a victory. Without realizing it, Ho had become the face of the global revolution to expand communism and stand up against the west.

There was little question that Mao and the other leaders were responsive to their people. They desired stability and loyalty from the masses. Ho could upset their aspirations with just a few strong words during one of the many speeches he was sure to give during his visit. Mao and the others would not want to risk angering him. Ho wondered if he had more power to negotiate than he had previously believed. Perhaps he needed to revise his thinking and demand more for his country. He disliked the idea of manipulating his friend Mao, but he had his priorities straight and Mao's feelings were not high on that list. He would do what he needed to help his people and reunite his country.

Ho and his delegation met with key leaders of the Chinese politburo in a large conference room with a huge wooden table. Ho was told by Mao that these men were the officials that controlled the various departments of his government. Ho was surprised. There were almost a hundred of them. There were formal introductions which took almost an hour. Ho grew weary and rubbed his eyes. "Are you okay, Uncle?" said Mao concerned.

"I am fine. Just… old," said Ho.

"I understand. Perhaps we should dispense with the formalities, and you can tell us why you have come?"

"I don't want to be rude to your ministers."

"Don't worry. They understand. And they are very curious about what brought the great Ho Chi Minh all this way. As am I."

"You tease me."

"No, Uncle. We are all impressed with what you have accomplished with so little. We fought the Americans in the mountains and hills of Korea. We lost one million of our best soldiers. What you did with the French at Dien Bien Phu was truly a miracle. And now, your Viet Cong are doing the same to the Americans. You are making progress against the most powerful nation on earth."

"I am afraid that is why we have come, Comrade Mao. We are no longer taking territory in South Vietnam. We are losing it. The Americans have increased their number of military advisors and are using their air force to support the ARVN ground troops. But the biggest change is the American helicopters."

"Yes. They used them against us in Korea to great effect."

"Then you understand the danger. They have the ability to transport an entire company, even two if they wish. They can land their troops in multiple locations all at once and surround the Viet Cong. As of yet, we have not found an effective way to combat this new technology. They are crushing us."

"Surely you will overcome such obstacles given time."

"Time. That is the problem. If the Americans continue to make progress, we fear they will enter the war and end the North."

There was a collective gasp in the room. Followed by whispered conversations. "You believe this is possible that the Americans would invade North Vietnam?" said one of the high-ranking generals.

"No. I believe is it probable."

"When?" said Mao.

"It is hard to say, but my guess would be next year after the monsoons, perhaps the following year if we are lucky."

"Then there still time to stop them."

"With your help, yes."

"We cannot commit Chinese troops to fight in Vietnam. That would only aggravate your situation and possibly trigger the American invasion."

"I see," said Ho, disappointed.

"But we can offer you much more than troops. How many battalions could you field if you had the supplies and weapons?"

"I am not sure. I had not considered it," said Ho, lying. "Two hundred, maybe a few more."

"Would that be enough to stop the Americans?"

"Perhaps. Such an army would surely make them reconsider any plans of invading. But the Americans also have aircraft."

"And so did the French, but you defeated them anyway."

"We did. But we lost many soldiers in the process."

"As did we. But such is the price of war. It may be possible to convey a message to the Americans that we will stay out of any war as long as their aircraft do not cross the border between North and South Vietnam."

"Why would they agree to that?"

"We took a beating from the Americans in Korea. But they also took a beating from us. I do not think they are anxious to tangle with us again so soon. The threat of such a war may be enough to keep their air force out of the North."

"That would help our cause a great deal."

"I need to consult with my ministers and military commanders before making a firm commitment. But I can assure you, Vietnam is not alone in this struggle. We will support our little brother. The revolution will continue."

Before Ho and his delegation left China, North Vietnam had a firm commitment from the politburo – arms and equipment for over 100,000 PAVN soldiers. The Chinese would do whatever was needed to ensure their southern border had a communist neighbor.

Saigon, South Vietnam

On the patio of the Presidential palace, Diem paced in front of his brother Nhu and Madame Nhu. "How can they do this? He is the only American I trust," said Diem upset.

"Why are you so sure that Lansdale didn't request it?" said Madame Nhu.

"He wouldn't do that. Not without talking with me first. No, this is Kennedy's doing. I am sure of it."

"Perhaps you are right," said Nhu. "But isn't that a good thing?

"What do you mean?"

"If Kennedy is recalling Lansdale to Washington, he must have a good reason. Lansdale knows more about the situation in Vietnam than anyone. I imagine President Kennedy wants to take advantage of Lansdale's knowledge and experience."

"How does that help us?" said Diem.

"Lansdale may be a lot of different things. Some good. Some bad. But the one thing I have always been sure of is his support and loyalty to you, my brother. If Kennedy is bringing Lansdale back so he can become his advisor on Vietnam, it will only help you that Lansdale will have the president's ear."

"I had not considered that. But who will replace him?"

"As I understand it, command of the two paramilitary teams will be transferred by to the CIA station chief John Richardson. He is a competent man and believes deeply in our cause."

"But he is not an advisor. I don't trust the CIA."

"Nor do I. I do not believe we need an American advisor now that Lansdale will be leaving. Your family will be your advisor when it comes to dealing with the Americans."

"That is the way it should be," said Madame Nhu, pleased. "We should have a going away reception for

Colonel Lansdale."

"I agree. I need to show my gratitude. Please see to it," said Diem.

On the eve of Lansdale's departure, Diem and his family hosted a lavish reception at the palace. The entire American embassy staff was invited. Diem wanted to ensure that the Americans remained on his side as his biggest supporter was leaving. Lansdale arrived dressed in a new brigadier general's uniform. "You have been promoted," said Diem as he offered his hand in the reception line.

"I have. It will not be official until I return to Washington, but I wanted to give you a preview before I left," said Lansdale. "After all, you are the one most responsible for my success here in South Vietnam."

"I am sure it is well deserved. Congratulations, General Lansdale."

"Thank you, Mr. President."

"I am very sorry to see you go."

"As am I to leave. But I was not given a choice. The president asked for me."

"Then you are to become his advisor?"

"Not directly. But I imagine I will be called in from time to time to consult on important matters concerning Vietnam."

"That is a good thing. I hope you will remember us as your friends."

"How could I not?"

"I don't know who they may send to replace you, but I am sure he will not fill your shoes. No one could."

"That is very gracious of you, Mr. President."

"It is the truth, especially in the early days when things were so uncertain. Your guidance saved my life and my country, General Lansdale. I shall never forget that."

Lansdale choked up and decided to change the subject. "I hope you will write or cable if you ever feel you need my advice. I will always be there for you, Mr. President."

"I will, General. I will."

Pentagon, Arlington, Virginia, USA

When Lansdale arrived back in the states, he was once again wearing his Colonel's uniform. He did not want to overstep his bounds or seem presumptuous until his promotion became official. He was surprised when the secretary for General Curtis LeMay, the Air Force Chief of Staff, asked him to come to the general's office in the Pentagon the next morning. It was unusual for the Chief of Staff to ask to see a colonel without others present. Lansdale had met with LeMay several times during his tours of Vietnam. He wondered if it was to congratulate him on his promotion, but he suspected it was something else.

When Lansdale sat down with LeMay the next morning, the conversation started with a friendly tone. LeMay congratulated him on the promotion and asked where he and his wife might live now that he was back in the states. After a bit more chit-chat the tone of the conversation changed, "Colonel, I am sure you recognize that there is a great divide in responsibility between a colonel in the field and a general assigned to the Pentagon."

"Yes, General. I do," said Lansdale.

"You have been engaged in a clandestine battle for several years now. Your experience and knowledge of the situation in Vietnam surpass almost everyone above the rank of colonel, including myself. You got your hands dirty with great success."

"Thank you, General."

"We expect you to put that knowledge and experience to use here in the Pentagon and Washington. I think you will find that your knowledge will be in great demand. It's why we brought you back. You are to be commended, Colonel. That being said, I want to advise you on the minefields you will now face. In an ideal world, generals would stay out of politics and only plan and fight wars. But we don't live in an ideal world. It's unfortunate, but a reality."

"I am not sure I understand, General."

"No. You wouldn't. You can only learn by stepping into the arena. My only advice is don't forget where your loyalties lie."

"With America, General. Always with America."

"That's a bit broad, Colonel. Because of where you have served and with whom, you are about to be tossed around like a seal between killer whales. You and only you will have the power to decide whose plans you should support... and whose you shouldn't. That is a very dangerous position for a new general if you don't mind me saying."

"So, what should I do?"

"Your best, Colonel. Always your best but plan your landing well. Killer whales have sharp teeth," said LeMay standing to shake Lansdale's hand. "Congratulations again on the promotion."

Lansdale left LeMay's office wondering what had just happened. He wasn't sure if LeMay was trying to help him or threaten him. Perhaps both.

# BLACKJACK

## Hanoi, North Vietnam

Le Duan met with the Viet Cong leadership at a government building in downtown Hanoi. "Comrades, we understand your struggles against the American helicopters and warplanes. I assure you, our top military leaders are working on strategies that will defeat the American technologies just as we defeated the French," said Duan. "You have our complete support. More and more weapons and supplies will be transported to you as we expand the Ho Chi Minh trail through Laos and Cambodia. Uncle has assured me that the Chinese are sending their latest weapons to replace the obsolete World War II weapons you have been using. In addition, they are sending ammunition to resupply the American weapons you have captured from the South Vietnamese military. All this and more will help you fight on to victory."

"What about PAVN troops?" said one of the younger VC leaders.

"We will continue to send you advisors to train your recruits, but it is still not prudent to deploy our troops into South Vietnam. We must avoid all strategies that might draw the Americans further into the war. Our forces are not yet ready to fight them."

"When will you be ready?"

"Soon. We must receive the arms shipments from the Chinese and Russians. And we must train our new army before engaging in battle with the Americans. You have been patient. But we must ask you to wait a little longer so that we may be assured of victory."

"We have waited long enough. The south will fall if we push Diem and his government."

"Perhaps. But such a move could also trigger the Americans into entering the war with their own troops to support the Diem government. It is a risk we cannot take."

"You are cowards."

The other VC leaders shouted down their comrade, rebuking him for his rude behavior.

"I suggest you watch your tongue," said Duan. "I have been fighting for independence since before you were born. Now that it is within our grasp, I will not just throw it away because of a child's taunts. We all must be patient. Just as we beat the French, we will beat the Americans."

Paris, France

Paris was Paris. Even in the Spring, the sky was grey, and the shadows were flat. It was easy to take a good photo in

Paris. The sunlight was dissipated by the clouds and soft like a giant lightbox. And when it rained at night, the streetlamps reflected off the pavement filling the tourists' viewfinders with magic.

Sitting in the backseat of a taxi, Coyle was not a tourist. He had lived in Paris for four years after the Indochina War. He had flown for the French military in Algeria. Although he missed Paris, he wasn't thrilled with the idea of asking Bruno for help. They had been friends and comrades in arms until Bruno stole Bridget from Coyle. The bastard. Coyle wondered why he even cared now that he had Bian. He just didn't think stealing away a friend's woman was something men should do. But then again, Bruno was French and so was Bridget. It seemed like a very French thing to do. After all, Coyle was in Paris, and he had to make allowances.

The taxi stopped in front of the apartment building Coyle once called home. He paid the driver, grabbed his bag from the trunk, and headed to the lobby's front door. He still had a key and used it. Tired from the long flight, he used the wrought-iron elevator, known for breaking down at the most inopportune moments, to ascend to the third floor. He exited the contraption and walked to the apartment door. He froze. He wanted to punch Bruno in the nose if he answered the door, but that was a bad idea since he needed Bruno's cooperation to save Bian's father. He wondered what he would say to Bridget if she answered the door. Calling her a "backstabbing whore" was probably not a good idea either. Clearly, he needed to take the high road.

He had procrastinated long enough and realized it was going to be awkward no matter what he did or said. He pressed the ringer in the middle of the door. Five seconds later, the door opened, and Bridget flung her arms around his neck and said, "Tom, it so good to see you."

She kissed him on each cheek leaving lipstick marks that made him look silly. How could he hate her? It was Bridget, the woman he had loved and had asked to marry. "Hello,

Bridget," he said in a low voice. Even now, he thought of winning her back from Bruno. He couldn't help himself. She was his and Bruno had taken her. The bastard.

As if on cue, Bruno appeared pushing Bridget to one side, giving Coyle a bear hug, and kissing him on both cheeks. "Coyle, good to see you. Come in and let's have a drink," said Bruno as if he had done nothing wrong. The bastard.

Coyle entered and sat down in the living room that was once his and Bridget's. It had changed little. Bruno, who just as soon sleep on the ground as a bed, didn't care what the place looked like as long as Bridget was there.

Somewhere in the middle of the second round of Pastis, Coyle relaxed, and it seemed like old times; laughing, telling stories, and teasing one another as only good friends can do. Coyle let go of the pain and forgave them. Bruno and Bridget had loved each other long before Coyle had entered the picture. They had fought the Nazis together during the occupation. It was Bruno's womanizing that had driven them apart. But Bruno had settled down and lost interest in other women. Now, he only wanted Bridget. Coyle was a sideshow for the main event of Bridget and Bruno. He was intermission. An excuse to make Bruno jealous that allowed him to finally come to his senses. Coyle realized that he never really stood a chance. They were destined to be together. They were French.

Later that evening, while Bridget was cleaning up from the fancy dinner she had made them, Bruno and Coyle went for a walk. Bridget had bought a dog, a French bulldog with cropped ears, and made Bruno take it for a walk every night before bed and early in the morning before he was allowed to exercise or eat his daily raw onion. To Coyle, it seemed like the dog had to pee every ten feet and shit on every lawn. Bruno just ignored the little critter. The French did not clean up after their animals. One had to watch where one stepped.

Coyle did not want Bridget to know about the mission.

Even though she loved both men at one point, she was a famous war correspondent. Her journalistic instincts and quest for fame often overruled her personal feelings. She could not be trusted to keep the mission a secret. Coyle felt slightly ashamed deceiving Bridget, but he needed to keep Bian and her father safe.

After the second dog shit, Bruno asked about Coyle's love life as Coyle knew he would. Bruno was not coy about such things and tended to blurt out whatever was on his mind. "So, are you still fucking the Vietnamese woman?" said Bruno.

"Her name is Bian," said Coyle annoyed.

"Do you have a photo?"

"No. I don't actually."

"Small tits, yes?"

Coyle just shook his head in disgust. "It's a legitimate question," said Bruno.

"I love her. That is all that is important."

"Well, I wouldn't say "all…""

"Get your mind out of the gutter, Bruno."

"No, no… that is where my mind belongs. It is very comfortable there."

"I'm not going to argue that point."

"You would be wise not to. So, Bian… where did you meet her?"

"I was choking on an aspirin in a coffee shop, and I drank her water."

"Subtle."

"No. Not really. But I got lucky. I ran into her again at the Royal Palace. She works there as a translator."

"Nice. You are a kept man then?"

"No. It's not like that."

"Not like what? There is nothing wrong with having a rich woman take care of you."

"For you maybe. We Americans see the world differently."

"Your loss. Did you ever figure out why she was lying to

you about her father?"

"Yeah, I did. You were right. He was captured by the Viet Minh and imprisoned in Hanoi."

"Ah, yes. So many were. Did they release him when the war ended?"

"No. He's still there."

"Why? That makes no sense."

"Bruno, what I am about to tell you has to stay between you and me. Not even Bridget can know. You have to give me your word."

"Alright. I promise."

"The North Vietnamese threatened to kill Bian's father unless she became an undercover intelligence operative."

It took Bruno a few moments to process what he had just been told. "And she now works at the Royal Palace?" said Bruno.

"She's Diem's personal translator," said Coyle.

"Holy shit. That's some prize for the North Vietnamese."

"Yeah."

"And you haven't told anyone?"

"No. If I do they will kill her and her father."

"A big pickle, yes?"

"A very big pickle."

"So, what are you going to do?"

"I don't know. My first inclination was to figure out a way to break the father out of prison."

"In Hanoi?"

"Yeah."

"Maybe it could be done."

"But even if I break him out and return him to South Vietnam, Diem's brother Nhu will kill Bian once he finds out she had been spying for the North Vietnamese."

"So, maybe you come with Bian and live in France?"

"She won't leave her father and I doubt her father will leave Vietnam. He's a patriot."

"I see. You have a problem, my friend. The solution is

simple.”

“What’s that?”

“You must kill the father.”

“I’m not going to kill the father of the woman I love, Bruno.”

“It would solve your problem. The North Vietnamese would lose their hold over Bian and Nhu would never find out she was spying for the North Vietnamese.”

“I’m not going to do it.”

“I could do it for you.”

“It’s a nice offer, but no.”

“What are friends for if they can’t kill someone for you every once and a while?”

“Did you get dropped on the head when you were little?”

“I don’t know… maybe. My mother was very clumsy.”

“I have half an idea of how I may be able to save Bian and her father, but I am still missing a few pieces.”

“I’m listening.”

“The way I figure it, Nhu will not kill Bian if he thinks she has vital information or that she is still useful. Maybe as a double agent.”

“Would she be willing to do that? …become a double agent?”

“Yes, once her father is out of danger.”

“But why would the North Vietnamese believe that Bian would continue to spy for them if her father is free?”

“Exactly. That’s the problem. But if they killed her father and didn’t reveal his death to her, they would believe nothing would have changed from her perspective and the information she is giving them is still viable.”

“So, you are going to fake the father’s death?”

“Yep. And the North Vietnamese have to believe that they killed him during his escape.”

“You have a very clever mind, Coyle.”

“Yeah, well… you won’t think that in just a minute.”

“There is a problem?”

“Yeah. Why would Americans break her father out of

prison?"

"Good question. I am sure the North Vietnamese will ask that."

"And there is another problem. If the North Vietnamese see that it is Americans breaking the father out of prison, they will assume that the Americans will tell Bian when her father was killed."

"Yes, yes. Of course, they will. And they will believe they no longer have a hold on her."

"Yep. And she can't be a double agent."

"So, what are you going to do?"

"I don't know. I have been racking my brain trying to find a way to make it all work and I keep hitting the same roadblocks."

Bruno considered for a moment, then asked, "How do the North Vietnamese guards know that you and your team are American?"

"I'm white and tall."

"Many nationalities are white and tall. The Russians are white and tall."

"Why would the Russians break a Vietnamese captain out of a North Vietnamese prison?"

"Yes. I see your point. Why would any nation want to break a Vietnamese soldier that fought for the…?"

It took Bruno a few moments to piece it all together. "You son of a bitch. You want me to break out her father because I am French."

"…and a well-known war hero," said Coyle. "When the North Vietnamese see that it is the infamous Bruno Bigeard breaking the father out of the prison, they will believe it is a covert French operation."

"You are very sly and manipulative, Coyle."

"Not really, but I have my moments."

"And why would I do such a thing?"

"Two reasons. The first is French honor. Bian's father fought for the French. It is your duty to free him now that you know he is still a prisoner."

Bruno grunted, "And the second?"

"You owe me. You stole Bridget, Bruno."

"I did not steal her, Coyle. She chose to go with me."

"You know, I imagine it has been eating away at you all these years."

"It has not. I sleep very well at night."

"Bullshit."

"If I do this, it is because of French honor, not because of Bridget."

"Alright."

"The North Vietnamese diplomats are sure to make a fuss. I'll probably be arrested once I return to Paris."

"Probably. But I doubt the French politicians want to see a war hero go to prison. The people wouldn't stand for it."

"No, they would not. The people love me."

"You'd probably be more popular than ever when they find out what you did."

"Perhaps," said Bruno falling silent for a few moments. "I will do it."

"For French honor?"

"Of course. But we'd be square on the Bridget thing too, yes?"

"Yes," said Coyle with an easy smile. "We would be even."


Border Mountains, Laos


High in the mountains near the North Vietnam and Laos border, SOG Sergeant Rivera, aka "Blackjack," sat with a group of Montagnard warriors. Gathered around a small fire, they were sharing a pipe, each taking a hit then passing it on to the man sitting next to them. When it was Blackjack's turn, he considered faking his toke on the pipe but knew that the warriors would probably see through his ruse and call him a pussy in their native language. As their leader, he could not afford to be thought of as a lesser man.

He took a deep pull on the pipe and watched the substance in the bowl glow red. Whatever the burning contents, he felt it immediately and his eyes rolled back for a moment. He was lost somewhere else… in his past… hunting boar with his older brother. The warriors smiled. They liked it when the Americans participated in their rituals, especially their leader.

Blackjack lay back and closed his eyes. He wanted to dream. He hadn't seen his brother in years. A distant bang woke him from his malaise. The enemy? Were they under attack? He grabbed his submachine gun, rose to his feet, and headed toward the noise. The warriors grabbed their weapons and followed the American into the surrounding jungle. They moved in silence, careful to avoid any dried leaves or fallen branches that might give away their position. Their eyes always surveyed the ground for tripwires and booby-traps. They heard laughing and voices in English.

Blackjack stepped into the clearing where he found a teenage Montagnard on the ground, motionless, with two of his team members standing over him. "What in the hell did you do?" said Blackjack.

"It's okay. He's not dead, just unconscious," said corporal Singer, a Navy Seal and the team's heavy weapons specialist.

"How is that okay? What happened?" said Blackjack kneeling to check on the young warrior.

"I was testing how much C4 it took to knock a man unconscious. After offering him some beef jerky and a pack of cigarettes, young Nung volunteered," said specialist Butler, the team engineer and explosives expert.

"Are you out of your fucking mind? You could have killed him."

"No way, Blackjack. We tried it on a pig first. He's fine."

Nung started coming around as the other warriors gathered in a circle. Nung laughed and held his head to stop the ringing in his ears. "See, no problem," said Singer.

The other warriors asked Nung what had happened.

There was a quick conversation followed by several young warriors stepping up to Butler to volunteer. "So, how much did you use?" said Blackjack.

Butler held up his thumb and said, "About half a thumb."

The SOC team had been given a grab and snatch mission originated by the CIA stationed in the American Embassy in Saigon. A covert Vietnamese agent in the north working as a typist in a military command center had discovered that a logistics captain stationed in Hanoi had been reassigned to the 559th Transportation Group in Laos. The 559th had 6,000 soldiers tasked with maintaining and expanding the Ho Chi Minh trail. The CIA believed the NVA captain knew a mountain of information that could be extrapolated to better define the North Vietnamese Army and its capabilities.

Blackjack knew it was a long shot that they would even find the captain as he headed down the trail to his eventual station at the end of the path. The Montagnard spies in the enemy camps would help with intelligence, but it was still a long shot. The Ho Chi Minh trail was thousands of miles long and had redundant branches all heading in the same direction. The team needed to figure out a way to grab the captain with minimal risk. As much as Blackjack hated to admit it, Butler had found the way.

When word came that an exhausted Vietnamese captain with huge blisters on his feet was heading their way, Blackjack was intrigued. The captain he was searching for had been working in an office and would not be accustomed to long marches. The captain was part of a platoon escorting a convoy of fortified bicycles loaded with weapons and supplies. He was not the commander of the unit and therefore appeared to be tagging along. Blackjack decided to strike the convoy on the off chance this was the guy he was looking for.

The ambush team was made up of six American SOG soldiers and twenty Montagnard warriors. They would be outnumbered, but not outgunned. The SOG team was heavily armed and the Montagnard had been given the latest American weapons with plenty of ammunition. And, of course, the team had the advantage of surprise on their side. Their goal was not to kill the North Vietnamese soldiers or even destroy the convoy but to capture the captain. If the convoy was destroyed or the enemy soldiers were killed during the ambush that was a bonus. Montagnard hated the North Vietnamese soldiers and loved killing them. The feeling was mutual.

Blackjack decided to set up the ambush on a trail that the North Vietnamese had been using for the past month. There were four parallel trails in the immediate area that the convoy could use, but the Americans knew that the North Vietnamese tended not to switch trails unless they were compromised by the enemy, washed out by a storm, or blocked by an avalanche. Since none of those events had happened on this trail, Blackjack felt the odds were good that the enemy convoy would use the current trail.

Butler set up his charge just off the side of the trail. The blasting cap he was using was almost as powerful as the explosive. He would trigger the explosion manually using a small plunger-type detonator that he always carried in his rucksack. He made sure the explosive was well hidden and used a half-buried boulder to direct the explosion toward the trail. He unspooled the wires attached to the charge and led them deeper into the jungle where he would be hiding as the convoy passed. He rechecked the wires to make sure they were well hidden and would not be tripped over should a North Vietnamese scout walk along the side of the trail before the convoy arrived. Butler tested the detonator by wetting his fingers and placing them on the terminals. He gave the detonator a short plunge which sent a painful shock through the terminals and into his fingertips. He hated that part of his job but recognized the necessity of it. Satisfied the detonator was working, he attached the wires and signaled Blackjack that he was ready.

The rest of the team took up positions on the same side of the jungle as Butler's position. Blackjack didn't want any of his team or the Montagnard killed or injured in the crossfire. He placed a few men up the trail in blocking positions in case the North Vietnamese attempted a breakout from the ambush. He also sent scouts down the trail to warn the team when the convoy was approaching. Once everyone was in position, Blackjack did a final check, sat down next to Butler in the jungle. Now came the hardest part… waiting.

It was late afternoon and clouds were gathering overhead for a pour. Rain would reduce the enemy's visibility and help hide the ambush. Just as the first drops pelted the leaves in the tree canopy above, a scout gave a signal that the convoy was coming. The ambush team tensed and hunkered down behind whatever cover they had chosen – a boulder, a tree trunk, an ant mound, or just a simple dip in the jungle floor. Their faces and bodies were camouflaged. Motionless, except for their eyes which probed the surrounding jungle for the enemy. They were invisible.

The scouts appeared first, North Vietnamese elite troops trained to spot booby-traps and ambushes. They found nothing and pressed on. Butler had done his job well. Next came the point man armed with a Fusil-mitrailleur Modèle 1924 M29 machine gun, a weapon captured from the French at Dien Bien Phu. He was followed by five soldiers carrying rifles.

The ambush team held their fire and kept hidden. The detonation of Butler's explosive was the signal to open fire. Butler and Blackjack examined each enemy soldier that emerged from the jungle trail. There was no sign of the captain.

Ten bicycles were next up the trail, each loaded down with 400 pounds of weapons and supplies. The bicycle frames were reinforced with iron rods and bamboo poles. Wooden side panels and saddlebags over the back tires were lashed with ropes and old bicycle innertubes to hold the cargo in place. Once loaded, the porter who supported and pushed the bicycle from the middle was unable to reach the handlebars so bamboo steering poles were lashed to the ends of the handlebars extending their reach. The weapons and ammunition were the heaviest loads and usually pushed by men, while women pushed bicycles loaded with rice, uniforms, and medical supplies. Flat tires and bent rims were common. Every porter knew the basics of bicycle repair and carried simple tools with spare parts. They would pull off to the side of the trail to repair damage to the bicycles. The convoy kept moving. Stragglers were defenseless until they caught up with their comrades and the North Vietnamese forces escorting them. The porters learned to repair their bicycles quickly.

As more and more of the convoy passed by the ambush team and the danger grew. Once the enemy soldiers passed the ambush position, they became a potential flanking force. The men that Blackjack had sent up the trail would not be able to hold them off for long and could be killed, wounded, or captured. Although Blackjack did not want to risk the lives of his men unnecessarily, he was mission-focused. The SOG and the Montagnard took great pride in accomplishing the tasks given to them by their commanders. Blackjack counted the enemy soldiers as they passed. If there was only a platoon as an escort, there were more soldiers up the trail than those that had not appeared. It was not an ideal situation.

Blackjack was considering not executing the ambush when the captain finally appeared through the jungle. The enemy officer was limping badly from the pain of his blisters and his uniform was drenched with the sweat of a man unconditioned. He looked miserable and exhausted. Sure that this man was their target, Blackjack exchanged a glance with Butler who also knew the danger of enemy soldiers up the trail. Blackjack considered for another moment as the captain approached the hidden explosive device. Blackjack nodded to Butler giving him the go-ahead. As the captain walked past, Butler pushed the plunger.

The explosion was more of a loud thud than a violent boom. The pressure wave hit the captain in the back of the head, knocking him cold. He collapsed on the trail. The ambush team opened fire mowing down the visible enemy soldiers. Bicycles crashed down spilling their cargo, as the porters ran for their lives disappearing into the jungle away from the firefight. Once the clearing was free of enemy troops, Butler and Blackjack ran forward, grabbed the unconscious captain by the arms and legs, and pulled him into the jungle on their side of the trail.

Blackjack knew that it would only be a matter of moments until North Vietnamese soldiers up and down the trail would flank his team on both sides. He wasn't going to give them that advantage. He had what he wanted. He ordered his men to fall back to the rendezvous point he had designated before the battle. The Montagnard were brave and disciplined. They leap-frogged backward into the jungle, an organized retreat that kept the enemy at bay. The Americans hurled grenades at the enemy soldiers that appeared within range. It was a strong deterrent. The North Vietnamese broke off their pursuit once they recognized that their convoy was no longer in danger.

For the Montagnard, it was another victory and Blackjack owed them a pig for their fires. The captain awoke a few minutes later, his hands and feet tied to a pole carried by two Montagnard. He would be carried to the Montagnard outpost, given a short rest and some food, then begin the long journey to the closest airfield. From there, he would be flown to a command center where two CIA officers would interrogate him, asking the same questions repeatedly to ensure his answers remained the same each time. Even though it was only logistics, the information he gave them filled out the picture of enemy forces throughout North Vietnam.

# A CHANGE OF COURSE

## July 12, 1962 - Washington DC, USA

In the west wing of the White House, Bob McNamara sat at his desk reading a cable from General Harkins. McNamara had learned to take Harkins' optimism with a pinch of pepper and a grain of salt. He knew to gauge Harkins' comments – if it was bad news, it was worse than the general reported, and if it was good news then it was exaggerated. The latest report on his desk stated that Viet Cong assaults, terrorist attacks, and incidents of sabotage had fallen from 550 to 350 per month and the number of Viet Cong defectors had risen. McNamara loved data. His associates at Ford Motor Company, where he had been president before joining Kennedy's cabinet, joked that if he ever cut himself, the chads from punch cards would fall out instead of blood. Harkin told McNamara that once the ARVN and Civil Guard had been fully trained and could effectively operate in the field, the Viet Cong presence in South Vietnam could be eliminated within twelve months.

Concerned about the public's perception of the growing number of US casualties, it was exactly what McNamara wanted to hear — the end of the war for America. And McNamara wasn't the only one that believed America was winning in the fight against communist expansion. Most Americans believed that non-communist South Vietnam was becoming stable and independent and that the United States should continue to support it. Even the New York Times reported that South Vietnam was "a struggle this country cannot shirk" and that America seemed to be winning the war. America was drinking the Pentagon Kool-Aid like a camel at an oasis. Americans loved to win and applaud their leaders when they delivered victory.

Bien Hoa Airbase – South, Vietnam

Originally designed for electronic countermeasures, the AD-1Q Skyraider was used by the 1st Air Commando Squadron to train South Vietnamese fighter pilots. Standing beside the aircraft, USAF Lieutenant Dean Adams coached his student, VNAF Lieutenant An Huynh on the aerial deployment of napalm. "Each MK-77 canister holds 110 gallons of the Napalm fuel gel mix and will spread over an area of up to 2,500 square yards. Anything or anyone in that area will be incinerated. The biggest difference in dropping napalm canisters rather than conventional bombs is that you can drop them at a much lower altitude and therefore be far more accurate in your targeting. There is no need to dive-bomb. The napalm ignites on impact with the ground or any hard object such as a tree, building or the ground. By flying low and horizontal over the target area, the napalm canister will break open and spread the incendiary liquid in whatever direction you are flying. So, when you line up your attack run you want to drop the canisters ahead of your target and let inertia carry the napalm to the target," said Adams wondering if Huynh understood a word he was saying. "Are you getting all this? It's important stuff. You don't wanna be killing your own guys."

Huynh nodded enthusiastically. Adams was still unsure but figured he could show the lieutenant what to do in the cockpit during their practice bombing runs. "Alright. The best way to learn is by practicing. Let's mount up."

Adams climbed up first and slipped into the backseat. Huynh followed and climbed into the pilot's seat in front. Huynh was already a trained pilot and went through the process of starting the engine and taking off without any help from Adams.

Once airborne, Adams directed Huynh to an unpopulated jungle twenty-three miles west of the airbase. The American pilots had often used the area as a practice bombing range. A nearby village was paid a monthly fee by the Americans for keeping people away from the area. "Do you see that little clearing off to one side of the grove of trees?" said Adams.

"Yes, Boss," said Huynh.

"That's your target. Remember, you need to drop your canisters in front of the target, not on it. You'll fly fast and low. No more than one hundred feet off the canopy. Once you've made your drop, you can turn to see how you did. You got it?"

"Yes, Boss."

As ordered Huynh banked the plane and lined up his run. The trees below were a blur as they passed underneath the Skyraider. Huynh dropped a canister fifty feet in front of the clearing. The canister disappeared through the canopy of trees, then exploded in a huge wall of flame that stretched one hundred and fifty feet through the jungle. Huynh was already turning the plane when the explosion occurred. He laughed and gave a whoop. "Good job," said Adams.

The jungle was an inferno. Everything was consumed by fire. As they passed over the area, a water buffalo broke from the trees. He was completely engulfed in flames and running blindly. "Ah, shit," said Adams appalled by the suffering of the animal.

Huynh laughed and said, "Good barbeque."

"Don't be an asshole, Huynh. That's somebody's rice bowl. Some poor family is not going to be able to plant its fields."

"They farmers. They not important."

"Shut the fuck up and put the damned beast down."

"I not understand."

"Kill it."

"Yes, Boss."

Huynh once again banked the plane and lined up his shot. As the Skyraider approached the water buffalo, Huynh squeezed the trigger. The four 20mm autocannon stitched the ground in front of the animal kicking up clods of dirt and rock, then blew the water buffalo to pieces. Its agony was over. "We go again?" said Huynh.

"No. You've had your fun. We're done for the day," said Adams. "Head back to base.

Disappointed and confused by the American's anger, Huynh turned the plane east and headed toward the airbase.

## July 16, 1962 – Saigon, South Vietnam

A Vietnamese man wearing black pajamas and carrying a rifle walked up to the lobby doors of the American embassy on Ham Nghi Boulevard. He laid down his weapon on the sidewalk and raised his hands as if surrendering. A few moments later, American marines opened the door, pushed him to the ground, confiscated his weapon, and searched him. They found nothing except a letter in English addressed to President Kennedy. Under heavy guard, they brought the man inside the embassy and the doors were once again closed.

Ambassador Nolting sat at his desk with the letter in his hand. He was deep in thought. He checked his watch it was almost 4 pm in Saigon which meant it was only 5 am in Washington DC. The president would still be sleeping, but Dean Rusk, the Secretary of State, would be awake and probably on his way to the White House. The contents of the letter were important, he considered using the phone to make a long-distance call but decided it would take too long and was not secure. He scribbled a message on a paper and headed to the secured telex room. He rarely went into the room where coded messages were sent, but on this occasion, he wanted to make sure the message was sent immediately, and he would wait in the room for a reply.

## White House - Washington DC, USA

JFK and Jackie were still asleep when Wilson Roosevelt Jerman, the president's butler, quietly entered their bedroom. He walked softly to the side of the bed and said, "Mr. President?"

There was no response. Jerman gently touched the president's arm and said again, "Mr. President?"

Kennedy awoke. He was groggy and said, "Wilson, what time is it?"

"Five forty-five, Mr. President. Secretary Rusk has asked to see you. He says it is important. He is waiting in your sitting room."

"Of course. My robe?"

Jerman held the president's robe as JFK rose and slipped into it. "Did he say what it was about?" said JFK heading to the door.

"No, Mr. President," said Jerman. "I will bring in some coffee."

"Thank you, Wilson."

JFK sat on a sofa across from Rusk and read the telegram. He looked a bit confused and said, "A Viet Cong soldier walked into our embassy with this letter?"

"After being thoroughly searched, of course," said Rusk.

"I should hope so. Do you think this is real?"

"I don't know. I suppose I do."

"The Viet Cong want a ceasefire?"

"Yes, Mr. President. Followed by the creation of a coalition government pending elections. South Vietnam would become a neutral country like Cambodia and Laos. No western or eastern support."

"Why did they bring this to us and not President Diem?"

"That had me a bit puzzled too. But it sort of makes sense. Diem might never show us the letter if it is not in his best interest. This way, the Viet Cong know that we read it. They'll want us to withdraw our advisors before the coalition government is activated. They need us to cooperate."

"...and put pressure on Diem."

"I would imagine that was their intent."

"What does Nolting think?"

"He's like me, skeptical but hopeful."

"I can't look like I'm negotiating with the communists."

"I understand, Mr. President. The negotiations will have to be back-channeled until we have confirmation that a deal has been struck."

"Tell Nolting to show the letter to Diem immediately. We don't need any more problems with him and his family."

"Yes, Mr. President. Should Nolting send a reply to the Viet Cong?"

JFK thought for a moment, then… "Tell Nolting to confirm to the Viet Cong that he received and read the letter, but nothing else. We need Diem to take the lead on this."

"And if he doesn't… take the lead?"

"Let's jump off that bridge when we come to it. Oh, and tell Nolting well done."

"Yes, Mr. President."

Presidential Palace - Saigon, South Vietnam

Diem was furious when Nolting delivered the Viet Cong message the next morning. "This is an obvious hoax," said Diem.

"I'm not sure it is, Mr. President," said Nolting.

"Why else would they deliver such a message to you and not me if it is not a hoax?"

"I don't know, Mr. President. I suppose they wanted us to read it."

"Has President Kennedy seen this?"

"Not the letter, but he was informed of its contents by secure telegram."

"Why would you discuss it with him before talking with me?"

"Mr. President, you know I respect you. But I work for President Kennedy."

"We are winning the war. Of course, they want a

ceasefire. These people have no respect. They should know their master," said Diem exasperated.

"What should I tell, President Kennedy?"

"Tell him whatever you wish, Mr. Ambassador. After all, you work for him."

## Valley of Ben Tuong – South Vietnam

Beginning with a pilot program in the Mekong Delta, the strategic-hamlet program was a counterinsurgency strategy in rural Vietnam. It gathered the Vietnamese population into fortified hamlets. As a key element in the program, the government would undertake political, social, and economic measures designed to gain popular allegiance through improved local services and better security.

By mid-March, Diem had ordered the expansion of the Strategic Hamlet program nationwide. Unlike the Americans who saw the program as a way to deny the Viet Cong recruits from the villages and to earn the trust of the people they were protecting; Diem saw the program as a way to control both non-communists and communists. Political leaders and spies inside each hamlet would report on any troublemakers or government naysayers. Brother Nhu's security squads would do the rest to weed out the Viet Cong and their sympathizers. Both the Viet Cong and ARVN compared the strategic hamlets to fish barrels where all the fish were gathered in one place for easy harvesting. Unable to invade the villages at night and gather supplies and recruits, the Viet Cong suffered. Recruits would need to sneak out of the strategic hamlets on their own without the encouragement of a VC bayonet. The number of enemy recruits dropped dramatically.

It was late summer when five American helicopters swooped in and landed next to a village near the Ben Tuong Valley. A company of ARVN troops disembarked and surrounded the village. The villagers were terrified. The village elders came out to talk with the company commander and were informed that the villagers were to pack their belongings. The entire village would be leaving for their new home – a strategic hamlet in a nearby valley. Each villager was given twenty US dollars as a relocation compensation fee.

Within the hour, the entire village of 221 men, women, and children along with their livestock was escorted away flanked by armed ARVN soldiers with orders to detain anyone that resisted or tried to flee. As an added incentive, the AVRN commander ordered the village torched. Black smoke rose over the village as the huts, mangers, and fences burned to the ground. The reeds having turned brown just before harvest, the rice fields were also set ablaze. There would be no returning to the village and farms that once were. It was all gone and so were their crops. To survive, the villagers would need to depend on the government to supply them food until the next harvest.

More than four million people living in the countryside, one-third of the population of South Vietnam, had been evicted from their villages and transported to strategic hamlets. Most of the farmers were angry at being required to abandon the fields they had harvested for generations. Families were forced to leave behind the graves of their ancestors. The program had the opposite effect desired by the South Vietnamese government and the Americans. With each forced eviction, Diem and his family became more unpopular and the Viet Cong grew in number.

September 11, 1962 – Saigon, South Vietnam

Deep inside the American embassy, key military advisors gathered to brief General Taylor, Chairman of the Joint Chiefs of Staff and Kennedy's most trusted military advisor. Taylor had flown in the day before and after a good night's sleep was anxious to get to the bottom of what was going on in the war against the Viet Cong. He and McNamara had read the reports from MACV – Military Assistance

Command Vietnam. Earlier in the year, MACV had taken command of MAAG which commanded most of the military advisors in Vietnam. Taylor had been sent by the president to figure out a strategy moving forward. In Taylor's mind, the reports and requests for additional military aid didn't match up. If South Vietnam was winning the war, why did they need more aid?

There was a consensus among many of the advisors in the field that General Harkins was not telling the entire story of what was happening in South Vietnam. He was conveniently leaving out the bad news and pumping up the good news. It wasn't exactly a lie, but it was close. According to Harkin, South Vietnam was winning the war against the Viet Cong and the military advisors would soon be recalled back to the United States. Taylor had requested that the military advisors from each of the ARVN areas of operation in South Vietnam attend the briefing and be given time to speak about what was happening from their point of view. Harkin didn't like the idea as he saw many of the advisors were caught up in the minutia and unable to see the whole picture. But he complied and brought the advisors in from the field to offer their points of view.

Somewhere during the middle of the briefing, Lieutenant Colonel Vann was asked to speak. Unlike most of the other advisors who did not want to raise Harkin's ire, Vann had decided to speak the truth and let the chips fall where they may. "Look, I only know what is happening in my neck of the woods," said Vann. "From where I am sitting, we are losing the war. And we are going to continue to lose it until we change course."

Taylor leaned in, interested in hearing what the young colonel had to say. Harkin was noticeably irritated. Vann went on, "General Harkins is correct in that we can win this war. Once trained and equipped with modern weapons, the ARVN are good fighters, but they have to be led by solid field commanders. The concept behind the fortified hamlet was to protect the local villagers from Viet Cong attacks and prevent the Viet Cong from recruiting young men. The problem is the Viet Cong own the night in the Mekong Delta. When attacks do occur, it is usually in the middle of the night and the commanders of the local ARVN forces refused to send units until the next morning. While it looks like cowardice, it is common sense. If the ARVN did send forces at night, there is little doubt they would be ambushed by the Viet Cong. In addition, most of the farmers are angry that they forced to uproot their lives and abandon their ancestors' graves to live in a hamlet. The modest amount of money we give them to relocate is of little consolation. The whole program is having the opposite effect from what it was originally intended. By forcing the villagers into hamlets, we are driving them into the arms of the Viet Cong."

"I think that is a limited view from a narrow part of the country," said Harkin. "The Mekong Delta where the Colonel is stationed is a hotbed of Viet Cong activity and is not representative of other areas where the hamlet program has been a great success."

"I understand," said Taylor. "But I would like to hear what the colonel has to say just the same."

"Of course. Colonel, please continue your list of grievances."

"Our air force bombs villagers indiscriminately whenever the ARVN commanders call for support. The ARVN commanders almost without exception will call in for air support before they ever send troops into suspected enemy villages. The results are that innocent villagers are killed with each air assault. A bomb doesn't distinguish between an enemy soldier and a child," said Vann.

"That is an exaggeration, Colonel," said Harkins, angry.

"With all due respect, General… no it is not. I have seen the results and it has turned my stomach. Every time we bomb a village, the people turn against the ARVN and join the Viet Cong. It's how they are growing so fast. Seventy percent of the Mekong region is now under Viet Cong control. They are going to continue to grow until we wise up."

"You would have the ARVN send in troops before air support is granted?" said Taylor.

"Absolutely, General. If the ARVN send in troops and the troops come under fire, then I say bomb and shell the hell out of the enemy positions. The ARVN need to feel that we support them and the villagers need to keep the enemy out of their villages or face the consequences."

"I see. What else?"

"The ARVN troops that I advise want to fight for their country. But most of the units are poorly led at the battalion level. It's demoralizing. When promotions are only given when the right bribe is paid, soldiers lose hope that they will ever advance in rank, no matter how brave they fight. That policy has to stop before we lose the entire South Vietnamese military. Rank should be awarded through merit, not bribes to their commanders or loyalty to the Diem family."

"We have discussed that particular problem at length. There is no easy solution," said Taylor.

"You've got to find one if we are going to turn this thing around."

"Colonel, do you still believe we can win this war?"

"If we turn things around and develop an effective strategy, then yes. We can win. Most ARVN soldiers respect their American advisors more than their own commanders. But we have to lead them, and we have to use discretion on when and where to use our technology to defeat the enemy. We can win. I'm sure of it."

Harkins squirmed in his chair. Vann had embarrassed him with the truth. He was not happy.

Taylor was impressed with Vann's observations and somewhat hopeful in the colonel's assessment that the war could be won. He felt the same. The Viet Cong were not boogiemen. They could be defeated if the right strategy was developed and if the South Vietnamese government cooperated.

September 12, 1962 - Houston Texas, USA

It was the development of the ballistic missile that drove humanity into space for the first time. The space race between the United States and the Soviet Union began on August 2, 1955, when the Soviets responded to the announcement that America would launch artificial satellites. The USSR would also launch its own satellite. The Soviets won the first leg of the race by launching Sputnik 1 on October 4, 1957. Just two months later, America responded by launching Project Vanguard on December 6, 1957. It was an epic failure. The American rocket exploded a few seconds after launch. The explosion appeared on the front pages of newspapers around the world with headlines like Flopnik, Kaputnik, Dudnik, and Stayputnik. To rub salt in the wound, the Soviets offered the Americans aid under their program for technical assistance to backward nations. That was a mistake that solidified American resolve. While the Soviets were laughing, the Americans got to work.

The Redstone team of Wernher von Braun's team got the go-ahead to launch their Jupiter-C rocket as soon as possible. The Jupiter rocket was based on the US Army's Redstone rocket. On January 31, 1958, the four-stage Juno I rocket was launched at Cape Canaveral. When the final stage achieved orbit, it released Explorer 1, a thirty-one-pound satellite holding instrumentation that proved the existence of the Van Allen radiation belt above Earth's magnetic equator. Within two months, the Americans launched a second satellite with more instrumentation to measure cosmic rays.

It looked like the Americans had caught up to the Soviets until April 12, 1961, when the USSR launched the first human, Yuri Gagarin into orbit around the Earth. It was heavy blow to the American space program.

Beneath a blue sky scattered with puffy white clouds, Kennedy sat on the stage deep in thought as the president of Rice University in Houston, Texas introduced him. When Kennedy had spoken to Congress five months previously, he knew he was taking a risk that might once again embarrass America if the program he announced failed. And yet, Kennedy believed that Americans could achieve great things if they focused their energy on one nation-inspiring objective – putting a man on the moon. Although somewhat inspiring, his speech to Congress was more about budgets and the mechanics of the moon program. He felt it fell short of conveying why he felt a moon mission was so important to America and the world. On that day at Rice University, he hoped to find the words that would inspire a nation.

Kennedy was slightly nervous but also enthusiastic. He was caught up in his own dream of excellence. The applause snapped him out of his thoughts and into the moment. He rose and walked to the podium. After thanking all the dignitaries that were on the stage with him and cracking a few jokes for the crowd of students, Kennedy said, "We choose to go to the Moon. We choose to go to the Moon in this decade and do the other things, not because they are easy, but because they are hard, because that goal will serve to organize and measure the best of our energies and skills, because that challenge is one that we are willing to accept, one we are unwilling to postpone, and one which we intend to win, and the others, too. It is for these reasons that I regard the decision last year to shift our efforts in space from low to high gear as among the most important decisions that will be made during my incumbency in the office of the Presidency."

The crowd roared and Kennedy finally had his moment. It was inspiring. The nation fell in line and focused its best efforts on reaching the moon before the end of the decade.

Kremlin - Moscow, Russia

On reading a translation of Kennedy's speech, Khrushchev realized that while the Soviets still had a few tricks up their sleeves, there was no way they could keep up with the Americans with their man-on-the-moon program. It was too much. Too expensive. Only America with its vast financial resources had the potential to reach the moon. Khrushchev's only hope was that the Americans would fail. They didn't. In fact, so many new inventions were created from the moon program that America leapt ahead of the rest of the world in scientific achievement and computer development. The continued development of the integrated circuit created massive American technology industries. Technologies that benefited the American military and civilians throughout the world. The moon program helped make the United States more formidable than any time in its brief history.

## Saigon, South Vietnam

Hanging out in the bars and lobbies of Saigon's luxury hotels was common for foreign journalists. Not only was it a sanctuary from the ever-pressing throng of Vietnamese that lived and did business in the streets of the capital, but it was also a way to keep track of the comings and goings of advisors, businessmen, and diplomats. High-ranking officers shirking their officer's clubs where they were forced to mix with lower-ranking officers, often gathered in the lobbies of the best western-style hotels, especially when meeting with embassy staff or diplomats. The Hotel Continental and Hotel Majestic were the most popular, mostly because of their patio and rooftop bars. A reporter could always count on a proper cocktail and a variety of whiskeys. The beer was always served cold, except for the British who requested it be served tepid, and each table had a bowl of peanuts or chips which provided the only nourishment for many of the journalists on many days.

Refusing to give up his quest, Halberstam once again approached a small group of American military advisors sitting at a table on the Majestic's rooftop lounge and said, "Good afternoon, gentlemen. David Halberstam, New York Times. Would any of you care to comment on–"

"Fuck off. You know we can't talk to journalists," said an Air Force major.

"Of course, you can. You're American citizens. You have the right of free speech."

"We're U.S. military. We don't have rights," said a captain.

"The American public wants to know what's going on here."

"No. They really don't. They want to be safe and free. They want two cars in their garage, a backyard swing set for their kids, and a lawn that they can mow on weekends. That's our job and we are doing it," said the major.

Halberstam glanced at the third soldier at the table who refused to say anything or even make eye contact. Halberstam decided to back off and said, "Alright, gentlemen. You win. Thanks for your time."

He walked off to the bar and ordered a gin and tonic. Nursing the drink for a few minutes, Halberstam avoided looking back at the officers but waited patiently. The silent officer walked to the bar and bought a pack of cigarettes. When the bartender turned to get the cigarettes, the officer said quietly, "Do you have a phone number?"

Halberstam didn't question the request. He just scribbled his number on the back of a napkin and slipped it to the officer who pocketed it. The ice had cracked, and persistence had prevailed.

Later that afternoon, Halberstam received a call from the officer. He was willing to talk off the record and answer Halberstam's questions if he knew the answers. Halberstam suggested they meet. The officer refused. Anything he had to say could be done over the phone. Halberstam was about to mention that the phone line could be tapped by South Vietnamese security forces but decided not to reveal the potential danger. He would settle for an over-the-phone interview. Halberstam had his first American military advisor willing to talk and hopefully reveal what was happening behind the military curtain. The officer refused to give any personal details about his assignment, but Halberstam could see that he was Air Force, so he asked about Farmgate. "We're flying over a thousand missions a month, mostly air support for ARVN ground operations in the Mekong Delta and the Central Highlands," said the officer.

"You mean the ARVN are flying the missions with American advisors in co-pilot seat?" said Halberstam.

"That's a joke. The ARVN trainees are lucky if they have a seat in the cockpit. They're window dressing in case we crash. American pilots are flying the missions."

"So, you're not training them?"

"They can learn by watching but that's about it."

"And the targets?"

"Viet Cong. The targets are legitimate… most of the time."

"What do you mean most of the time?"

There was a long silence on the phone after Halberstam's follow-up. "Sometimes we target villages occupied by Viet Cong."

"How do you know Viet Cong are there?"

"Intelligence… if you can call it that. Plus, the VC in the villages fire back when we pass overhead."

"Couldn't it just be villagers firing back trying to protect themselves?"

"I suppose it could be. But where did they get their weapons? We don't know exactly what is happening below when we're flying missions. We have to trust others to ensure the targets are legitimate."

"Do you think you have ever been ordered to kill innocent civilians?"

"Who is innocent in this mess? Viet Cong have children too and when they grow up they become Viet Cong."

"Do you think you have bombed children?"

"… and pigs and chickens. When we drop our bomb load on a village everything goes up in flames. We don't get to pick and choose who lives and who dies. That's not how it works."

"You said everything burns."

"That's right."

"Are you dropping napalm on villages?"

There was another long silence, then… "You're not using my name in your story, right?"

"I don't know your name."

"Right. You're right. You don't know me."

The line went dead. The interview was over. Halberstam had pushed it too far, but he wasn't sorry he had done it. The truth needed to be revealed. He knew he had a major story on his hands, but he couldn't publish it without confirming the details in the interview. It had taken him several months to find someone to talk to. He couldn't imagine waiting another couple of months to get someone to confirm the story. He decided on a shorter route. He called Neil Sheehan.

After hearing Halberstam's notes from the interview, Sheehan agreed to ask his military advisor contact, Colonel Vann, if the details were true. Halberstam wanted to be there when the questions were asked. Sheehan refused. He had worked hard to win Vann's trust. He wasn't going to introduce him to a competing journalist. Halberstam understood and admitted he won't do it either if he had someone like Vann. He would settle for Sheehan asking the questions.

Sheehan waited until he and Vann had returned from another mission. As they disembarked the helicopter and walked back to Vann's office, Sheehan broached the subject of the interview and asked Vann if would consider confirming the details if he could. "Look, Sheehan, I'm not some pussy flyboy dancing around the truth. If I know, I'll tell you. But keep in mind, I can get my ass canned for revealing shit like this. Then where will you be?"

"I won't quote you directly. You're just confirming the details of the original answers for the journalist's questions," said Sheehan.

"Who is the journalist?"

Sheehan was hesitant, then said, "David Halberstam of the New York Times."

"Halberstam? He's a good journalist. I've read his stuff."

Sheehan had never considered that Vann would ask the journalist's name and wondered if he had just given up Vann to Halberstam. "Ask your questions? I'm hungry and I want to hit the base chow line before they close for the evening."

"Okay. So, the way this works is you just speak up if anything I say is wrong," said Sheehan.

"Yeah, yeah. I didn't just fall off the turnip truck yesterday. Get on with it."

Sheehan went through the interview notes point by point. Vann said nothing. In fact, Vann was so silent, Sheehan wondered if he was still paying attention when he reached the last point. "Are you still with me?"

"I'm walking right next to you, Sheehan. Of course, I'm still with you."

"I mean the story."

"I know what you meant. You said to speak up if anything was inaccurate. It ain't."

"Have you witnessed this stuff firsthand?"

Vann stopped walking and turned to Sheehan. "What did you think was going on out there in the countryside? You've seen what we're facing. We don't know who the good guys are and who are the bad guys. There is no way to tell the difference until it is too late and you have a bullet in the back of your skull. When in doubt we drop a bomb or call up an arti strike. It's the sad truth of war, but it is the truth. Everyone needs to grow up and put on their big boy pants. We are in a fight for our lives."

Vann continued toward the mess hall. Sheehan stood dumbfounded. Halberstam had his story.

Royal Palace – Saigon, South Vietnam

Sitting down to a formal dinner in the Royal Palace, General Harkin talked with President Diem and his family in between bites of a melt-in-your-mouth lamb shank navarin followed by a decadent pastry ring of Paris-Brest and Vietnamese coffee. "You cannot expect to win the war against the Viet Cong with your army sitting in its barracks or outposts. You must attack, attack, attack. Get the Viet Cong running and keep them running," said Harkin.

"General, with all due respect, our military's primary mission is to protect our cities and capital. The cities are what matter most. These skirmishes in the countryside are of little consequence," said Diem.

"I don't understand how you can say that when seventy percent of your population live outside the cities in areas that the Viet Cong control."

"That number is an exaggeration," said Brother Nhu.

"I won't argue the point except to say the South Vietnamese civilians living under Viet Cong control are significant in number. But it is also the way you choose to fight. When they finally do muster their men from their barracks, your generals prefer large-scale sweep operations using multiple battalions. Such operations can hardly be kept secret and rarely encounter the enemy."

"Our troops are safer in large operations where they can dominate any enemy they encounter and use artillery and air power to soften the enemy positions," said Diem.

"And get the general's names in the newspaper," said Harkin.

"Perhaps. But beyond the headlines, my generals have their priorities straight – preserve our forces in preparation for the coming invasion from the North."

"That invasion is already here, your excellency."

"And we are fighting it in our way."

"The North is choosing not to engage your forces. You must deploy smaller-sized units to attract the enemy, then bring in American firepower to destroy them."

"We will not allow the Viet Cong to slaughter our troops," said Madame Nhu. "They must survive to protect President Diem and his government."

"General, we are winning the war and we will continue to do so until the enemy is vanquished from our lands. Every day our forces are getting stronger and more aggressive. To save our country and its people, we must continue on our path, no matter what our American advisors admonish," said Diem.

Harkin was exasperated and knew he had little chance of convincing Diem while he was surrounded by his family. The South Vietnamese government had dug in their heels. They were immovable. The Americans would need to find another way to fight the communists in Southeast Asia.

## White House - Washington DC, USA

When National Security Advisor Walt Rostow and Chairman of the Joint Chief General Taylor returned from a two-week tour of South Vietnam, the tone of their conversations with President Kennedy had changed dramatically. Neither Rostow nor Taylor believed the South Vietnamese could win the war on their own even with America's financial support. "Diem is not promoting officers based on their performance, but rather their loyalty to him and his family," said Rostow.

"It's not just demoralizing to the ARVN troops, it's dangerous. Incompetent leaders are being elevated into high positions commanding large portions of the military and major areas of the country," said Taylor. "Diem has colonels that have never seen combat in charge of brigades. If there was ever a recipe for failure, Diem is following it hook, line, and sinker."

"So, what are you suggesting?" said Kennedy.

"We need to change the relationship between South Vietnam and the United States," said Rostow. "It needs to be less about advice and more about a limited partnership."

"You are talking about putting our troops on the ground."

"We are," said Taylor. "It's the only way to win at this point."

"And if we are not going to commit troops, we need to consider pulling out before things get really bad and America is blamed for the fall of South Vietnam," said Rostow.

Kennedy considered their advice for a long moment, then said, "I have always said that the South Vietnamese can only win if it's their war. They are the ones that will need to rule their country when we finally leave. They will never value their freedom unless they are forced to fight for it. I'm not putting American troops on the ground in Vietnam. It's a slippery slope and once we start, I feel it will be impossible to stop the demand for more and more troops."

"Then pull our military advisors and pilots out. Diem has been given plenty of ultimatums and he refuses to listen to our advice. We shouldn't have our men in harm's way unless we control them."

"I can't pull out. Promises have been made. I swore to defend our country and allies against communism. If we pull out the world will see it for what it really is – a failure to meet our commitments to our allies. American global influence will tumble, not to mention what will happen here in the states."

"It will be by far better for America if we pull out now rather than be part of the downfall of South Vietnam," said Rostow.

"You don't know if that will happen, Walt."

"It's gonna happen, Mr. President. Believe me, it's gonna happen."

"I agree," said Taylor. "Diem may be able to fight off the communists for another year or so, but he will fall eventually. His own military is turning against him."

"Do you think his generals will try another coup?" said Kennedy.

"I don't know. Maybe. There's a lot of infighting. That's for sure," said Rostow.

"Look, we are stuck between a rock and a hard place. Diem can't win and we can't leave. I am willing to substantially increase our military aid commitment and our number of military advisors to train the ARVN troops if that is what it takes," said Kennedy.

"I don't think more weapons or advisors are going to make a difference if Diem and his generals continue to take the defensive," said Taylor. "There needs to be a fundamental change to what is happening on the ground."

"Alright. So, we need to convince Diem to change his strategy," said Kennedy.

"We've already tried that many times, Mr. President. It doesn't work. His family has him convinced that he is winning the war. He's not. But it doesn't seem to matter while he is under their influence."

"So, let's work on kicking Nhu and his wife out. I'm all for that. We could threaten to end financial and military aid until they leave the country."

"I suppose that might work," said Rostow. "But it's risky. It's really gonna piss off Nhu and Madame Nhu. There is no telling what they will do or say. These days they are more in control of the day-to-day operations of the country than Diem."

"Well, we've got to do something. Let's start with that."

"Yes, Mr. President."

"I'll talk to Nolting and see what he thinks," said Kennedy. "In the meantime, you two come up with a suggestion for military advisors required to train all of South Vietnam's forces and new weaponry that can make a real difference. Anything short of nuclear warheads is on the table."

"More armored personnel carriers might help the ARVN commanders be more aggressive if they know their men are protected," said Taylor. "The APCs are impervious to small gunfire and the Viet Cong still only have a few armor-piercing weapons that can stop them.

"Well, that's something to hang our hat on. Give me your recommendation and let's get that plan in motion."

"We could also change our policy on military advisors not directly engaging the enemy. If they are allowed to shoot at the enemy, they can take more of a command role in the field. Most of the ARVN troops seem to be willing to follow our advisors more than their own commanders," said Rostow.

"Alright, but I want to keep any policy changes in the field away from the American press. The American people do not need to know our advisors are taking a more active role in the war. Not yet anyway."

Hanoi, North Vietnam

Le Duan had arranged for his first wife, Le Thi, to take their children to visit their grandparents. He wanted some time alone with Suong. Surprised, yet grateful for the romantic gesture, she prepared a dinner of Duan's favorite dishes — pig feet soup with potatoes and carrots, braised and caramelized catfish, egg rolls, and, of course, rice. After dinner and a glass of ruou can, Le Duan guided Suong into the bedroom and made love to her. When finished and glistening from sweat, Le Duan turned to her and said, "We need to talk."

"Well, you've had your way with me. Go ahead," said Suong.

"The ethics committee has suggested a new mandate that would prohibit polygamy. A man will only be allowed one wife starting at the beginning of next year."

"Okay, but that won't apply to us, will it?"

"Why won't it? We are no better than anyone else."

"You are the leader of the party. Surely you can see there is a difference?"

"Perhaps. But setting a good example is paramount."

"You are going to break up our family over a mandate?"

"It's not what I want. It is what must be done for the good of the nation."

"That's bullshit."

"Suong, you know I love you."

"Then you have already decided who is to go and who is to stay?"

"There is no decision. Le Thi is my first wife and the mother of my children."

"Will you divorce me?"

"Yes."

"When?"

"By the end of the year. You will be given another place to live and will be well taken care of. I will see to it."

"You stupid man. If you should have learned anything from our time together it would be that I can take care of myself. I will go back to my home in the hills."

"I cannot allow that. You will be the former wife a first secretary. Our soldiers cannot properly protect you in the hills."

"I don't need their protection."

"Suong, the revolution cannot risk you being captured or kidnapped. You know too much."

"So, that's it? You're not worried so much about my welfare as much as the secret I hold?"

"There are some in the politburo that have expressed that concern."

"Get out of my bed."

Le Duan complied and left the bedroom. Suong fought back the tears. She wasn't afraid of the future without Le Duan and she wasn't even upset that her husband had picked his first wife instead of her. She was a mother herself and understood that the needs of Le Duan's children came first. What she really hated was how he had accepted the ethics committee's mandate without a fight. For the first time, she saw how cowardly he had behaved. He had fallen from the throne she placed him on and there was no going back.

# TINDERBOX

October 14, 1962 - Washington DC, USA

Vietnam was not the only hot spot on the president's plate. Kennedy had known for weeks that the Soviets were up to no good in Cuba. At the end of September, a US Navy reconnaissance aircraft photographed the Soviet ship Kasimov, with large crates on its deck the size and shape of Il-28 jet bomber fuselages. Intelligence reports from anti-Castro operatives had been describing large construction projects with Russian engineers in charge. Another reconnaissance flight revealed that Cuban surface-to-air missile sites on the northern end of the island were arranged in a pattern similar to those used by the Soviet Union to protect its ICBM bases. But without concrete evidence and a clear understanding of what it was that the Soviets were doing Kennedy thought it unwise to reveal his hand. After the Bay of Pigs, America had a credibility problem with the press and the international community. Kennedy didn't want to make it worse by going off half-cocked.

CIA Director John McCone had scheduled several reconnaissance flights over Cuba, but each time cloud cover prevented the U2's camera from capturing clear images. Something was going on below the clouds, but they didn't know what. Kennedy could imagine as well as others. It was a nightmare scenario.

The president had requested contingency plans from the military and diplomatic options from the state department if his worse fears came true. It was the first day of clear weather over the island and the CIA had been processing the film and performing its analysis of the photos the U2 had finally captured. If his suspicions were realized, Kennedy felt he would need to act quickly and wanted to be ready.

McCone entered the Oval Office with a large brown envelope under his arm marked "Top Secret." He opened the envelope and spread the photographs out on Kennedy's desk for the commander and chief to examine. The president used the magnifying glass that McCone retrieved from his briefcase to study the photos. Kennedy's heart sank when he saw a close-up of the missiles next to a construction site. "How many?" said Kennedy.

"About twenty missiles that we can verify, but there could be more," said McCone.

"And they're nuclear?"

"No way to tell for sure without examining the weapon's payload, but yes… The R-12s you are seeing in the photos are medium-range ballistic missiles, capable of carrying thermonuclear warheads. They also have R-14s in other locations which are intermediate-range missiles also capable of carrying nuclear warheads."

"What's the difference?"

"The R-12s have a maximum range of 1,200 miles while the R-14s have an effective range of 2,400 miles."

"Jesus, they'll be able to reach almost the entire continental United States."

"Except for Pacific Northwest and Alaska, of course. As far as we can tell, they are building three sites for the R-14s and six sites for the R-12s."

"How did they do this without us knowing?"

"What can I say? They were very fast and sneaky."

"How long before they're operational?"

"At this point, we don't know."

"Well for God's sake, find out, Bill… and fast."

"Yes, Mr. President. We are already working on it. If you want my best guess at this point, I'd say early November."

"We should never have put our missiles in Italy and Turkey. It was too provocative. It upset the balance."

"That's true, Mr. President. But we had to do something if we were going to save Berlin."

"I agree but now we've got to save America."

"Yes, Mr. President."

"What are the Soviets saying?"

"They're denying any Soviet weapons in Cuba are offensive."

"A ballistic missile with a thermonuclear warhead is not offensive?"

"I didn't say anyone was believing them, Mr. President. I think they have a real public relations fiasco on their hands."

"And we have a major new threat on ours. We have men in Cuba?"

"Yes, Mr. President. We have a team of about twenty men hiding in the hills above Havana."

"Get them to take some photos. We need a closer look. Something the people can understand."

"Right away, Mr. President."

"I want everyone on my staff with the appropriate security clearance to see these before this afternoon's cabinet meeting. The Joint Chiefs too."

"It's gonna be hard to keep it a secret with that many eyes."

"I don't think we want to keep this a secret. At least not much longer."

"We may be able to get more intelligence on the Soviet's intentions without the photos becoming public knowledge."

"I think their intentions are very clear, don't you, Bill?"

"I see your point, Mr. President."

"You'll excuse me, Bill. I need to think."

"Of course. Do you want me to leave this set of photos? I have another set."

"No. I've seen enough. I'll reach out if I have more

questions."

McCone gathered the photos and left Kennedy deep in thought. The president was now facing the biggest challenge of his presidency with the lives of 100 million Americans at stake.

At 6:30 pm, Kennedy summoned a meeting of the nine members of the National Security Council and five other key advisers, in a group he formally named the Executive Committee of the National Security Council (EXCOMM). They were the best and brightest JFK had at his disposal. It would be their job to find a way out of the precarious situation now facing America. For the following two weeks, few in that room would get much sleep. The fog created by their lack of sleep would make the situation even more dangerous, but it couldn't be helped. Everyone knew the stakes on the table and the thought that one wrong move could start a nuclear war didn't help make things clearer.

Without informing the members of EXCOMM, President Kennedy tape-recorded all of their proceedings during what would become known as "The Cuban Missile Crisis." He was the president. He didn't need their permission. JFK understood the importance of the moment and wanted to capture it for posterity. He also didn't want anyone changing their story if it all went bad. Of course, in the worst-case scenario, he wouldn't need an audio record of the proceedings. There would be nobody left to listen to them.

The events unfolding in Cuba and the USSR were like a chess match with each player taking a turn. Kennedy needed to decide on his next move. The president informed the group that he was convinced Russia was building launch sites and missiles were already in Cuba. The Russians and Cubans needed to be convinced to pull back from the brink and stop construction immediately. After a discussion over options, JFK decided to send his brother, Attorney General Robert Kennedy, to contact the Soviet Ambassador,

Anatoly Dobrynin. More than anyone, JFK trusted his brother to handle Dobrynin and not let him wiggle out of the truth.

Soviet Embassy - Washington DC, USA

Protocol required that the Soviet Ambassador be summoned to the White House. Robert Kennedy knew that a summons would allow the Soviets to stall for at least a day while schedules were juggled. There was no time. The Attorney General went directly to the Soviet Embassy unannounced and asked to see the Ambassador. The guards at the front gate didn't know the president's brother and prevented him from entering. Kennedy stood outside the gate until an apologetic diplomat came out and escorted him inside.

Meeting Dobrynin in his office, Robert Kennedy was straightforward with the Soviet Ambassador and said, "You're building missile launch sites in Cuba. Why?"

"Cuba has a right to defend itself," said Dobrynin.

"Not with thermonuclear missiles."

"They are not nuclear missiles. They have conventional warheads and are designed for surface-to-sea defense. Castro has good reason to believe America may attempt another foolhardy attack on his homeland."

"You need to tell Khrushchev to knock it off and pull the missiles out."

"Secretary Khrushchev gave me strict instructions that I was to assure your president that he has no intentions of upsetting the balance of power between our two nations. There will be no surface-to-surface missiles installed in Cuba."

"And yet, that is exactly what you are doing."

"You are imagining things."

"We have reconnaissance photos."

"May I see them?"

"No. We only had the one set and they are currently

being reviewed by our generals and admirals."

"How can I refute your claims if you will not show me your evidence?"

"You are just going to have to trust me. Khrushchev is treading on very thin ice. We know what he is doing and it will not stand."

"I will convey your concerns, Mr. Attorney General. By the way, why did Secretary Rusk not ask for a meeting? That is protocol."

"My brother wanted you to understand the gravity of the situation, so he sent me."

"Duly noted."

Kennedy rose, shook hands politely, and left.

White House – Washington DC, USA

When Robert returned, he reported directly to his brother. After a quick recap of the meeting at the Soviet Embassy, JFK called another meeting of the EXCOMM and asked Robert Kennedy to report what was discussed with Dobrynin. "So, Khrushchev is just going to deny the whole thing?" said the president's National Security Advisor, McGeorge Bundy.

"It seems that way," said Robert.

"We can't let them do that. The American people would never stand for it," said Vice President Johnson.

"Obviously not. But how do we stop them?" said JFK.

Over the next several hours, the members of EXCOMM and the president discussed the possible courses of action. Secretary of Defense Robert McNamara made a list on a large sheet of paper that he pinned to the curved wall of the oval office, so everyone was clear on the options being considered. There were six options:

1.  Do nothing: American vulnerability to Soviet nuclear missiles was not new.
2.  Diplomacy: Use diplomatic pressure to get the

Soviet Union to remove the missiles.

3. Secret approach: Offer Castro the choice of splitting up with the Russians or being invaded.
4. Invasion: Full force invasion of Cuba and overthrow of Castro.
5. Airstrike: Use the US Air Force to attack all known missile sites.
6. Blockade: Use the US Navy to block any missiles from arriving in Cuba.

"An airstrike is the only way to ensure that those missiles do not become operational," said General LeMay. "Plus, it sends a clear message to both Castro and Khrushchev that it's our backyard and we're not fucking around."

"I think there is little question that an airstrike would be seen as an overt act of aggression against Cuba. The international community might side with Castro. We are already in hot water because of the Bay of Pigs. An airstrike could be seen as an extension of that conflict," said Secretary of State Dean Rusk.

"Who cares how it's perceived? Those are one-megaton nuclear missiles ninety-miles off our coast. They can hit before we have time to retaliate. If they become operational; Khrushchev will have our nuts in a vice," said General Taylor.

"A blockade would prevent further missiles and warheads from being delivered to the island," said McNamara.

"Isn't that like fetching the horse from the barn after it's burnt down?" said Johnson.

"I suppose. But if we can contain their deployment, we might be able to negotiate the removal of the missiles through diplomatic means," said McNamara.

"The Soviets will see that as weakness," said Taylor. "We must show strength and determination when dealing with Khrushchev."

"An airstrike shows strength and determination," said LeMay.

"So does an invasion," said Taylor. "With should start with Navy and Air Force strikes on defensive positions along the coast followed by Marine and Army units in a full amphibious assault. Seizing the launch sites before they become operational is the only sure way of ensuring the missiles are secured and America stays safe."

"Airstrikes? Invasion? Let's take a step back for a moment," said McNamara. "What are we really talking about here? Twenty, maybe forty nuclear warheads. The Soviets have over 300 nuclear missiles pointed at America and its allies. What's forty more? I say it's a threat we can live with. We should negotiate our way out of this mess. Maybe get some concessions on West Berlin or Vietnam."

"When the time is right, I think we should use our back channels to offer Castro a choice. When the drums of war start beating, he's gonna realize that he's bitten off more than he can chew," said Bundy. "We can live with Castro. We can't live with Soviet missiles off our coast. Let's give him a choice between breaking off relations with the Russians or being invaded by the greatest military in the world. Aside from his politics, I'm pretty sure he is gonna pick survival."

For the next few days, President Kennedy listened to his wise men argue their positions back and forth. He asked more questions than made comments. He wanted all options on the table to deal with the situation. At times, he gave the group space by not attending a meeting. He knew that his advisors and cabinet members would often change their recommendations to align better with his position when he was in the room. It was natural. They were there at his pleasure and believed deeply in their leader. But the strategies being discussed were far too important than the appearance of loyalty. He knew in the end, they would fall in line with whatever decision he chose. But in the meantime, he wanted their ideas thrashed about. These men, more than all others, were capable of defending their positions with strong arguments.

After several days of debate and as matters in Cuba turned from bad to worse, the EXCOMM formed a consensus – airstrikes and full invasion. Not everyone in the group agreed whole-heartedly, but they did agree. It was the only way to extinguish the threat to America for sure. Without judgment, President Kennedy asked to go around the room and have each member explain why he believed this was the best option. Some argued more passionately than others. For some, it was more of a concession because they were unable to find a better way.

It took almost an hour. When they were done Kennedy took a long moment to consider. "Gentlemen, as I had hoped, you have thoroughly examined the issues at hand. I am impressed, reassured, and grateful. No stone has been left unturned and that is what our nation needs at this hazardous moment in our history. Having heard each of your positions explained in both public and private, I believe I understand your reasoning," said Kennedy. "However, I cannot in good conscious take this country to the brink of a nuclear war that a full invasion could potentially bring to fruition. With our nuclear capacity outnumbering the Soviets more than twenty to one, I know some of you believe that the Soviets will not choose war to protect Cuba and I believe you are correct in that assumption. But we could also be wrong about the Soviet's defense of Cuba, and I cannot take that risk. Too much is at stake. Hundreds of millions of lives, both Soviet and American, could be lost if our missiles and bombers are unleashed. And that is a future I cannot bear to consider. I have decided to take one of two different paths – airstrikes only and a blockade. I ask you now, to dig deeper and continue your debate on which of those two options would be the best for our country."

There were grumbles around the room but no outbursts. Things were far too serious for conjured drama. Kennedy rose and left the room. After a few moments, the arguments continued. The Joint Chiefs were united and lobbied for airstrikes while McNamara and his followers petitioned for the blockade. Most were somewhere in between and needed to be convinced one way or another.

Central Leadership Compound – Beijing, China

Inside Huairen Hall, the meeting place of the Chinese Politburo, the seven members of the standing committee were not happy with the events in Cuba and Moscow. They supported the revolution in Cuba and thought Fidel Castro a great hero of the people. But over the last few years, Castro had chosen the Soviets as his main sponsor even after the Chinese communist party had made him generous offers of support. The seven would not go directly against Moscow for something so trivial as Cuba and decided it was prudent to let things play out. There could be opportunities in the future to realign alliances in favor of China.

But the immediate action of placing nuclear missiles in Cuba concerned them deeply. The Soviets had created an imbalance of power between themselves and the Americans. It was a dangerous position and could bring about nuclear war. The Chinese communists knew that if the Soviets went to war with the United States and their allies, China would have little choice but to side with the Soviet Union. If the Soviets lost, so would China. Nobody was sure what that would mean, except it would not be good for the Chinese people or the communist party.

The standing committee could not publicly criticize the Soviets or the Cubans during the crisis. As always, the communists must stand united and support one another if the revolution was to be successful. But diplomats and spies were sent to uncover the Soviet's true plans and place the cork back in the nuclear bottle if possible. In the meantime, the rhetoric and actions between the Chinese and the Americans stationed in Vietnam were tempered. Miscalculations were to be avoided. There was no sense in antagonizing the enemy until the crisis was over.

Hanoi, North Vietnam

Hearing of the US and USSR standoff over Cuba, Le Duan once again went to Ho Chi Minh for advice. While he didn't always agree with Ho, Duan knew his experience in dealing with the west was vast and he sought his opinions during times of crisis. Ho was appearing less in public and staying at his house with its large pond. He enjoyed feeding the hundreds of colorful carp that swam to him whenever he appeared by the water's edge. The two statesmen walked along the pond while they talked. "I am not sure why I am concerned. Moscow and Washington DC are far away. Any hostilities, even nuclear, would likely not affect Vietnam," said Duan.

"You are wise to be concerned. The Americans carry their nuclear weapons in their back pockets like a thug carries a knife. They are the only nation in the world that has used such horrific weapons against civilians, not once, but twice," said Ho.

"Do you believe they may use them against us?"

"I doubt it. The shame would be great. But the possibility is always there… lingering. I am more concerned about the Americans using ground troops and their air force against the north. We must not push the Americans too much."

"So, you do not believe the conflict in Cuba will affect us?"

"Depending on its outcome, I imagine both sides to become more cautious or aggressive. If the Soviets and Americans avoid war, I doubt they will want to rush back to the brink. But once another nuclear weapon is used, it will be hard for the nations processing them to stop using them to solve other problems they face."

"What if the Soviets bring the Americans to their knees or even destroy them?"

"It is a wishful thought, but not based in reality. The Americans have vast resources and are far more powerful than the Soviets or the Chinese. And let's not forget the American allies. They have sworn to defend the United States if it is attacked. A nuclear war would not end well for our revolution. It would mean 'the gloves would come off' as the Americans say. They would be unrestrained."

"As would we."

"That is true. My biggest concern is that, after witnessing American aggression and power, the Chinese will grow timid and decrease or even cut off the arms and supplies they send us."

"The Chinese fought the Americans in Korea. I do not think they fear the west."

"The Chinese have long memories. They have no interest in losing another million soldiers to American military might. This conflict in Cuba will serve as a reminder of what they have sacrificed, especially if the Soviets lose."

"Is there anything we can do to determine the outcome is in our favor?"

"No. This is out of our hands. We can only wait and watch with the rest of the world."

"With the Americans occupied elsewhere, shouldn't we press our advantage?"

"When the tiger is awake and hunting, it is wise to stay out of sight and not tempt him with more prey."

The Kremlin – Moscow, Russia

Khrushchev had his hands full with more than the missiles in Cuba. There were those in the Politburo that believed that with this latest move war between the United States and the Soviet Union was now unavoidable and that the Soviet military should strike first in hopes of crippling the American leadership and avoiding a retaliatory strike. It was foolish thinking but sounded like a logical approach to the uninformed. He needed the politburo united for the hard times ahead. Decisions would need to be made quickly to avoid calamity. He would make those decisions unilaterally, if need be, but since the events of WWII and the death of Stalin, dictators were frowned upon, even in the Soviet Union.

At least his generals were happy. With the deployment of missiles in Cuba, they would soon be able to strike the US within minutes. This was seen as a great deterrent that would allow the Soviet military leeway in other arenas. The generals were also pleased that control of the missiles was still in Soviet hands. They did not want Castro and his followers to make a rash decision and attack another country with such a powerful weapon. The Americans might interpret the situation incorrectly and blame the Soviets for Cuba's actions. Everyone, including the generals, wanted to avoid World War III if possible. But the generals weren't afraid to bluff when necessary. A dangerous trait.

## White House – Washington DC, USA

The president was lying down on the floor behind his desk. The stress and sleepless nights brought about by the crisis were wreaking havoc on his back. He could only sit for an hour before the pain overwhelmed him. Pacing helped a bit. Eventually, he would need to lie down for thirty minutes to take pressure off his lower spine. He felt like an invalid and was concerned about how it might look to the public and his enemies if his condition was ever revealed. His family did their best to explain away any visits to the hospital as routine checkups. They weren't.

Addison's disease, the condition that had plagued him most of his adult life, was catching up to him. His autoimmune system was a wreck. Kennedy was dying. Slowly. But dying just the same. He refused to give in to it and worked through the pain whenever possible. But there were times when the stress was so high that the pain came in waves, like lightning down his spine. The only remedy, albeit temporary, was to rest and let his autoimmune system catch up enough to fight the disease.

The president's secretary peeked through the doorway and said, "Mr. President, your brother and Secretary Rusk asked for a few minutes."

"Of course. Send them in," said Kennedy as he rose to his feet like an old man that had fallen – first rolling over on his stomach, pushing his body up with his arms, then tucking knees beneath him. Using the edge of the desk to pull himself up to his feet, then straightened his back until he was completely erect. The facade was complete. He looked normal as Robert and Rusk walked in. "We got a problem," said Robert.

"Only one?" said Kennedy.

"Okay. You're right. We got another problem."

"And what's that?"

"The term 'blockade' is problematic. According to international law, a blockade is an act of war."

"Well, we don't want that. What do you suggest?"

"We were thinking quarantine," said Rusk.

"Quarantine? It sounds like Cuba's got the small pox."

"Yes, but it does not mean war. We could say that our actions are a quarantine of offensive weapons."

"Hmm... sounds softer than a blockade. I'm not sure that's the message we want to send to the Soviets or Castro."

"We realize it's not perfect. But it does give us some wiggle room for other countries to support our actions."

"And, since the blockade will be in international waters, it will not be a blockade in the traditional sense of cordoning off a port or harbor," said Robert.

"I like it. Quarantine it is," said the president. "Anything else?"

"Yes, but we'll handle it."

"What is it?"

"The Joint Chiefs are digging their heels in on an airstrike."

"I expected as much. To a hammer, everything is a nail."

"So, what are you going to do?"

"Nothing. They'll fall in line if I decide on a blocka—, excuse me, quarantine."

"You really think so?"

"I'm the Commander and Chief, gentlemen. They work for me. Besides, in the end, they are all patriots and will set their own opinions aside to do what is best for our country. If there is one thing drilled into a soldier throughout his career in the military, it's respect for the chain of command."

"Yes, Mr. President. Thank you for your time."

Robert and Rusk left.


The next day, the president decided to go with a quarantine. As he predicted, the Joint Chiefs grumbled for a moment and even tried to talk him out of it with their final arguments, but when they realized that the boss was resolved, the generals and admirals fell in line. They would execute Kennedy's wishes to the best of their abilities. Besides, he could always change his mind later if things got out of hand. Invasion was always on the table, even when the president took it off. It was just a matter of timing.


October 22, 1962 – White House, Washington DC, USA


The oval office was packed with people and television camera equipment. JFK sat at his desk. It was hot. Someone suggested face powder to keep the sheen on his forehead to a minimum. His mind elsewhere, Kennedy didn't object. A light bit of powder was used sparingly. JFK knew this would probably be the most important speech of his life. He could not imagine a more important matter to inform the American public. He wasn't nervous. That wasn't his style. He was focused. There would be no humorous moments in the speech. Nothing to take away from the seriousness of the speech's content.

As part of his obligation to consult with Congress, JFK had spent several hours before the broadcast with the top leaders in both houses. The congressmen were not pleased with the quarantine. They thought it soft and wanted a stronger response to what they saw as blatant communist aggression. Kennedy stood his ground and informed them that the decision had been made and would not change unless future events required further actions. They protested but accepted it. America only had one commander and chief.

At the top of the hour, the light on one of the television cameras turned red and the speech began. Kennedy was live on national television. Eighty-seven percent of Americans had televisions in their homes and those that didn't watched from restaurants, bars, and offices. But the Americans were not alone. Millions from around the world watched with deep interest. What happened between the Soviets and the Americans would have a profound effect on other nations, especially in Europe and South America. It was almost as if the world had stopped to listen and watch. The cameras recorded the speech using large spools of film held in lightproof canisters. Kennedy looked into the camera in front of him and said, "Good evening, my fellow citizens:

This Government, as promised, has maintained the closest surveillance of the Soviet Military buildup on the island of Cuba. Within the past week, unmistakable evidence has established the fact that a series of offensive missile sites is now in preparation on that imprisoned island. The purpose of these bases can be none other than to provide a nuclear strike capability against the Western Hemisphere.

Upon receiving the first preliminary hard information of this nature last Tuesday at 9 a.m., I directed that our surveillance be stepped up. And having now confirmed and completed our evaluation of the evidence and our decision on a course of action, this Government feels obliged to report this new crisis to you in fullest detail.

The characteristics of these new missile sites indicate two distinct types of installations. Several of them include medium-range ballistic missiles capable of carrying a nuclear warhead for a distance of more than 1,000 nautical miles. Each of these missiles, in short, is capable of striking Washington, D.C., the Panama Canal, Cape Canaveral, Mexico City, or any other city in the southeastern part of the United States, in Central America, or in the Caribbean area.

Additional sites not yet completed appear to be designed for intermediate-range ballistic missiles—capable of traveling more than twice as far—and thus capable of striking most of the major cities in the Western Hemisphere, ranging as far north as Hudson Bay, Canada, and as far south as Lima, Peru. In addition, jet bombers, capable of carrying nuclear weapons, are now being uncrated and assembled in Cuba, while the necessary air bases are being prepared.

This urgent transformation of Cuba into an important strategic base—by the presence of these large, long-range, and clearly offensive weapons of sudden mass destruction—constitutes an explicit threat to the peace and security of all the Americas, in flagrant and deliberate defiance of the Rio Pact of 1947, the traditions of this Nation and hemisphere, the joint resolution of the 87th Congress, the Charter of the United Nations, and my own public warnings to the Soviets on September 4 and 13. This action also contradicts the repeated assurances of Soviet spokesmen, both publicly and privately delivered, that the arms buildup in Cuba would retain its original defensive character, and that the Soviet Union had no need or desire to station strategic missiles on the territory of any other nation.

The size of this undertaking makes clear that it has been planned for some months. Yet only last month, after I had made clear the distinction between any introduction of ground-to-ground missiles and the existence of defensive antiaircraft missiles, the Soviet Government publicly stated on September 11, and I quote, 'the armaments and military equipment sent to Cuba are designed exclusively for defensive purposes,' that, and I quote the Soviet Government, 'there is no need for the Soviet Government to shift its weapons . . . for a retaliatory blow to any other country, for instance, Cuba,' and that, and I quote their government, 'the Soviet Union has so powerful rockets to carry these nuclear warheads that there is no need to search for sites for them beyond the boundaries of the Soviet Union.' That statement was false.

Only last Thursday, as evidence of this rapid offensive buildup was already in my hand, Soviet Foreign Minister Gromyko told me in my office that he was instructed to make it clear once again, as he said his government had already done, that Soviet assistance to Cuba, and I quote, 'pursued solely the purpose of contributing to the defense capabilities of Cuba,' that, and I quote him, 'training by Soviet specialists of Cuban nationals in handling defensive armaments was by no means offensive, and if it were otherwise,' Mr. Gromyko went on, 'the Soviet Government would never become involved in rendering such assistance.' That statement also was false.

Neither the United States of America nor the world community of nations can tolerate deliberate deception and offensive threats on the part of any nation, large or small. We no longer live in a world where only the actual firing of weapons represents a sufficient challenge to a nation's security to constitute maximum peril. Nuclear weapons are so destructive and ballistic missiles are so swift, that any substantially increased possibility of their use or any sudden change in their deployment may well be regarded as a definite threat to peace.

For many years both the Soviet Union and the United States, recognizing this fact, have deployed strategic nuclear weapons with great care, never upsetting the precarious status quo which insured that these weapons would not be used in the absence of some vital challenge. Our own strategic missiles have never been transferred to the territory of any other nation under a cloak of secrecy and deception; and our history—unlike that of the Soviets since the end of World War II—demonstrates that we have no desire to dominate or conquer any other nation or impose our system upon its people. Nevertheless, American citizens have become adjusted to living daily on the Bull's-eye of Soviet missiles located inside the U.S.S.R. or in submarines.

In that sense, missiles in Cuba add to an already clear and present danger—although it should be noted the nations of Latin America have never previously been subjected to a potential nuclear threat.

But this secret, swift, and extraordinary buildup of Communist missiles—in an area well known to have a special and historical relationship to the United States and the nations of the Western Hemisphere, in violation of Soviet assurances, and in defiance of American and hemispheric policy—this sudden, clandestine decision to station strategic weapons for the first time outside of Soviet soil—is a deliberately provocative and unjustified change in the status quo which cannot be accepted by this country, if our courage and our commitments are ever to be trusted again by either friend or foe.

The 1930s taught us a clear lesson: aggressive conduct, if allowed to go unchecked and unchallenged ultimately leads to war. This nation is opposed to war. We are also true to our word. Our unswerving objective, therefore, must be to prevent the use of these missiles against this or any other country, and to secure their withdrawal or elimination from the Western Hemisphere.

Our policy has been one of patience and restraint, as befits a peaceful and powerful nation, which leads a worldwide alliance. We have been determined not to be diverted from our central concerns by mere irritants and fanatics. But now further action is required—and it is underway, and these actions may only be the beginning. We will not prematurely or unnecessarily risk the costs of worldwide nuclear war in which even the fruits of victory would be ashes in our mouth—but neither will we shrink from that risk at any time it must be faced.

Acting, therefore, in the defense of our own security and of the entire Western Hemisphere, and under the authority entrusted to me by the Constitution as endorsed by the resolution of the Congress, I have directed that the following initial steps be taken immediately:

First: To halt this offensive buildup, a strict quarantine on all offensive military equipment under shipment to Cuba is being initiated. All ships of any kind bound for Cuba from whatever nation or port will, if found to contain cargoes of offensive weapons, be turned back. This quarantine will be extended, if needed, to other types of cargo and carriers. We are not at this time, however, denying the necessities of life as the Soviets attempted to do in their Berlin blockade of 1948.

Second: I have directed the continued and increased close surveillance of Cuba and its military buildup. The foreign ministers of the OAS, in their communique of October 6, rejected secrecy in such matters in this hemisphere. Should these offensive military preparations continue, thus increasing the threat to the hemisphere, further action will be justified. I have directed the Armed Forces to prepare for any eventualities; and I trust that in the interest of both the Cuban people and the Soviet technicians at the sites, the hazards to all concerned in continuing this threat will be recognized.

Third: It shall be the policy of this Nation to regard any nuclear missile launched from Cuba against any nation in the Western Hemisphere as an attack by the Soviet Union on the United States, requiring a full retaliatory response upon the Soviet Union.

Fourth: As a necessary military precaution, I have reinforced our base at Guantanamo, evacuated today the dependents of our personnel there, and ordered additional military units to be on a standby alert basis.

Fifth: We are calling tonight for an immediate meeting of the Organ of Consultation under the Organization of American States, to consider this threat to hemispheric security and to invoke articles 6 and 8 of the Rio Treaty in support of all necessary action. The United Nations Charter allows for regional security arrangements—and the nations of this hemisphere decided long ago against the military presence of outside powers. Our other allies around the world have also been alerted.

Sixth: Under the Charter of the United Nations, we are asking tonight that an emergency meeting of the Security Council be convoked without delay to take action against this latest Soviet threat to world peace. Our resolution will call for the prompt dismantling and withdrawal of all offensive weapons in Cuba, under the supervision of U.N. observers, before the quarantine can be lifted.

Seventh and finally: I call upon Chairman Khrushchev to halt and eliminate this clandestine, reckless, and provocative threat to world peace and to stable relations between our two nations. I call upon him further to abandon this course of world domination, and to join in a historic effort to end the perilous arms race and to transform the history of man. He has an opportunity now to move the world back from the abyss of destruction—by returning to his government's own words that it had no need to station missiles outside its own territory, and withdrawing these weapons from Cuba—by refraining from any action which will widen or deepen the present crisis—and then by participating in a search for peaceful and permanent solutions.

This Nation is prepared to present its case against the Soviet threat to peace, and our own proposals for a peaceful world, at any time and in any forum—in the OAS, in the United Nations, or in any other meeting that could be useful—without limiting our freedom of action. We have in the past made strenuous efforts to limit the spread of nuclear weapons. We have proposed the elimination of all arms and military bases in a fair and effective disarmament treaty. We are prepared to discuss new proposals for the removal of tensions on both sides—including the possibility of a genuinely independent Cuba, free to determine its own destiny. We have no wish to war with the Soviet Union— for we are a peaceful people who desire to live in peace with all other peoples.

But it is difficult to settle or even discuss these problems in an atmosphere of intimidation. That is why this latest Soviet threat—or any other threat which is made either independently or in response to our actions this week— must and will be met with determination. Any hostile move anywhere in the world against the safety and freedom of peoples to whom we are committed—including in particular the brave people of West Berlin—will be met by whatever action is needed.

Finally, I want to say a few words to the captive people of Cuba, to whom this speech is being directly carried by special radio facilities. I speak to you as a friend, as one who knows of your deep attachment to your fatherland, as one who shares your aspirations for liberty and justice for all. And I have watched and the American people have watched with deep sorrow how your nationalist revolution was betrayed— and how your fatherland fell under foreign domination. Now your leaders are no longer Cuban leaders inspired by Cuban ideals. They are puppets and agents of an international conspiracy which has turned Cuba against your friends and neighbors in the Americas--and turned it into the first Latin American country to become a target for nuclear war—the first Latin American country to have these weapons on its soil.

These new weapons are not in your interest. They contribute nothing to your peace and well-being. They can only undermine it. But this country has no wish to cause you to suffer or to impose any system upon you. We know that your lives and land are being used as pawns by those who deny your freedom.

Many times in the past, the Cuban people have risen to throw out tyrants who destroyed their liberty. And I have no doubt that most Cubans today look forward to the time when they will be truly free—free from foreign domination, free to choose their own leaders, free to select their own system, free to own their own land, free to speak and write and worship without fear or degradation. And then shall Cuba be welcomed back to the society of free nations and to the associations of this hemisphere.

My fellow citizens: let no one doubt that this is a difficult and dangerous effort on which we have set out. No one can see precisely what course it will take or what costs or casualties will be incurred. Many months of sacrifice and self-discipline lie ahead—months in which our patience and our will will be tested—months in which many threats and denunciations will keep us aware of our dangers. But the greatest danger of all would be to do nothing.

The path we have chosen for the present is full of hazards, as all paths are—but it is the one most consistent with our character and courage as a nation and our commitments around the world. The cost of freedom is always high—and Americans have always paid it. And one path we shall never choose, and that is the path of surrender or submission.

Our goal is not the victory of might, but the vindication of right—not peace at the expense of freedom, but both peace and freedom, here in this hemisphere, and, we hope, around the world. God willing, that goal will be achieved. Thank you and good night."

The red light on top of the camera turned off and the film canisters stopped rolling. It was over. The room was dead silent as those inside tried to absorb what they had just heard. There was no clapping or patting on the back. There was little doubt that the world was on the brink of war… and this time it could mean the loss of hundreds of millions of lives in America, Cuba, the Soviet Union, and potentially

China and Europe. The Soviet Union had been caught red-handed in a lie and deception of the most serious nature. Kennedy had held nothing back and revealed all to the world. He had told the brutal truth.

After a few more moments to collect his thoughts, Kennedy rose and stepped from his office so the technicians could pack up their gear. He made little eye contact on his way out. What he had just said affected him too. Putting it in a coherent argument made it more real. He could hardly believe that things had spun so far out of control in such a short amount of time. This was not what he wanted.

During the speech, a directive went out to all US forces worldwide, placing them on DEFCON 3. The heavy cruiser USS Newport News was designated flagship for the quarantine. The most dangerous showdown in world history had begun.

The public would be sitting on pins and needles during the crisis. Few Americans got any sleep. Most would just stare into the darkness and wonder if that moment would be their last. Not knowing the extent of damage and when it might come was too much for the mind to handle. It drove more than a few to insanity and even suicide.

October 24, 1962 - Caribbean Sea

Over the next two days, US Navy ships sailed to their assigned positions. At 2 pm, the surface quarantine was established in the Caribbean Sea. 12 destroyers from US Second Fleet's Task Force 136 stretched in a shallow arc 500 miles from Cape Maysi, Cuba. The ships were just out of range of the Soviet IL-28 bombers based in Cuba. The line would grow as the crisis intensified until there was a total of two cruisers, twenty-two destroyers, and two guided-missile frigates. In addition, the USS Essex aircraft carrier group patrolled the area in front of the quarantine line making it the lead ship. The anti-submarine warfare squadrons based in Puerto Rico and Bermuda anchored the north and south flanks. The United States military had enough firepower on station to obliterate any ship that disregarded the quarantine line. It was a strong and effective response to the Soviet and Cuban weapon deployments. It was clear the Americans meant business.

Although an end-run around the quarantine line was possible it was unlikely that any ship would slip through without being discovered. There were just too many civilian eyes on islands and ships in the area watching the seas during the crisis. The US Navy monitored civilian radio transmissions to pick up any friendly reconnaissance reports.

To avoid mistakes, strict instructions on the rules of engagement were drilled into the troops aboard the US vessels. US Naval officers knew what their commander and chief expected and were determined to carry out Kennedy's wishes.

## Virginia, USA

Having just explained the procedure of "duck and cover" during a nuclear attack, Janet Scarborough stood in front of her classroom of high schoolers. Some listened intently, while others looked bored. "Do not look at the blast," said Janet. "Flying glass from shattered windows could cut you, not to mention the third-degree sunburn you would get on your face. Keep your head down and stay under your desk. Look at the floor until the danger has passed."

She spotted the class wiseass slouched in his chair, making a paper airplane. She said, "Michael, why don't you put that down and listen for a change. It might save your life."

"I doubt that," said Michael.

"What do you mean?"

"My dad is in the aircforce. He says that if a nuclear missile hits a city it'll kill anyone within a five-mile radius and those that don't die in the blast will suffer from radiation poisoning that's worse than death. Nobody is gonna survive."

One of the girls in the class burst into tears. Janet gave Michael her "now look at what you have done" look and said, "That's enough, Michael."

Several more students including a couple of boys started to tear up and sniffle. A wave of fear rolled through the classroom as the students considered the very real danger they and their families faced. Janet knew she could not coddle these kids. They were too old and knew too much. She decided to tell them the truth. "Everyone, listen up. My father and husband were in the military too. The one thing I can promise you is that our soldiers will do everything in their power to protect us and so will President Kennedy. America is the strongest nation in the world. The Soviets would be crazy to attack us. They know the consequence they would face."

"You don't know that for sure, Mrs. Scarborough," said one of the girls sobbing.

"No, I don't. Nobody does. They're communists. They think differently than we do. Their revolution is more important than the freedom we value so much."

"So, maybe it's good that we duke it out with them," said Michael. "Get it over with before they overrun more countries and become too powerful. That's what my dad says."

"I am sure there are a lot of people that feel that way. But I've seen war and what it can do to people. I don't want to see another. I pray our leaders find a way out of this and that the Soviets see reason. After all, they have families too. They're mothers and fathers just like we are. They want the best for their children and loved ones. They want to keep them safe, just like we do. We do these duck and cover drills as a precaution against nuclear war, not because it is inevitable."

"Are you scared, Mrs. Scarborough?" said another girl.

"Sure. These are serious times. But I don't let my fear

control me and neither should you. We need to be brave and use our heads. And on that note, let's practice the duck and cover drill… When you hear an air raid siren, you immediately get on the ground wherever you are. Find something strong to get under that will protect you in case a ceiling cave's in or a brick falls from a building. If you are in the classroom, you should use your desk. Just curl up in a ball beneath it and cover your head with your arms. Remember to look at the floor, not the windows. Alright, let's try it," said Janet making an all too real sound of a siren. The class followed her example as she hit the deck and crawled beneath her desk. Then Michael, tucked under his desk with his arms over his head like the other students, farted loudly. Everyone laughed, including Janet as she shook her head in mild annoyance. *He'll probably grow up to be a general,* she thought. *I suppose I should be grateful.*

When Janet returned to her home that night, she parked her car in the driveway as usual and walked to the front door. She was surprised to find it was unlocked. Living alone, Janet was careful to always lock her doors even though she lived in a nice neighborhood. Janet considered going to a neighbor's house and calling the police, but she ruled out the idea. It was her home and she would protect it. She was her father's daughter. She entered her house and left the front door open in case she encountered an intruder and needed to escape quickly. "Hello," she called out. There was no response.

She moved into the kitchen and opened a cabinet drawer. Inside was her father's air force sidearm – a Smith & Wesson Model 15 revolver. She pressed the release button and opened the cylinder as her father had taught her. It was fully loaded with six .38 special shells. She hadn't fired the weapon in years, but she was still pretty sure it would work. Guns tend not to malfunction if left undisturbed in a drawer. She closed the cylinder. It was a double-action revolver; she only needed to point at the target and pull the trigger to fire the weapon. She kept her finger off the trigger. She knew she could reach it fast enough if she needed. Her father had taught her to shoot and how to safely handle a gun. The beer bottles and pie tins they brought to the woods never stood a chance. Janet was a natural shootist. She often wondered if she could shoot another person. She supposed she was about to find out and steeled herself.

She searched all the rooms downstairs and found nothing. She walked up the stairs, down the hall, and into her bedroom. Still nothing. She moved back down the hall and then saw the door to her daughter's room ajar. Her heart leapt. She kept the bedroom doors of her son and daughter closed to cut down on the monthly heating bill. She moved slowly forward and pushed the door open with one hand and held her revolver at the ready with the other. Fighting her instincts, she kept her finger off the trigger as she had been trained. As the door swung open, she saw a young woman curled up on the bed – it was her daughter, Karen. Janet breathed a sigh of relief and broke into tears. Karen stirred and turned to see her mother. They hadn't spoken in almost a year. "Hey, mom," said Karen as if nothing was wrong. "Are you gonna shoot me?"

Janet realized she still had the revolver in his hand. She moved to the bed and set the revolver on the side table pointed away from Karen. She hugged her daughter and said, "What are you doing here? Why didn't you call?"

"I don't know. It was kind of a last-minute thing," said Karen.

"I'm so glad you're home."

"Me too. It's been too long," said Karen starting to cry.

"What's wrong, Sweetheart?" said Janet holding her close as she used to when Karen was a little girl and much less argumentative.

"It's just… everything that's happening. The world's gone crazy. I just wanted to come and be with you."

Hearing those words, Janet's tears came with heaves of joy. Her little girl was back. Whatever would happen in the coming days, they would face it together. "I wish Scott was here," said Karen.

"Me too, Sweetheart. Me too."

Over the next week, school was canceled so children could stay home with their parents. Janet was grateful. She and Karen would stay curled up on the couch with their eyes glued to the news on the television. Karen made two dozen chocolate chip cookies with walnuts as her mother had taught her. "Aren't you worried what those will do to your hips?" said Janet taking a bite of the fresh-from-the-oven cookies.

"At this point… not really," said Karen.

"Yeah, I suppose your right. It would be a shame to leave an unopened bag of chocolate chips in the cupboard."

"My thinking exactly," said Karen.

The same scene played out across America. Families huddled together in their living rooms. Small children were oblivious to the danger. Parents explained to the older children what it meant and what the family would do if the worse happened. The family dog feeling the stress and offering a few licks of its tongue to soothe its masters' fear. There was nothing anyone could do. Their fate was in the hands of Khrushchev and Kennedy.

## White House – Washington DC, USA

A telegram from Khrushchev to Kennedy was received at 10:52 pm EDT and brought directly to the Oval Office. In the message, Khrushchev stated, "If you weigh the present situation with a cool head without giving way to passion, you will understand that the Soviet Union cannot afford not to decline the despotic demands of the USA" and that the USSR viewed the blockade as "an act of aggression." Khrushchev indicated that their ships had been instructed to ignore the American blockade and proceed on course to Cuba.

In response, President Kennedy sent a message making

known his intention of a possible airstrike followed by an invasion of Cuba. The United States would not allow nuclear weapons of any kind to remain in Cuba. America would respond militarily if the missiles and warheads were not removed immediately.

## Kremlin – Moscow, Russia

Reading Kennedy's cable, Khrushchev knew he had overplayed his hand. "He's a madman," he said to himself. Kennedy was far more aggressive and self-assured than Khrushchev had previously believed. While the two superpowers had entered the era of mutual destruction, the USSR was not ready to fight its western adversary. Even though the Soviet military would inflict great harm on America and its allies, it would quickly exhaust its most powerful weapons and lose a nuclear war. If that happened, the USSR would be at the mercy of its most formidable enemy. Khrushchev knew he must avoid war at all costs. But even in that dark moment of realization, he wondered if it was still possible to negotiate some outcome that could look like a victory to the members of the politburo and allow him to stay in power.

## United Nations – New York, USA

Kennedy was determined to keep the pressure on the Soviets from all fronts until the missiles were removed. JFK had US Ambassador to the UN Adlai Stevenson request an emergency meeting of the UN Security Council. During the meeting, Stevenson confronted Soviet Ambassador Valerian Zorin and challenged him to admit the existence of Soviet nuclear missiles in Cuba. Zorin refused to answer which spoke volumes to the international diplomats listening to the contest.

In response, the US raised its readiness level to DEFCON 2. It was the only time in US history when B-52 bombers went on continuous airborne alert. B-47 medium bombers were dispersed to various airfields throughout the world and made ready to take off on fifteen minutes notice. Each bomber carried enough nuclear weapons to completely obliterate several large cities. One-eighth of SAC's 1,436 bombers were on airborne alert and 145 intercontinental ballistic missiles stood on ready alert. One hundred sixty-one nuclear-armed interceptors were repositioned and placed on a fifteen-minute alert. Tactical Air Command had 511 fighters deployed to face Cuba. Short on airlift resources for a major airborne drop, TAC requested the call-up of twenty-four Reserve squadrons. The US was ready for any response from the Soviets. But there was none.

Fearful of triggering a nuclear war that they would lose, the Soviets stood down and didn't make a move. They did not increase their alert status or air defense posture. Their aircraft stayed in their hangars. The Soviet military froze in place. It was a wise move on Khrushchev's part. The US generals and admirals were chomping at the bit. They would not flinch to bring the whole weight of America's military down on Cuba and the USSR should the president order it. Their fingers were on the triggers that could bring about World War III.

What made the moment even more precarious was that at that point in time President Kennedy had decided that America would need to go to war to abolish the threat of Soviet missiles in Cuba. The tables had turned. It was now his advisors and cabinet members holding him back and asking him to give the Soviets more time to withdraw their missiles before attacking. With the quarantine line now in place and the Soviets seemingly standing down, they believed a peaceful solution was still possible. Kennedy was not so sure, but heeded their council and waited. Was it acting for the benefit of the Soviets or was the president's new resolve real? Nobody knew except Kennedy, and he was holding his cards close to his chest. Not even Robert knew his brother's true mind and that scared the hell out of everyone in the White House.

## Quarantine Line - Caribbean Sea

The Soviet Tanker Bucharest sailed toward Cuba. The American ships were still adjusting their positions to ensure the quarantine line was impassable. It wasn't... not yet. A patrol aircraft from the USS Essex spotted the Bucharest a few miles from the line of American ships and notified their command center. The American destroyer USS Gearing was ordered to intercept the Soviet ship.

As the Gearing raced toward the Bucharest, the Soviet ship slipped through the quarantine line. Unable to stop the Soviet tanker, the Americans performed several flyovers of the Bucharest inspecting the ship with each pass. Not seeing any signs of large crates on the deck, the reconnaissance pilots were convinced the Bucharest was only carrying oil and not any military cargo. To save face, the Americans decided to let the Bucharest continue to its destination without an inspection.

The US Navy knew that the intrusion made them look weak and were determined not to let it happen again. More ships were ordered to sail to the quarantine line. To shore up the quarantine line, two lines known as Walnut and Chestnut would be formed by the US Navy ships. Additional military ships and port facilities were provided by multiple South American and Caribbean nations.

Later that day, the Lebanese freighter Marucla approached the outer line of American ships and was detected by a Navy aircraft. The Americans needed to make an example and show that the quarantine line was effective. The destroyer USS Joseph P. Kennedy Jr. was ordered to intercept and board the freighter.

As the American destroyer approached the Marucla, the US Navy seamen were ordered to battle stations and manned the bow and stern twin five-inch gun mounts and the triple Mark 32 torpedo tubes on either side of the ship. Over the radio, the American commander ordered the freighter to stop and prepare to be boarded for inspection. The Marucla slowed to a stop.

The civilian crew aboard the Marucla watched in awe as the destroyer pulled alongside and its gun swung around to point at the Lebanese ship. The Americans didn't need to ask twice. The unarmed crew aboard the Marucla fully cooperated with the Americans. Once the Americans were satisfied that the freighter carried no military cargo, the Marucla was cleared to continue its journey. Word quickly spread through the shipping lanes that the Americans meant business.

## Cuba

The Soviets and Cubans realized that no further missiles or military equipment would make it to Cuba unless the balance of power was shifted. The Cuban workers continued to prepare the missile launch sites. The missiles currently on the island were seen as the only way to force the Americans and their allies to break the quarantine line and let the Soviet freighters through. The Soviets were quickly running out of options and it was a dangerous gambit.

## White House – Washington DC, USA

Aerial photographs from CIA reconnaissance flights confirmed that the work on the missile site was continuing unabated. In response, President Kennedy authorized the loading of nuclear weapons onto American military aircraft under the command of SACEUR, which had the responsibility of carrying out first strikes against the Soviet Union. Kennedy knew that the Soviets would most likely respond by escalating their own preparations for the use of nuclear arms as first-strike weapons. The world watched in dismay as the two superpowers squared off and primed their militaries for global nuclear war.

As preparations continued, the Americans received word from British intelligence that an intercepted and decoded message indicated that the Soviets had ordered fourteen of their freighters to change course and return to the Soviet Union. President Kennedy and his staff breathed a sigh of relief. The confrontation was not over, but the message was a welcome reprieve from the building tension in the White House and Pentagon. But President Kennedy was not about to take his foot off the pedal. He ordered reconnaissance flights over the missile launch construction sites to be increased to one every two hours. He also ordered plans for an intermediate government to be installed should the Americans invade Cuba. With the full weight of the US military behind them, there was little doubt the Americans would win this time around.

Kennedy made no effort to keep his preparations for war a secret. He knew the Soviets and Cubans had an array of spies in the US and that they would report the Americans' progress to their leaders. Kennedy felt it needed to be clear what his enemies were facing in hopes that they would back away from a war they could not win and could potentially destroy their nations.

Word came that Castro was prepared to use nuclear weapons against an American invasion of his country even though it meant destroying Cuba and killing millions of his people. Kennedy was not deterred. In Kennedy's mind, Castro had created this problem by turning to the Soviets and allowing the deployment of nuclear weapons on Cuban soil. JFK did not want war, but he would do what was necessary to keep America safe… even if it meant the destruction of Cuba and its people. If the Soviets and Cubans chose war, they would have it.

Kennedy could see that Khrushchev was biding his time. The longer the Americans did nothing, the closer the missile sites moved to becoming operational.

When faced with nuclear missile ninety miles off his coast and ready to launch at a moment's notice, Khrushchev was certain Kennedy would change his tune and back down from his war footing.

All during the crisis, Khrushchev and Kennedy communicated through diplomats and secured cables. At times, communications were threats. Other times, compromises were suggested. Neither leader wanted war, but nor would they back down without concessions. Having slept little during the crisis, they both were exhausted. Khrushchev's messages became particularly disturbing as he became more belligerent, and he rambled off-topic. He began repeating himself as if his memory of what had been said was failing. Kennedy's back pain was aggravated by the stress and lack of rest. His pain it made it difficult to focus.

One of the issues faced by the Soviets and Americans was that only the Cubans could agree to inspections on their territory. Even though Khrushchev was leaving Castro out of the loop, that didn't prevent Khrushchev from using missile site inspections as a negotiating point. After negotiating a deal with the Americans, he could always leave room for renegotiating by saying it was the Cubans that would not agree to the inspections.

As American and Soviet diplomats tried frantically to come up with solutions that would avoid armed conflict between the superpowers, disaster struck... twice.

October 27, 1962 – Bane, Cuba

A Korean War Veteran, USAF Major Rudolf Anderson loved flying the Dragon Lady, the nickname for the Lockheed U-2F high altitude reconnaissance aircraft. He was part of the 4080th Strategic Reconnaissance Wing which had been given the duty of aerial reconnaissance over Cuba. Earlier in the day, Anderson had taken off from McCoy AFB, a forward operating air base ten miles southeast of Orlando, Florida. It was his sixth mission flying over Cuba.

With a 103-foot wingspan and only one engine, the U-2 was not particularly fast for a jet aircraft. What made it special was its high-resolution camera and the aircraft's ability to reach an altitude of over 70,000 feet which was thought to be the outer envelope of the Soviet's anti-aircraft missiles. The altitude was so high and the air so thin, the pilots were required to wear partially pressurized spacesuits.

With over 1,000 hours of flying the U-2 under his belt, Anderson was considered the top pilot in the 4080th and a vital component in the reconnaissance effort over Cuba during the crisis.

As his aircraft approached the target site, two Soviet-made S-75 Dvina surface-to-air missiles were launched toward his aircraft high over Banes, Cuba. Two Soviet generals stationed in Havana had ordered the anti-aircraft battery commanders to shoot down any American reconnaissance aircraft if they were found within range. One of the two missiles exploded close to Anderson's U-2. Shrapnel from the missile pierced the cockpit and Anderson's spacesuit. Both the cockpit and the spacesuit depressurized, and Anderson lost consciousness from lack of oxygen. With no one at the controls, the aircraft tipped over on its side and crashed into the ground at over 400 miles per hour. Anderson was killed instantly.

White House – Washington DC, USA

When President Kennedy was informed by Robert McNamara of the crash of the U-2 and the use of the Soviet anti-aircraft missiles, he fell silent. "Well…" he finally said, "… we are in an entirely new ballgame."

It would be several weeks before Major Anderson's body was recovered by the Cubans and returned to the United States. Kennedy ordered that Anderson be posthumously awarded the first Air Force Cross, as well as the Air Force Distinguished Service Medal, the Purple

Heart, and the Cheney Award.

Strangely, it was not the shooting down of Anderson's U-2 that was the most dangerous event of the day that would become known as "Black Saturday."

## Caribbean Ocean

The USS Cony was a Fletcher-class destroyer assigned to the quarantine line. The Cony was one of eight antisubmarine warfare destroyers assigned to the hunter-killer Task Group Alpha along with the USS Randolph antisubmarine aircraft carrier.

In the late afternoon, the Cony sonar operator acquired a solid contact. The ship proceeded swiftly to where their commander believed a submarine was attempting to pass underneath the quarantine line. Determining the submarine's approximate depth and bearing, Commander William Morgan had no way of contacting the submarine's commander. It was too deep for radio contact. The American commander did not want to sink the submarine, but he could not allow it through the quarantine line either. He had no choice but to force it to the surface. He ordered his crew to launch signaling depth charges which carried an explosive with the power of a grenade. The signaling depth charges would not breach the submarine's hull but would give those inside terrible headaches.

Inside B-59, a Soviet Foxtrot-class diesel submarine, the sonar shouted, "Depth Charges in the water." The submarine's commander, Captain Vitali Savitsky picked up the intercom microphone and ordered his crew to brace for depth charges. Eight depth charges exploded shaking up the crew but doing no damage. Having no way of knowing that the depth charges were not lethal, the Soviet captain assumed that they were under attack and that World War III had started. He ordered his crew to arm its nuclear torpedoes.

On the surface, the Americans aboard the Cony had no idea they were tangling with a submarine armed with nuclear weapons. Intelligence reports had indicated that the Soviets were focused on their missile technology and had not yet developed nuclear torpedoes. The intelligence analysts had miscalculated. The Soviet nuclear torpedoes were armed with fifteen kilo-ton nuclear warheads similar in size and destructive power to the bombs that destroyed Hiroshima and Nagasaki. If detonated, the Soviet torpedo would destroy the submarine that launched it, the USS Cony, and potentially any ships within the extensive blast radius. It would also start a war between the superpowers. Unaware of the danger below his destroyer, Morgan ordered another group of depth charges dropped. Moments later, white water boiled up and blew into the air from the explosions. The hunt continued with more explosions below the surface.

In B-59, the explosions drove the submarine's crew crazy. It wasn't physical damage as much as psychological. There was no way to know what was happening on the surface or back in Mother Russia. For all they knew, their country and their families had already been destroyed.

After the depth charges stopped, the sonar assault began. The American destroyer's sonar dome pounded the Soviet submarine with ultra-high frequency sound waves. Whenever the submarine tried to run, the American destroyer chased after it and quickly caught up with it. The Soviets had no choice but to take the punishment or surface. Several crew members passed out from the pain. The air-conditioning equipment broke down and the temperature inside the vessel soared to 140 degrees Fahrenheit. Sweat soaked the crew's uniforms and stung their eyes. The assault continued for four hours. Seeing his crew exhausted to the point of collapse, Savitsky broke from the stress and screamed, "Maybe the war has already started up there.

We're going to blast them now! We'll die, but we will sink them all. We will not disgrace our navy."

To fire a nuclear weapon, the Soviet navy required the agreement of the vessel's commander and the political officer. Both agreed that World War III had begun, and it was their duty to destroy as many American military ships as possible. It was only luck that a third officer was onboard B-59 that day. Commander Vasyli Arkhipov was the officer in charge of the submarine squadron of which B-59 was a part. As Soviet naval regulations dictated, while he was on board he too had to agree to launch the nuclear torpedo at the American ship. He didn't agree. In Arkhipov's mind, it was still possible that the war had not begun, and the Americans were simply attempting to drive the Soviet submarine to the surface. He agreed that the submarine commander would be within his rights to fire the nuclear torpedo if the Americans continued to assault the Soviets once they had surfaced.

Savitsky and the submarine's political officer didn't like it but acknowledged that Arkhipov was within his rights. Savitsky wanted to surface with the torpedo doors open and pointed toward the American destroyer. Arkhipov again disagreed. The Americans would see such an act as aggressive and might fire upon the submarine. The argument continued for several minutes each side trying to convince the other of the correct course of action. Arkhipov held his ground and finally won out. The submarine would surface with its torpedo doors closed but could immediately open them and fire if the Americans fired first. The captain ordered his crew to prepare to surface.

On the Cony, the sonar operator informed Morgan that the submarine was filling its ballast tanks with air and rising to the surface. Morgan ordered the ultra-high frequency assault from the Cony's sonar dome to stop immediately.

It was night as Morgan made his way out of the bridge to the deck. He ordered the ship's lights and gun turrets to turn to the port side. He also ordered the guns' barrels to remain level and not point down toward the water. He watched as the dark sea next to the destroyer turned white and B-59 surfaced 200 feet off the port side. The submarine's diesel engines started and began recharging its batteries. The hatches opened and the crew poured out onto the submarine's deck, stripping off their sweat-soaked uniforms.

Trained in communicating with the Russians and following Morgan's orders, Ensign Tomer used a flashing light to signal in morse code. He asked the submarine captain to identify the Soviet vessel.

Savitsky replied through his own flashing-light operator, "Submarine is Soviet ship X."

Tomer asked for the submarine's status.

"On the surface, operating normally," the Soviet captain responded.

"Do you require assistance?" flashed Tomer.

"Nyet," was Savitsky's terse response.

As the conversation continued, the Americans and the Soviets relaxed. There was a sense that neither meant the other harm if it could be avoided. As they continued to communicate, Savitsky and Tomer heard the deep thrum of approaching aircraft engines. An American P2V Neptune appeared and roared overhead dropping incendiary devices to light up the submarine and activate its photoelectric camera. As the flares popped, the light was blinding. Savitsky thought the flares were precursors to an aerial assault on his vessel. He wheeled his submarine bringing his forward torpedo tubes to bear on the American destroyer. The torpedo doors opened.

Seeing the submarine captain's intention, Morgan ordered Tomer to apologize for the American reconnaissance aircraft's aggressive conduct. No harm was meant by the Americans, only photos.

After sending the message, Morgan and Tomer watched for a tense minute as the Soviet submarine remained motionless and there was no response. Morgan ordered his gunners not to move their barrels from their current positions or make any sudden moves. Everyone on both vessels remained motionless. At that moment in history, the simplest misunderstanding by either side could easily have started World War III. The standoff ended with B-59 closing its torpedo doors and wheeling back to its original position away from the Cony. Morgan and Tomer were visibly relieved. "Keep that Russian captain happy, ensign," said Morgan.

"Will do, commander," said Tomer.

Tomer nodded to Savitsky. Savitsky nodded back. A moment later, another message flashed from the submarine, "We could use some fresh bread and American cigarettes."

"We will transfer supplies by high-line," signaled Tomer.

Once the Soviets received the requested supplies, Savitsky signaled his thanks, and the Soviet submarine began its long journey back to Russia. Cony followed along until B-59 had recharged its batteries and submerged. Cony gave the submarine a wide berth and returned to station. It wasn't until years later during a briefing that Morgan was informed that the Soviet submarine B-59 had been armed with nuclear torpedoes. He wondered how that information, had he known it at the time, would have changed the course of history. It was the image of B-59's torpedo doors opening as it turned to bear on the Cony that stood out most in Morgan's mind. Would he have opened fire if he had known the contents of the torpedo's warheads? It wasn't the first time, or the last time ignorance had saved the world.

October 28, 1962 - White House Washington DC,
USA

There was no defining moment during the Cuban Missile Crisis when either side felt the crisis had passed and their nation was safe. Instead, there was a series of ratcheting down events that occurred. The first significant event was Khrushchev's public announcement that the Soviets would dismantle the missiles and ship them back to USSR. In addition, the Cubans would allow UN inspectors to examine the launch sites to ensure the Soviets complied.

What Americans and the rest of the world did not know was that Kennedy and Khrushchev had come to a secret agreement. The American president had agreed not to invade Cuba unless the Cubans attacked first and to pull American missiles out of Turkey and possibly Italy if the Soviets pulled their missiles and bombers out of Cuba. The Soviets would need to make their withdrawal of their missiles and bombers public while the Americans would proceed with their withdrawal once the Soviet missiles were no longer a threat. At Kennedy's insistence, the American terms in the agreement would not be made public. Khrushchev would just have to take Kennedy's word that the American missiles would be withdrawn. Being in a far worse position to negotiate, the Soviets had agreed.

What the Soviets failed to realize was that the Americans no longer wanted nuclear missiles in Turkey or Italy. Since the deployment of submarine-launched Polaris nuclear ballistic missiles or SLBMs, the American military no longer needed land-based nuclear missiles to reach Moscow. Using the SLBMs with a range of 2,500 miles, American submarines could easily hit multiple targets in the USSR, including Moscow, without exposing themselves to first-strike attacks by their enemies. They simply maneuvered into position underwater and fired their missiles while still submerged. Each SLBM had three one-megaton nuclear warheads that would separate on reentry into the atmosphere and land one mile apart so as not to interfere with each other's radiation pulse. With the deployment of the SLBMs, land-based nuclear weapons like those in Turkey and Italy had become obsolete. Kennedy had negotiated away a weapon that America no longer wanted.

The next day, USAF reconnaissance photos showed that the Soviets were disassembling the missiles on Cuba and transporting them to Soviet freighters waiting in a nearby port. The Americans did not immediately stand down but watched closely.

What the Americans did not know was that the Soviets already had 162 nuclear warheads in Cuba. Since the Americans did not know about the warheads, Khrushchev considered leaving the warheads with Castro to be used if the Americans ignored the secret agreement and invaded the island. But Khrushchev knew that if Castro used Soviet-made nuclear weapons against the US or any of its allies in the surrounding area, the Soviets would be blamed and held responsible. To Khrushchev, leaving nuclear weapons with Castro meant losing control and control was what Khrushchev wanted most of all. While he initially left the nuclear warheads in Cuba under Soviet military control, Khrushchev ordered the weapons returned to the USSR within the year.

November 9-20, 1962 – Caribbean Ocean

After the last Soviet missile had been loaded on the freighter that would carry it back to the USSR, there was still the matter of the Soviet IL-28 bombers that were stationed in Cuba. It would be another ten days before the Soviets agreed to remove their aircraft from Cuban soil. Concurrent with the Soviet agreement on the bombers and as a show of good faith, Kennedy ordered US Navy to redeploy the vessels in the quarantine line. The status of Worldwide US Military forces was once again downgraded from DEFCON 3 to DEFCON 4. The crisis was over.

The American public, having stood on pins and needles throughout October and early November, let out a great sigh of relief and finally got some much-needed sleep. They had survived and America was still standing tall. With American and the world's perception that he had outplayed the Soviets and won the peace, Kennedy took his victory lap.

With two confrontations with the communists under his belt, few conservatives publicly questioned Kennedy's commitment to containing the red tide. Germany and Vietnam would be the new battlegrounds in the struggle against communist expansion. Kennedy was convinced that the Soviets would make a play to overrun Berlin before the end of the year.

For the moment, he felt the Chinese were being held at bay in Vietnam. They were supplying weapons, advisors, and money to the North Vietnamese and secretly to the Viet Cong, but no Chinese troops were in North Vietnam. His generals were telling him that with America's help Saigon was winning the war against the Viet Cong. It wasn't great, but it was something Kennedy could hang his hat on. It was also a lie that would be exposed...

# MANSFIELD

Like Congressman John Kennedy, Senator Mike Mansfield had been an early supporter of Diem when he was serving as prime minister under Bo Dao. That support continued as Diem became president and led the fight against communist expansion in South Vietnam. With like minds on many issues, Kennedy and Mansfield became good friends during their time in the senate. President Kennedy often asked Mansfield's opinion on Vietnam throughout his presidency. It wasn't until Mansfield's first visit to South Vietnam in 1962 that his opinion changed. He had undertaken the fact-finding tour at the request of the president. Kennedy had visited Vietnam previously during the Indochina War and knew that few could reveal the truth more than an inquisitive member of Congress with the president's backing.

Like most visiting dignitaries from the United States,

Mansfield received the red-carpet treatment from Diem and his generals. He inspected battalions of fine-looking soldiers that seemed ready to fight the communists on a moment's notice with the latest American-made weapons. He attended rallies filled with cheering spectators waving signs of support, hoping to get a glimpse of President Diem or a member of his family. He spoke with General Harkin, the commander of MACV, and was shown dozens of maps and charts that showed that South Vietnam with America's help was winning the fight against the Viet Cong. According to Harkin, US military advisors could be called home by the end of next year if the persecution of the war proceeded on schedule. The South Vietnam military would soon be fully trained, armed with the latest technology, and able to defend its nation on its own. It was enough to make any American feel proud… and it was all a not-so-clever facade.

As the end of Mansfield's tour drew near, he decided to strike out on his own. He secured a car and driver from the American embassy and drove to the various news outlets around Saigon. He interviewed foreign journalists and asked their opinions about what was happening in the country and the war. While their opinions varied, they all said the same thing when it came to the war – the senator needed to talk with Lieutenant Colonel Vann.

Mansfield drove out to the airbases and interviewed several of the military advisors who were more than willing to talk. After all, Mansfield was a US senator and had the ear of President Kennedy. He saved his interview with Colonel Vann for last. The journalists had been right. Nobody knew what was happening in the field better than Vann. More than anyone he had his mind wrapped around the military situation and what needed to be done. Mansfield was thoroughly impressed with Vann. The colonel knew his stuff and had a strong esprit de corps. Vann was a true warrior and wanted to win with all his heart. Vann told Mansfield the truth as he saw it – South Vietnam was losing the war. Vann articulated the problems and even offered solutions, the biggest of which was to get rid of Diem and his family before they destroyed the country and the military. Mansfield didn't like what Vann had to say, but he believed him.

It was a long flight home for Mansfield. He didn't sleep. His world had been tipped on end. He now saw that everything he had believed about Vietnam was wrong. He like so many had been fooled by generals like Harkin. He was determined to set it right.

Mansfield met with President Kennedy on December 2, 1962, in the oval office. He reported what he saw and what he had heard. He didn't embellish or hold back. He believed that it was vital that the president be told the truth as far as the senator knew it. At the end, Kennedy asked Mansfield his opinion of the war and the senator and friend answered, "Diem and his family are squandering most of the financial aid we are sending. He is using our money to pay off the generals and officials that keep him in power. The strategic hamlet program we funded seems like a complete failure and is driving the people further away from their government and Diem. As far as military aid, Diem is siphoning off the best weapons and supplies for the forces loyal to him. Few of the weapons and supplies make it beyond the bases in the biggest cities. The units in the field get little beyond new rifles and machine guns. It feels like he is starving sections of the military on purpose; to keep them weak."

"Can you blame him? He has survived two coups and two attempted assassinations, one of which bombed the palace."

"Diem and his family bring these things upon themselves, Mr. President."

"So, what are you recommending, Mike?"

"We cut our losses and end further involvement in Vietnam."

"I can't do that."

"You can and you should. The consequences of South

Vietnam falling to the communists would be devastating to our country. We would lose all credibility with our allies."

"We will lose our allies if we pull out."

"I am not sure that is true, especially if we explain the situation."

"We are damned if we do and damned if we don't. Even I can see that."

"Yes, Mr. President. It is a pickle, but I honestly believe that supporting Diem and his family will only make matters worse and hasten the fall of the country."

"So, what are you suggesting? How do we get rid of Diem?"

"That I don't know. I am still reeling from the revelations you send me to uncover. I'll need time to consider the possibilities, as will you. What I can tell you is this... we are no closer to winning this war than when it started. We are back at the beginning. Nothing has been gained. Our old friend Diem has withdrawn and is becoming a recluse sitting in his palace and barking out commands. More and more he is withdrawing from reality and only listening to those that offer him good news. It is his brother Nhu and his sister-in-law that are seen in public and the people hate them. Madame Nhu in particular doesn't know when to keep her mouth shut. It's a public relations disaster if there ever was one."

"Well, I can't say I am completely surprised by your report, Mike. Most of my advisors and cabinet are for the war effort but cracks are starting to show. What does surprise me is the tone of your report. You used to support my positions on Vietnam."

"I still support you, Mr. President. It's why I went to Vietnam and why I am standing before you now. This nation needs to change course before we get sucked down by Diem and his family."

"I doubt Diem and his family can suck down the United States."

"Don't doubt it, Mr. President. He will be your ruin if

you don't do something and quick."

For the first time, Kennedy began to consider that the survival of the Diem regime and the survival of South Vietnam were not inseparable.

While Kennedy and the senator remained friends, Mike Mansfield was the first high-level government official to openly criticize US involvement in Vietnam and the first to hammer a nail in Diem's coffin.

# LONG SHOT

### Saigon, South Vietnam

Coyle, Granier, and Bruno sat in the middle of a warehouse used by the CIA for supplies. It was the only place they were sure would not be bugged. There were maps of Hanoi, schematics of the prison, and aerial photographs of the prison laid out on a foldable card table. Granier finished going over the plan he and Coyle had developed. Bruno listened without comment until the end, then said, "This is a joke, yes?"

Coyle watched as Granier's expression sharpened. He thought for sure Granier would deck Bruno. Granier and Bruno were in excellent shape. It would be hard to say who might win, except that Granier was younger by a few years. The one thing Coyle was sure of was that if a fight broke out Bruno would be on the next flight back to Paris and the mission to save Bian's father would be over before it started. "Bruno, I think you are exaggerating," said Coyle.

"Exaggerating? If we follow this plan, we will all end up in the prison with the girl's father or dead. I am not sure which is more likely," said Bruno.

"This is not my first covert mission in Hanoi," said Granier grinding his teeth.

"Really? I am surprised you made it this far. God must

like you or you are very lucky."

"Alright, smart-ass. What would you change?"

"Change? All of it. It is trash. We should start from scratch."

Granier turned to Coyle and gave him an "if-you-don't punch-him-I-will" look. Coyle turned to Bruno and said, "Granier and I spent a lot of effort collecting reconnaissance on the prison. I'm sure there is something we can use."

Bruno riffled through the photographs, drawings, and maps. "Perhaps," he said. "How many guards are at the prison?"

"A company. We figure there are fifty troops on duty at any one time."

"And the number on our team?"

"You're looking at 'em, bub," said Granier.

"So, you are purposing we three take on a company of NVA? It is ludicrous."

"We will have the element of surprise," said Coyle. "That's got to count for something."

Bruno shook his head and said, "You really must learn how to fight, Coyle. I have already fought my Dien Bien Phu. I do not want to fight another."

"Look, if you're too much of a chicken-shit, Coyle and I will go it alone. We'd probably be better off without you," said Granier.

"No, we wouldn't," said Coyle. "None of this will work without Bruno."

"I am not a chicken-shit as you say. I just don't want to die if it is not necessary. I suggest you leave me with these materials and let me come up with a plan that will work," said Bruno.

"We'll do that, Bruno. Take all the time you need," said Coyle pulling Granier away. "We'll get you a café to help you think."

"Yes, yes. Café would be good."

Once out of carshot from Bruno, Granier turned to

Coyle and said, "I ain't going with that guy. He's an arrogant asshole like Conein. He's gonna get us killed."

"No, he won't. He's very good at planning. But you're right. He's cut from the same cloth as Conein. And just like Conein, he's a hell of a fighter. We need him," said Coyle.

"This is not what I signed up for."

"Yeah, but it's what we got. We need to make it work."

Granier considered for a moment, then… "Alright. It can't hurt see what he comes up with, but if I don't like it, I am out."

"Okay. That's fair."

When they returned with Bruno's café, he had already worked out the broad strokes of his plan. He presented it to Granier and Coyle. Coyle kept glancing at Granier to make sure he was on board. He was. Although he hated to admit it, Bruno's plan was better than his own. Bruno seemed to consider all elements and used the results of actions several times to take full advantage of any effort that was expended. The only flaw in Bruno's plan was that all three of them must survive to make the plan successful. That was not probable against the forces they were facing and all three of them knew it. "The odds of success have improved but are still long. Do we go anyway?" said Bruno.

"We go," said Coyle.

"We go," said Granier.

"I agree. We go," said Bruno. "Now, let's work out the details."

It took another week to gather all the supplies and weapons they would need to carry out the covert mission. The biggest problem was Coyle locating an aircraft that they could use to cross the border and fly to Hanoi without raising suspicion. He finally settled on a de Havilland Canada DHC-4 Caribou. It was a twin-engine transport/cargo aircraft similar to an American-built C-47 Skytrain but smaller. What made it ideal for the mission was that the

North Vietnamese had captured several of the aircraft over the past few years and put them to use in their own fledgling air force. The North Vietnamese military would not question a DHC-4 displaying their insignia and flying over their territory. Coyle had tracked down a South Vietnamese Air Force Caribou in Hue. His plan was simple. He would steal it. Right before takeoff, he would change the insignia to the Vietnam People's Air Force. The tricky part was flying an enemy aircraft in South Vietnam airspace without getting shot down. Coyle figured they could take off early in the morning while it was still dark and cross the border before sunrise.

The first leg of the mission was to fly to Hue from Saigon. Coyle had arranged to fly a supply mission to Hue. Garnier and Bruno sat in the cargo hold with their gear stowed in duffle bags. When the plane touched down in Hue, Coyle faked the flu and requested that his co-pilot fly the plane back to Saigon. He would follow later when he was feeling better. Once the aircrew had taken off, Coyle began his search for the Caribou. He found it in a hangar being worked on by a mechanic. Concerned, he inquired about the aircraft. It was just routine maintenance and would be finished by the end of the mechanic's shift. Coyle and his team of two went to a nearby hotel. They ate, slept, and ate again before leaving at 3 am. They didn't know when they would have a chance to eat and sleep again. Such was a soldier's life.

When they entered the hangar, the aircraft was gone. Coyle didn't panic. It was common to move aircraft around an airfield, he just had to find it without raising suspicion from the South Vietnamese guards that protected the airfield. The best way to avoid the guards was to hide in plain sight and look like you owned the place. Bruno, Coyle, and Granier each carrying two duffle bags walked along the tarmac joking with each other and telling stories. They passed two sets of guards until they finally found the Caribou in front of a warehouse ready for loading. Coyle started his preflight check as Granier and Bruno loaded the plane including a fuel bladder they had borrowed from the mechanic's hangar. Granier hijacked a fuel truck and filled the fuel bladder.

One hour before sunrise, Granier and Bruno replaced the South Vietnamese insignia with North Vietnamese insignia as Coyle started the engines. Granier and Bruno climbed in, and Coyle taxied to the runway. He had not filed a flight plan but radioed the tower anyway hoping to bullshit his way through. It worked. Ten minutes later, they were in the air and on their way to North Vietnam.

Having crossed the border between North and South many times, Granier knew the best places to cross without being detected. Coyle flew as low as he dared as they approached the border. At one point one of the props clipped the top of a tree. No damage was done. He pulled up slightly to give them a bit more room. The moment the aircraft crossed the border Coyle hoped that nobody was watching. A suspicious report to superiors could bring a world of hurt down on the team. Granier had been right. No patrols were in the area when they crossed. Coyle immediately gained altitude, corrected his course, and headed for Hanoi.

With a range of 1,307 miles, the aircraft could easily reach Hanoi without refueling. The biggest problem was where to land. Coyle had identified several utility airfields and a couple of country roads that would make good landing strips. The DHC-4 was a rugged aircraft capable of making short takeoffs and landings (STAL) when required. What concerned Coyle, Granier, and Bruno was that for the mission to remain covert they would need to land without anyone taking notice. Coyle decided on a country road a few miles outside of Hanoi's outer ring of suburbs.

Coyle did a quick pass to ensure they had privacy. Nobody was in sight. He lined up his landing on the road and lowered the landing gear. As the wheels touched down on the dirt road Coyle looked over and saw a peasant farmer walking out of the jungle followed by his water buffalo. "So much for secrecy," said Coyle to Granier sitting in the co-pilot's seat.

"I'll take care of him," said Granier.

"You can't kill him. He didn't do anything."

"I'm not gonna kill him."

As the plane rolled to a stop, Granier moved into the cargo hold, opened one of the duffle bags, pulled out a coil of rope, and cut two lengths. He hopped out of the aircraft and ran back to the farmer in his field. The farmer seeing the tall foreigner running toward him panicked and tried to run back into the jungle. Granier grabbed the farmer. The water buffalo bellowed his objection. "Calm down. I'm not gonna hurt him," said Granier escorting the farmer to a nearby tree away from the road.

He sat the farmer down in the shade of the tree and tied him securely to the tree with the rope. He walked back out into the field, slipped the second piece of rope into the buffalo's nose ring, and led him to where the farmer was tied up. Granier tied the buffalo's rope to the farmer. "There. You can keep each other company," said Granier, then turned and walked back to the aircraft.

Bruno was returning from a quick recon of the area by the road. He found a flat area and guided Coyle as he turned the aircraft off the road and into a nearby cove within the jungle. All three men covered the aircraft with leaves, branches, and shrubs until it was well camouflaged. Using the fuel bladder, Coyle refilled the aircraft's fuel tanks so it was ready for a quick takeoff. The three-man team removed their weapons from the duffle bags and checked their gear. Everything was in order. They stowed their weapons and gear back in the duffle bags. They smeared mud and dirt on their skin and changed out of their uniforms into the clothes of peasants with conical hats to hide their faces. Coyle and Granier were too tall to be mistaken for Vietnamese, but Bruno was in the ballpark. A quick check of the map and they took off down the road. "He's going to escape," said

Bruno looking over at the farmer as they passed. "We should shoot him."

"He's not going to escape," said Granier. "I know how to tie a knot."

"What if someone comes looking for him?" said Coyle. "I'm not saying we should kill him. I am just saying he's probably got a family that's expecting him for dinner."

"So, what do you suggest?" said Granier.

"I don't know. Maybe we should take him with us."

"You are too soft, Coyle. It has always been your problem," said Bruno turning to Granier. "He's always been a lover, not a fighter."

"I know," said Granier.

"Fuck off, both of you," said Coyle.

Bruno stopped and opened one of his duffle bags. He pulled out a bottle of Napoleon brandy. "A little early don't you think?" said Granier.

"I brought it to celebrate our victory," said Bruno. "One must always be prepared."

Bruno walked to where the farmer was tied up, opened the bottle, and gave him a drink. It was strong like his rice wine but the farmer shirked from the flavor. A few more swigs and the farmer was guzzling the brandy. Bruno fed him the entire bottle until the farmer was very drunk and mumbling to himself. Bruno pulled out his knife and cut the ropes from the tree freeing the farmer and the water buffalo. "What good will that do?" said Coyle.

"After finishing the bottle, I doubt he will remember his name let alone an aircraft landing on the road. And even if he did, nobody will believe him."

"That's kind of clever," said Granier.

"Yes, I am."


Hanoi, South Vietnam


The team made it to the outskirts of Hanoi without being detected. They rested in a grove of trees while they waited for darkness.

Once it was sufficiently dark to hide their faces, they set out for the center of the capital. It felt like descending into the belly of the beast. There were NVA troops everywhere. If they were found out there was little doubt they would be killed or captured. They stuck to alleys whenever possible and avoided the firelight from street vendors' barbeques. All three men were in shape and made good time. Except for pistols in their waistbands and a just-in-case grenade tucked in a shirt pocket, they kept their weapons hidden in the duffle bags, one carried on their backs like a pack and the other carried with one hand which they would trade off when their arms got tired.

Just before midnight, they came to the prison. They looked for an empty building across the street that would give them a good view of the prison while performing their last-minute reconnaissance. They broke in quietly, did a quick search to ensure they were alone, then moved to the window and stared out at their target.

There was no need for the prisoners or their captors to worry about fire; the prison was all metal and rock. The exterior of Hoa Lo prison was painted French yellow as it was in colonial times. The green shutters on the second floor were closed over the barred windows which made the air inside the buildings stifling and stale. There were no windows and few doorways on the first floor. It was a compound surrounded by long, twelve-foot masonry walls capped with broken shards of glass encased in cement and multiple coils of razor-sharp barbed wire. The prisoner cell blocks were arranged in a trapezoid away from the outer walls. Over the front gate were the words "Maison Centrale" in an arc. The heavy doors were wooden on the outside with steel plates on the inside. They were painted black as were the flat iron bars above the doorway. The roof was tiled and covered with black mold. It was French-built to stand hundreds of years. It was a fortress of dismay and, at times, terror.

Pairs of guards patrolled the outer perimeter. There were always two guards on the outside and two guards on the inside of each block-long wall. Inside were North Vietnam's most dangerous criminals – political prisoners condemned by the People's courts. Not allowed to communicate with anyone from the outside, they had no voice that could be heard by the public. They were silenced. Most were forced to attend reeducation classes in hopes they would be reformed when they finally left. But the reality was that few would ever leave. There was a French guillotine in the dining hall. No longer used, it remained as a reminder of French justice and made the North Vietnamese look merciful. It was maintained in working order and tested out once a year in full view of the prisoners. Lard greased the channels to ensure the blade slid fast and sure. Watermelons were sliced in half by the heavy blade, then served to the prisoners as a macabre treat.

There were iron boxes that kept misbehaving prisoners in a squatting position unable to straighten their legs for days on end. There were interrogation rooms with iron doors and hand-cranked generators to produce electricity on demand to prisoners' testicles and nipples. There were dungeons with no light and little air where prisoners could be locked away for months or even years at a time. There were rooms with long iron shackles that clamped down on a dozen prisoners' ankles at a time. The hallways were dark and narrow allowing little airflow. There were trees and even a gazebo in the courtyard to protect the well-behaved prisoners from the hot sun. There was no escape and little hope in Hao Lo prison and that was just the way the North Vietnamese liked it. "It sure is a monster," said Coyle starring at the walls.

"Yes. We, French, know how to design buildings that last," said Bruno.

"How thick are the perimeter walls?"

"Three feet of stone and rock."

"Where are the guards patrolling the exterior walls?" said Coyle.

"I don't know. It's strange. The reconnaissance report said guards were patrolling outside the prison," said Granier.

"We are not going to find out sitting on our asses," said Bruno. "Let our show begin."

They nodded in agreement, then opened their duffle bags and unloaded their weapons and gear.

Twenty minutes later, a hot-wired scooter motored down the street in front of the prison. It was Granier with a backpack on the step floor between his legs. As he approached the main gate, he pulled a ring attached to a wire extending from the top of the pack. It began to smoke. He tossed the pack at the bottom of the metal-reinforced wooden doors and sped off. As Granier disappeared around the corner, the satchel charge inside the pack exploded blowing the front doors off their hinges. One of the trees on the sidewalk in front of the prison caught fire lighting up the night.

Heavily armed NVA soldiers poured out of the breached gate and took up defensive positions up and down the block. Two light machine guns were set up just outside the gate, each facing opposite directions down the street.

Across the street from the prison, Granier climbed to the roof of a three-story building where his sniper rifle was waiting. A large tree camouflaged his position, but he could still see the front and down one sidewall of the prison through the leaves and branches. He waited until a large number of soldiers deployed in front of the prison before radioing Coyle and Bruno. Granier kept the NVA soldiers in his sights but held his fire. Any shots from his weapon would reveal his position and force him to move. He needed to stay put so he could cover both the front of the prison and the side perimeter wall.

Outside the prison wall on the intersecting street,

Granier was covering from his rooftop position, Coyle and Bruno used grappling hooks with ropes to scale the perimeter wall. When they reached the top of the wall, they threw thick blankets over the broken glass and barbed wire then climbed on top of the wall. It was awkward but it worked. Coyle jumped down into the narrow alley between the outer wall and a cell block. Two NVA guards heard his boots hit the stone floor and turned around to see the intruder. Raising their rifles, they moved to capture them. Still on top of the wall, Bruno used a silenced pistol to shoot and kill both guards as they approached. Bruno jumped down to join Coyle. "Granier's operative said the captain was being held in one of the outer cell blocks on the north side. There should be a door on this end of the building," said Coyle.

They moved around the corner. Most of the guards were protecting the breached front gate but two guards remained at the entrance to the cellblock. Even silenced, Granier's pistol would make too much noise and bring unwanted attention. "Give me your knife," said Bruno.

Coyle knew better than to ask questions and handed Bruno his knife. Bruno pulled out his own knife with his empty hand. "Okay. You're bait again. Go pee on that wall over there, but don't turn your face to the guards no matter what," said Bruno.

"And if they shoot me?" said Coyle.

"They won't. Besides, this was your idea."

Coyle shrugged, set down his weapon, walked to the wall with his back to the guards, and urinated. Seeing Coyle, the guards called out and moved to append him. As they moved past the corner of the building Bruno stepped out and plunged a knife into the Adam's apple of one of the guards. He released his hold on the knife and grabbed the barrel of the second guard's rifle. He stepped forward into the guard and thrust the second knife into the left side of the guard's chest. Both men fell dead. Coyle and Granier dragged their bodies around the corner to keep them out of sight.

They moved to the doorway and entered the cell block. It was quiet. Too quiet. There were no guards inside the building. Coyle and Bruno exchanged an uneasy look. Coyle moved to a desk up against a wall and searched the drawers. He found a set of keys and moved to the first cell door as Bruno kept watch. Coyle didn't need the keys. The door was ajar and the cell was empty. "Oh, shit," said Coyle.

He moved to the next cell and it was the same. He moved down the hallway hoping to find a secured door. There were none. The cells were empty. "What the hell is going on?" said Bruno.

"They moved the prisoners," said Coyle deflated.

"To where?"

"I don't know, but we need to check the other cell blocks. It's possible they just moved the prisoners within the prison."

"This was not the plan. The longer we stay, the more chance we will be caught."

"I understand. You go while I check the other cell blocks."

"You know I won't do that."

"Then shut up and let's get moving."

"Alright. It is what it is. We're gonna need another distraction."

Coyle radioed Granier and explained the new situation. "You realize this is all going to shit," said Granier over the radio.

"Yeah. But what choice do we have?" said Coyle. "This is the only shot we are going to get at this thing. Let's not waste it with chit-chat."

"I agree. You get moving. I'll create your distraction."

Upon the rooftop, Granier, a master of chaos, aimed his scope and put a bullet in the head of the NVA company commander. He fell dead. Shots rang out in all directions as the NVA laid out random suppressing fire hoping to keep the hidden enemy from firing again. Granier knew two things – one, the NVA would need a couple of minutes to get reorganized under the second in command, and two, the NVA were going to come looking for him. He wasted no time and left the rooftop.

Reaching the street, Granier knew he could easily escape before the NVA arrived and surrounded him. But that wasn't what Coyle and Bruno needed. More mayhem was required. He moved to the corner of the building and peeked around. He saw a squad of NVA running toward him. He reached into pockets and pulled out two grenades. Pulling the safety rings, he pitched the two grenades around the corner, then made a run across the street toward another building.

The twin explosions killed one NVA and wounded three others with shrapnel. The unharmed soldiers hit the deck and laid down more suppressing fire like that was the key to surviving.

Before the dust and smoke of the explosions settled, Granier forced his way through a door into what he imagined was an apartment building. He entered the closest apartment and moved to the front window. A bedroom light came on and he heard footsteps. He pulled out his pistol and fired two shots into the wall without even looking. The footsteps receded and a door shut. The apartment's occupants got the message. Granier peered out through the open slats of the closed shutters.

The NVA squad had ceased fire and were climbing to their feet. They advanced toward the sound of the gunshots in the building across the street straight at Granier's position.

Granier aimed and fired through the window and shutters breaking the glass and shattering the wood slates. He emptied his clip and moved off for a new position in another building.

Two more NVA lay dead and three more were wounded. They called up for reinforcements. More guards within the prison compound were called up to protect the breached front gate allowing Coyle and Bruno to continue their search.

Coyle and Bruno moved through the cell blocks checking the doors and cells. It seemed like nobody was left in the prison. After checking another cell block, they saw the reason the prison was empty. A large section of a side wall had been torn down to expand the compound and build new cell blocks. The compound was no longer secure. "So, why are there so many guards?" said Bruno.

"To prevent anyone from tampering with what is left," said Coyle. "It's obviously empty. What are we going to do?"

"Leave quickly," said Bruno.

"Yeah, I suppose that's the only option that makes sense."

Outside the prison walls, troop trucks rolled up and the second half of the company guarding the prison unloaded. The captain in charge of the company listened to the officer on duty explain what had happened. The captain realized what was happening outside the prison was a diversion. He wasn't sure why since the prison was empty, but it didn't matter. The enemy was inside, and he meant to find them. He ordered the officer to continue the pursuit of the sniper and send a squad to cover the outside of the prison where the wall had been torn down. At the same time, he took the rest of the company inside the prison to find the intruders.

Coyle and Bruno moved to escape through the open wall section. They heard the stomping of boots and watched as a squad of NVA rounded the corner outside the prison. Unwilling to be caught in the open, Coyle and Bruno pulled back inside the prison and searched for another way out. They moved back through the cell blocks toward the opposite side of the prison where Granier had planned to cover their escape. Bruno had a satchel charge in his backpack to breach the wall as they had planned originally. Coyle radioed Granier who was moving to this next snipping position and told him that they were coming out.

Granier acknowledge that he would cover their exit.

Coyle and Bruno entered the next cell block when they saw NVA pouring in the opposite side of the cell block searching for intruders. They pulled back. The trap was closing. Bruno moved to the alley between the outer wall of the cellblock and the perimeter wall at the back of the prison. He peeked around the corner and saw more NVA advancing toward his position. "We need a plan and quick," said Coyle.

"Yes, yes. Never panic," said Bruno pulling off his backpack. "Radio Granier and tell him we are changing our egress point to the back perimeter wall."

As Coyle radioed Granier, Bruno pulled the ring on the satchel charge. Smoke rose from the charge, but Bruno held it. "Are you going to throw that thing?" said Coyle.

Bruno waited until the NVA in the alley closed on their position before pitching the satchel charge around the corner. When the charge landed against the base of the perimeter wall, the NVA saw the smoking backpack and knew immediately what it was. They retreated down the alleyway. Reverberating off the walls of the alley, the explosion was deafening and concentrated. Smoke and dust filled the alley.

From his position outside the prison, Granier could see the smoke rising from Coyle and Bruno's position. He spotted a building overlooking the street they would exit on and decided on his next sniper position. He took two shots at the NVA on the street, killing one soldier and wounding another, before moving to the new building down a back alley.

Another group of troop trucks pulled up and more troops disembarked. More NVA reinforcements joined the search for the sniper. The commander of the search heard and saw the explosion on the backside of the prison. He realized what the sniper was doing – a distraction and covering fire for an escape. He ordered his men to leapfrog past some of the buildings and enter the building overlooking the back street of the prison where Granier was headed.

Inside the prison, Bruno turned to Coyle and said, "Time to go."

Coyle nodded and peeked around the corner of the alleyway. It was filled with dust and smoke. Bruno moved into the cell block doorway and sprayed the hallway with bullets from his submachine gun. The NVA inside took cover.

Coyle moved down the alley through the dust and smoke to where he thought the charge had exploded. There was a tar-like smell in the air from the explosives. He couldn't see more than a foot in front of his face and his eyes stung. He felt the wall. It was hot and the stone was rough from where the explosion had blown away the wall. He was in the right place, but he couldn't find a hole. He kept searching. Bruno moved up beside and fired blindly down the alleyway where the NVA had been. "What are you waiting for?" said Bruno.

"I can't find the hole in the wall," said Coyle.

Bruno joined him feeling the wall. Nothing. The charge had not breached the thick stone wall. Bullets zinged through the smoke and dust. The NVA were closing in on their position. "We gotta go," said Bruno.

"Where?" said Coyle.

"Anywhere but here," said Bruno as the gunfire increased.

They moved back toward the cellblock door around the corner. NVA poured out and opened fire. Coyle and Bruno moved back into the alley. They were trapped with the enemy closing in on both sides.

Outside the prison, Granier climbed the last steps of a four-story building. He burst through the rooftop doorway and moved to the edge overlooking the prison. He glanced down and saw a squad entering the building on the first floor. He didn't have much time. He turned and surveyed the building. There was an electrical cable strung over the gap between the rooftop of the building next door and the building he was on. That would be his escape route. He unshouldered his rifle and sat resting his elbows on his legs for stabilization. He peered through this scope to see the street behind the prison and panned over to where the smoke was rising. There was no hole in the wall. "Oh, shit," said Granier to himself.

He wasn't sure what to do. He could hear distant yelling from the NVA troops climbing the stairs as they searched for him. He didn't have long. He set his rifle down, jumped up, and ran to the doorway. He pulled out his Ka-Bar and jammed it between the door sill and the edge of the door. It was tight, but he knew it would only slow them down for a few moments. He moved back to the edge, picked up his rifle, and peered through the scope. No sign of Coyle or Bruno. He glanced back at the electrical cable and decided he could cut the cable once across to prevent the NVA from following him so easily. It would buy him time to take another look at the back street and hopefully cover Bruno and Coyle.

Inside the prison, Coyle and Bruno had turned over a concrete table and bench to use as cover. They fired their weapons sparingly conserving their low ammo. "We can still get out through the open wall or the front gate," said Bruno.

"I don't know. They've got them covered pretty good," said Coyle.

"If we stay here, we die."

"Where in the hell is Granier?"

"It doesn't matter. He can't help us. We're on our own until we reach the outside."

They both heard the sound of an engine starting. "What in the hell is that?" said Coyle.

A bulldozer used to knock down the sidewall for the expansion appeared from behind a building. With its shovel lowered to protect the driver and the unit of NVA that followed behind the machine, the bulldozer pivoted and advanced on their position. Unyielding, Bruno shot at the steel beast with his submachine gun. "You're wasting ammunition," said Coyle.

"You got a better idea?" said Bruno reloading.

"Yes. We live to fight another day. Dying isn't going to save Bian or her father."

"You give up if you wish, Coyle. I am a paratrooper. I will fight until I run out of ammunition or die."

As the bulldozer moved within ten feet of the table and stopped, two grenades arched over the top of the shovel and landed on Bruno and Coyle's side of the cement tabletop. With the grenades between them, they scrambled around to the front of the table's slab for cover. The grenades exploded. When the dust settled, a half-dozen NVA pointing their rifles had surrounded Coyle and Bruno. There was no place to run. They set down their weapons and raised their hands. It was over.

On the rooftop, Granier still had not seen Coyle or Bruno. He didn't know what had happened, but he had an idea. He heard the first NVA soldier reach the rooftop door and pound on the door with the butt of his rifle. Granier's time was up. He slung his rifle over his shoulder, moved to the cable, pulled himself up with two hands, lifted his legs, and wrapped them around the cable. He shimmed his way across the gap. He heard more rifle butts pounding against the metal. Reaching the other side of the gap, he dropped down on the adjacent rooftop. The rooftop door he had jammed burst open and five NVA soldiers poured out of the doorway onto the roof. They pointed their rifles at Granier. He considered drawing his sidearm but knew that would only give them a reason to kill him. He glanced around the rooftop for a way to escape. There was none. As much as it went against his nature, he raised his hands in surrender.

Ten minutes later, Granier was thrown in a cell inside Hao Lo Prison. He was not fond of the irony. The guards inside the cell blocks carried no firearms to prevent prisoners from overpowering them and taking their weapons. They did carry wooden Billy clubs with wrist straps which they used frequently on the prisoners to keep them in line. Once Granier heard the guards' footsteps fade away, he moved the small, iron-barred opening in the door and said, "Coyle, are you here?"

"Yeah, I'm here, Granier," said Coyle.

"What about Bruno?"

"He's here too. He's just sulking."

"I'm not sulking. I'm thinking," said Bruno.

"Separate cells?" said Granier.

"Yeah," said Coyle.

"So, what in the hell happened?"

"The satchel charge didn't breach the wall. Then the NVA assaulted our position with a bulldozer."

"A bulldozer?"

"Yeah. They're surprisingly effective."

"I imagine."

"So, what are they going to do next?"

"They'll interrogate us. It's not going to be pleasant. Once they're done, they'll probably split us up and transport us to different locations."

"I guess it's over. We failed."

"Yep… for now."

Bruno sat on the floor surveying his cell. The floors and walls were made of concrete. He had already checked the bars on the windows. They were unmovable and the iron was not heavily rusted. There was a mat on the floor and a handleless metal bucket to relieve oneself. Not much to work with. He studied the bucket for a couple of minutes until something occurred to him. He stood up and moved to the door. "Gentlemen, we've got to get out of here," said Bruno.

"Oh, that's helpful," said Granier.

"I mean we must get out of these cells. I think I know a way we might escape."

"How's that?" said Coyle.

"Shit."

"Shit?"

"Where does the shit go for hundreds of prisoners? They must have some sort of sewer system. That's a lot of shit."

"You want us to escape through the sewers?" said Granier.

"Why not?"

"I'm sure they thought of that and barred up the channel."

"Then we break through. The iron bars are probably corroded from the acid in the prisoners' urine. I doubt they check them very often."

"I suppose it's better than just sitting here," said Granier.

"It's suicide and disgusting," said Coyle. "But I agree… anything is better than sitting here. So, how do we get out of these cells?"

"They'll start interrogating us soon. Maybe then…" said Granier.

"If they have figured out who I am, they will start with me," said Bruno.


Several hours later, Bruno heard the guards coming down the hallway. He could not tell how many by their footfalls on the concrete, but he imagined they would be three if they didn't know who he was and five if they did. He heard the rattling of chains – shackles. The guards stopped in front of his cell door and a small door for serving food opened in the middle of the door. "Bigeard, put your hands behind your back and put them through the opening," said the team commander in French.

They knew him. *It would be five or more*, thought Bruno. If they were well trained, they would be prepared with riot gear. It made his job more difficult. He thought for a moment, then turned around and put his hands through the opening. He felt the guard grab his left hand leaving his right hand free. That was a mistake. As the guard placed the first manacle on his wrist, Bruno reached over with his free hand and grabbed the guard's wrist. The guard dropped the shackles and attempted to free himself from the prisoner's grasp. Too late. Bruno used both his hands to pull the guard's arm through the opening. Bruno twisted his body around while extending the guard's arm reversing it, then released one of his hands and used his elbow to come down on the guard's elbow like a hammer. There was a loud crack and the guard screamed in pain; his elbow shattered. One down. Bruno held onto the guard's arm putting pressure on the broken elbow. He wanted the rest of the guards to enter his cell before reinforcements could arrive. As the cell door swung open, Bruno released the disabled guard's arm. The man crumbled to the floor in the hallway.

Bruno could see that there were five more guards wearing helmets and holding Billy clubs in the hallway lined up to enter his cell. The lead guard also carried a wooden shield in front of him. If possible, Bruno wanted to take them on one at a time as they entered the cell. Bruno knelt on one knee. As he entered the cell, the lead guard lowered his shield slightly but kept it in front of him. Bruno waited until he was close, then leapt up and kicked the bottom of the guard's shield. The shield was launched upward smashing into the bottom of the guard's head breaking his jaw along with several teeth. The guard fell to the floor releasing his shield. Two down. Bruno considered picking up the shield but decided against it. He was better at fighting with his hands unencumbered, even when he was outnumbered.

The next guard came in holding his wooden Billy club up and to the side ready to strike the prisoner. When the guard was close, he swung his club at Bruno's head. Bruno pitched back avoiding the club. The guard wasted no time as the club came back toward his chest and swung again in a reverse move. Bruno ducked this time and the club swung over the back of his head barely missing him. When his head rose again, Bruno reached out with his hand and wrapped it around the guard's arm like a snake coiling around a branch. With the guard's club arm tangled in Bruno's arm, Bruno used his free hand to punch the guard's fingers wrapped around the club handle. Loud cracks of fingers breaking and the guard released the club. The lanyard tied to the base of the club kept it from falling. Bruno hit the guard in the face with his elbow knocking him unconscious. Three down, three to go. As the unconscious guard fell, Bruno slipped the lanyard off the guard's wrist. Bruno was armed with a Billy club and more dangerous.

The next guard entered with his club in front of him ready to protect himself against Bruno's club. Instead of swinging for the guard's head, Bruno simply hit the guard's hand holding the club breaking his grip, then on his backswing, Bruno hit the guard in the side of the head. The unconscious guard went down in a lump. Four down.

Bruno retrieved the guard's club as the last two guards entered and moved to opposite sides of the cell surrounding Bruno. Bruno turned around and stepped backward through the open doorway into the hallway forcing the guards to come through one by one. As the first guard stepped into the hallway, Bruno swung one club. The guard used his own club to deflect the blow as Bruno used the other club to hit the guard in the side of the jaw. Another load crack and the guard fell·wailing in pain.

The next guard wasted no time and stepped through swinging wildly at Bruno. Bruno waited until the guard's club arm was across his body, then smacked the guard's head with both clubs at once. He crumbled straight down, his skull cracked on both sides. Bruno turned to face any more guards coming down the hallway. There were none. "Bruno?" said Coyle.

"Yes, yes. I am finished. I'll be right there," said Bruno retrieving the cell door keys from one of the guards. He clubbed the guards on the floor that were still conscious knocking them out.

Bruno opened the cell doors freeing Coyle and Granier

as they looked down at the six broken guards on the floor. "Six?" said Granier impressed.

"A personal best, I think," said Bruno.

Bruno, Coyle, and Granier made sure each guard was unconscious or dead, then carefully searched the cell block for more guards. They were alone. "Now, what?" said Coyle.

"Now we escape as planned," said Bruno.

"You make it sound easy," said Granier.

"Easy, no. Doable, yes. The plan will work."

"And if it doesn't?"

"We improvise, yes?"

"Yeah, sure. Any idea how we get down into the sewer?"

"They must empty the buckets somewhere."

They moved through the cell block and into the dining hall. Still no guards on the inside of the prison. Reaching almost to the ceiling, the French guillotine loomed large in the hall. They moved to the doorway leading to the courtyard, opened the door, and peered out. It was daytime. They could see thirty NVA, some patrolling, some sitting in the courtyard. There was no way to slip out without being seen. With only Billy clubs, they wouldn't stand a chance against the armed enemy troops. "Well, that's not going to work," said Granier.

"Hang on. I've got an idea," said Coyle staring at the guillotine.

He moved to the deadly contraption and shimmied up one of the two posts that held the blade channels. Although it had been maintained well, the guillotine had been in use for almost twenty years and many of the mechanical parts were well worn. The latch that held the blade at the top of the posts was particularly worn and was struggling to hold the heavy blade in place as Coyle climbed further up. As he reached the top, the blade was released and slid toward Coyle's legs still wrapped around the channel. Seeing the blade moving, he opened his legs and dangled with one hand as the blade dropped, finally crashing into the wooden block below. Still in one piece, Coyle pulled himself up. "I bet you have a few nightmares from that one," said Granier.

"A few?" said Coyle.

Coyle climbed up and stood on top of the crossbar. He used a Billy club to bash a man-sized hole in the ceiling's plaster revealing the support joists and roof tiles. Trying to be as quiet as possible, he carefully pushed on the bottom side of the tiles until one came loose. He grabbed the tile, pulled it through the hole, and dropped it to Granier waiting below to catch it. He continued grabbing each loosened tile and dropping it to Granier. With the hole big enough, he pulled himself up onto the rooftop. "What do you see?" said Bruno.

"Everything," said Coyle poking his head back through the hole. "I think I may have a way out. We're gonna need that guillotine rope and some sort of grappling hook."

Granier and Bruno looked around the hall for something they could use as a grappling hook. Nothing. Granier looked up at the light and notice there were no electrical wires which meant the wires were beneath the plaster. He moved to the wall and used his Billy club to crack the plaster and pull it away. After several large pieces of plaster fell away, Granier found what he was looking for – a metal conduit tube inside the concrete wall. Granier wrapped his fingers around a section of conduit and pulled it away from the wall chipping away more plaster and creating a shower of sparks when the electrical wires inside were severed. He was temporarily shocked but kept going, removing the section of conduit. He removed the wires inside, then bent the conduit back and forth using his knee and hands until it broke into two pieces. Again, using his knee and hands he bent one of the pieces of conduit into a giant fishhook. "It ain't a grappling hook but it'll have to do," said Granier. Bruno slipped the fishhook in one of the belt loops on his trousers, climbed up the guillotine, loosened the knot holding the rope, coiled it, and slipped it over his shoulder.

He climbed through the hole in the ceiling and disappeared.

After a couple of minutes, Granier grew antsy. The NVA could come into the hall at any moment. He moved toward the guillotine and started to climb up when Coyle poked his head back through the opening in the ceiling and said, "We're short. We need more rope."

"We ain't got any more rope," said Granier.

"Improvise."

Granier climbed back down and surveyed the hall. He pulled more conduit off the wall, then pulled the electrical wires from the conduit. He twisted four wires together to make an eight-foot length that he thought could hold a man's weight. He coiled it, threw it over his shoulder, headed up the guillotine, and up through the hole in the ceiling.

On top of the roof, he handed the coil of wires to Bruno. Bruno tied them one end of the rope. The other end had the fishhook. Bruno whirled the rope and fishhook around like a cowboy roping a steer. His target was a power cable strung between poles on the opposite side of the perimeter wall. He threw the fishhook and missed. It clattered as it fell against the wall. He pulled it back and it caught on the barbed wire on top of the wall. He yanked at it but couldn't free it from the tangle. Granier joined him pulling the rope. The barbed wire pulled free and they reeled in the fishhook with barbed wire attached. They pulled off barbed wire freeing the hook. Bruno coiled the rope. "Give me that," said Granier taking the rope and hook away from Bruno.

"I have engineers that do this," said Bruno, frustrated.

Granier took aim, whirled the rope and hook, hurled it and it caught the electrical cable the first time. "Beginner's luck," said Bruno.

"American know-how," said Granier.

Coyle was busy pulling away more tiles to expose the roof joists lower down on the roof. Granier handed him the twisted wires. Coyle tied them to a joist. All three heard yelling in the courtyard. "I think they figured out we've escaped," said Coyle.

"Coyle, go," said Granier. "Bruno you're next."

Coyle wrapped his hands and legs around the rope and headed across. Bruno steadied the rope and kept watch. The shouting was joined by the sound of boots running on concrete. Granier moved back to the hole above the hall and look down. It was filled with NVA, some climbing the guillotine. "We're out of time. Go, Bruno," said Granier as he pulled up several tiles and hurled them at the soldiers shimming up the guillotine.

One tile hit the lead soldier in the shoulder causing him to fall and hit another soldier on his way down. It would only buy them a few more moments. The NVA below fired their rifles into the ceiling. Granier moved away from the hole as bullets punched through the roof tiles. He turned to Coyle climbing past the wall. Coyle released his feet and jumped down to the sidewalk. Bruno wasn't far behind. Granier moved down the roof and looked over to see NVA rounding the corner of the building and taking aim with their rifles. It was now or never for Granier. He leapt off the roof and grabbed the rope as he fell. "What in the hell are you doing?" said Bruno almost falling from the wobbling rope.

Rifles fired from below. A bullet whizzed by Granier. "Getting shot at," said Granier pulling his feet up and wrapping them around the rope, then pulling his body along the rope as fast as he could.

Bruno cleared the wall and dropped down. Granier kept moving along the rope.

An officer popped his head out of the hole in the roof and saw Granier escaping. He unholstered his pistol, took aim, and fired multiple times.

The officer's bullets missed Granier but hit the rope in front of him. Granier watched as the rope's strands snapped one by one. "Oh, shit," said Granier to himself.

The rope broke. Granier fell. He was over the wall, but his pants caught on the barbed wire on top of the wall. His upside-down body slammed against the wall knocking the wind out of him. He tangled helplessly. Bruno and Coyle ran to his aid and pulled him down. His pants ripped, but he was free. They ran into the nearest alley with Bruno in the lead.

They ran over a mile twisting and turning through streets and alleys until Coyle finally stopped and sat on the pavement in an alley to catch his breath. "Enough. We lost them," said Coyle huffing and puffing.

"For the moment," said Bruno.

"I can't believe that actually worked," said Granier.

"Why not? We have luck on our side, no?" said Bruno.

"I don't know that I would call this luck."

"It is luck, fate, or whatever you wish. We are alive and free. We should make it back to the plane by sunup."

"I'm not going back. Not without Bian's father," said Coyle.

"Now you are being stupid, Coyle. There is no way to find him. The mission is over."

"Actually, there might be a way," said Granier.

"Are you thick in the head too, Granier?"

"No. I just hate to lose."

"So, do you have a gypsy's crystal ball or are you going to just search the whole city assuming he is still in the city?"

"Look, if Mohamad can't find the mountain, maybe the mountain can find Mohamad?"

"What the hell are you talking about? Why can't you Americans just talk straight?"

"Nah. Then we wouldn't piss you off as much."

"I'm curious what you have in mind, Granier," said Coyle.

"We need to kidnap someone important and offer a swap."

"Great. Who did you have in mind?" said Bruno.

"Le Duan, the chairman of the communist party. I'd bet they'd trade him for a few ragtag prisoners."

"And how do you propose to do this?"

"Well, we're gonna need some weapons."

"I've still got my Billy club," said Coyle.

"I was thinking about something with a little more range… like a bicycle."

"Idiots. I am in a cabal with complete idiots," said Bruno shaking his head.

In the darkness, Granier walked down an alley in a residential neighborhood. Bicycles, motorbikes, and foot carts were parked in front of two and three-story houses. Most were locked with chains through the wheels. Granier kept up his search until he found a bicycle with the chain through the front wheel only. Making sure he wasn't being watched, he felt under the seat in search of a tool bag. Nothing. He searched several bicycles in the alley until he found a tool bag. He moved back to the bicycle with the chain on the front wheel and used a small wrench from the tool bag to loosen the wheel nuts. He pulled the bicycle's frame from the front wheel and wheeled down the alley on its back tire.

Keeping out of sight, Coyle and Bruno were waiting in a small field behind a dilapidated lean-to that was once somebody's home. Granier laid the bicycle down and handed Coyle a spoke wrench. "You guys remove the spokes and the tire. I need the innertube," said Granier.

While Coyle and Bruno worked on the back of the bicycle, Granier went to work removing the chain, then the key (a round steel rod) in the crankset. The key had been hammered in place and was difficult to remove. Granier used a nail he removed from the lean-to and a rock he found in the field to hammer out the key. He used the tail of his shirt to muffle the sound of hammering. Once the key was out, Granier removed one of the pedals and its crank arm from the crankset. What remained was the crank set's gear with a hole in the middle and a crank arm with a pedal attached. "What are you going to do with that?" said Bruno.

"A slingshot bow," said Granier.

"I've never seen anything like that," said Bruno.

"Give me the innertube and I'll show you."

Bruno pulled the inner tube from the tire and handed it to Granier. Granier used the nail to score and cut the innertube in half. He tied the ends of one half to the outer ring of the crankset. He pulled the inner tube half back like a slingshot to check it. It worked. "You have done this before?" said Bruno.

"Yeah. Where I grew up. We'd use these gadgets to go fishing," said Granier.

"You can't be serious. Did you ever shoot anything?"

"Mostly carp, but occasionally we'd get a bass or catfish," said Granier as he turned to Coyle. "How many spokes do you have?"

"Nine," said Coyle handing him the loose spokes.

"That should be enough. I need six long strips of rubber and nine short fat ones with one edge frayed like a feather spit down the middle."

"Fletchings?" said Bruno helping Coyle.

"Exactly."

Once Coyle and Bruno were finished, Granier bundled three spokes together to form one shaft and tied each end with a strip of rubber to hold them together. He used the tire patch glue to affix each of the rubber fletchings Coyle and Bruno had created to the makeshift arrow shaft. After completing all three arrows, he loaded one in the center hole of the slingshot crankset. A rat scurried across the field. "Anybody hungry?" said Granier as he drew back the arrow in the sling, took aim, and let it fly.

The arrow skewered the rat. "Impressive," said Coyle.

"A rat is one thing. An armed soldier is another," said Bruno.

"How far can you shoot that thing?" said Coyle.

"Accurately? Maybe thirty feet," said Granier. "The 5th bureau has a weapon stash about three miles to the south in a cemetery. If we can reach it, it should have everything we need."

"So, why the slingshot bow?" said Coyle.

"There is a pretty good chance the NVA will have guards at the cemetery. They've figured out that we use them to stash weapons, but they don't know which graves. So, they post guards."

"Alright. So, once we rearm ourselves, how do we find Le Duan?" said Bruno.

"We follow him home from the politburo. There will be fewer guards."

"And how do we find the politburo?"

"I know where it is. We have our operatives keep pretty good tabs on it."

"You realize the plane we hid has probably been found by now. We were never supposed to stay here this long," said Bruno.

"Yeah, I've considered it. If the plane is still there and I can get my hands on a sniper rifle, it shouldn't be an issue. In the meantime, we'd better get moving."

Granier, Coyle, and Bruno set out to cross the city. The only one armed, Granier took the lead. They stuck to alleys when possible and used the shadows from the moon when moving on streets. The open ground was the real problem. Nowhere to hide. So, they split up and simply walked across one at a time as if there was nothing suspicious to see.

When they finally came to the cemetery, they found Granier was right. There were two armed guards. It was getting close to sunrise. Time was running out. Granier waited until the guards moved to opposite ends of the cemetery before making his move. The guard he decided on was young. He followed him at a distance. When the guard stopped to urinate on a gravestone, Granier moved up behind him closing the distance between them. He drew his arrow as he walked. At twenty-five feet, the guard heard footsteps behind him and turned. Granier released the homemade arrow. The arrow hit the guard on the left side of the chest. It went all the way through punching through his back. The guard fell dead. Granier grabbed his rifle, handed it to Bruno, and said, "Feel better?"

"Much," said Bruno checking the chamber to ensure it was loaded with a round. It was. Granier moved off and the others followed as he searched for the gravesite where the weapon stash was buried. It had been several years since the weapons had been placed, but he thought he remembered the name of the grave and roughly where it was located. "We're looking for the headstone of Nguyen Van Quyet," said Granier as they entered the area of the cemetery where the weapons were buried. "I'm gonna go see if I can find us a pick and shovel in the groundskeeper's shed."

Granier moved off as Coyle and Bruno kept up the search. After of few minutes of stumbling around, Coyle found the gravestone. "Where is Granier?" said Bruno.

"He'll be along," said Coyle.

Across the cemetery, Granier found the groundskeeper's shed. It was locked. He thought about bashing it with the bicycle slingshot but thought it would make too much noise. He heard footsteps behind him and a man speaking in Vietnamese. He drew his arrow back without raising it. He twisted around, found his target, and fired the arrow from his hip. The arrow hit the soldier in the shoulder wounding him. The soldier raised his rifle to shoot. Too late. Granier ran toward the man closing the distance and swung the edge of the crankset across his throat. It was a gruesome sight – more gash than cut. Blood flowed and the guard fell on his face, then died. Granier picked up his rifle and broke the lock on the shed using the butt of the gun. He retrieved a pick and a shovel and headed back to find Coyle, Bruno, and hopefully the stash of weapons.

It took them fifteen minutes to dig up the crates holding the weapons. They were untouched and intact. Pulling the first one out and opening it, Bruno and Coyle each grabbed a submachine gun and several clips already loaded with bullets. Digging a little further produced another crate with two dozen grenades, a satchel charge, and several bayonets. They each took two grenades, a bayonet, and Coyle took the satchel charge. The last crate at the bottom of the grave was a narrow crate. Granier lifted it out and opened it. It was a sniper rifle. Granier grinned.

The meeting place of the politburo was "Dragon House," deep within the Thang Long Imperial Citadel. It was well protected with an entire battalion of crack NVA troops patrolling the grounds outside and within the perimeter walls of the compound. Once the seat of power in Vietnam, the Imperial Citadel was originally built over 900 years ago during the Ly dynasty. Most of the imperial palaces, temples, and administration buildings had become dilapidated over the centuries and were finally demolished by the French at the end of the 19th century. Even though the walls and the main gate remained intact, the great pagoda that stood in front of the emperor's palace was torn down to its foundations. One of the buildings that was saved from destruction was Dragon House named because of the twin ornate stone dragons on the stairs leading to the building. It was not a large building compared to the great palaces that once graced the citadel, but it didn't need to be. Unlike the massive Chinese politburo, the North Vietnamese politburo was small and efficient. The ministers were given broad areas of responsibility that required full days and many late nights.

Even though he was the first secretary to the communist party, Le Duan was no exception. He had more responsibility than anyone and took it seriously. It seemed the more Le Duan took control over the politburo, the more politburo took control of him. As he assumed his new role, the NVA commander in charge of guarding him insisted that he move from his house into the citadel where he and his family could be better protected. He refused. His home was a refuge from the political shenanigans that plagued him throughout the day. His family was a welcome relief from the smoke-filled rooms and hallways filled with ministers impatient to talk with him about their latest program requiring his approval for additional funds or resources. It seemed everyone smoked, and everyone wanted something from him. Among those ministers seeking to book an appointment with him, it was a competition of the worse kind. He didn't want his children growing up around such divisiveness.

But the commander of the guard was persistent and not unwise. Many would do him harm if given the opportunity including but not limited to the South Vietnamese and the Americans. To protect his family, Duan agreed to relocate closer to the citadel. A wealthy French merchant was expelled from his villa to make room for Le Duan and his family. The villa was only a block away from the citadel and surrounded by a high wall. Although his first wife, Le Thi, was pleased with the enormous house filled with European furniture, a huge kitchen with copper pots and pans, and a walled backyard where the children could play safely, Duan thought it was too much. He was worried that it set the wrong example. To convince him not to reject the generous gift, Le Thi reminded him that he was expected to entertain the other ministers and foreign dignitaries. "Even the great and humble Ho Chi Minh has a palace," said Le Thi.

"It's not his palace. It's the Presidential palace and it belongs to the people. It's used for diplomatic functions. He doesn't even sleep there," said Duan.

"Just because he refuses the generosity of his people, doesn't mean you have to. This is what the people want, Le. We should graciously accept it and use it for the nation's benefit. Besides, don't you want your children and me to be safe?"

"Of course, I do."

"Then it's settled."

"Be careful what you ask for. It is going to be hell to clean."

"Surely it must come with servants."

"I refuse to have servants. If you want the villa, you have to clean it."

"Suong can do it."

"I doubt it, but you have my blessing if you can convince her."

The first secretary's residence became one of the country's most closely guarded secrets.


Granier went into the citadel alone even though Bruno and Coyle argued that they could keep watch while he attempted to locate Le Duan. He worked better alone and was sure of his skills when it came to stealth. Locating the Dragon House was not a problem for Granier, finding a safe position where he could observe was. NVA soldiers were everywhere. He wasn't sure if the guard had been increased because of the team's escape from Hao Lo prison, but he imagined it was probable. The North Vietnamese weren't stupid. A covert foreign snatch team breaks into an empty prison; it could have been a diversion for a bigger mission. And now it was. He went in unarmed except for the bayonet and carried the scope from the sniper rifle. If he was caught with any weapons, he had little doubt the NVA would shoot first and ask questions later. The NVA battalion's mission was the protection of the ministers, and they were the best the North had to offer.

Coyle and Bruno took up overwatch positions on the roof of an office building across the street from the citadel. They could not see over the high walls and trees, but they did have a view of the citadel's back gate which was the only opening wide enough for a car. It was up to Granier to find Le Duan.

It was still dark when Granier entered the citadel. He planned to find his observation position in the predawn light before the ministers arrived, then wait all day until they left and follow Le Duan. Climbing the perimeter wall wasn't difficult. There was no barbed wire capping the wall. The

NVA commander's strategy for guarding the ministers was more about an overwhelming guard force than obstacles. They did not want to disrupt the ministers, many of which enjoyed walks through the gardens within the citadel. It seemed more like a park than a massive fortress with thousands of trees, bushes, fishponds, and acres of lawn edged with hedges. Hundreds of huge ceramic pots holding miniature sculpted trees decorated the dozens of plazas within the walls. Some of the original foundations of buildings long gone were sunken a few feet and fashioned into stepdown parks with stone paths, picnic tables, and dozens of shade trees. Many of the ancient buildings were surrounded by waist-high walls and steps protected by stone serpents, oddly-shaped tigers, and grotesque monsters. It was good cover that Granier took advantage of as he made his way toward the Dragon House.

As the sky turned purple and lightened, Granier settled on a watchtower overlooking the plaza where Dragon House was located. The NVA had placed a machine gun position on the second story of the tower and had blocked off the stairs leading to the top of the tower on the third story. Granier figured once he was past the machine gun team, no guards would patrol the rest of the tower and he would be safe. The most dangerous part would be climbing into position. He couldn't use the stairs without being seen. He moved to the side of the tower facing away from the plaza and climbed up the plaster walls using a drainpipe.

On the second story, he took a peek around the corner to observe the layout of the machine gun position and the makeup of the fire team. It was straightforward with a gunner, a loader, and an ammunition bearer. The team's ammunition boxes were stored inside the sandbag wall that protected the team and weapon. The ammunition bearer doubled as a guard to protect the team's rear. The machine gun was a Chinese belt-fed Type 67 mounted on a tripod. It fired 7.62×54mm rounds at a rate of 700 per minute and had a range of 1000 feet. It was more than enough to cover one side of the plaza. Granier surmised that there was another machine gun position on the opposite side of Dragon House. The NVA weren't taking any chances.

Granier climbed up the third story and into a small, roof-covered space surrounded by a decorative half-wall made of ceramic ventilation tiles. It was such a good spot to covertly overlook the plaza, he wondered if the tower had been used by the emperor and royal family to spy on the members of the royal court. He pulled out the sniper scope and surveyed the area.

There was a Type 63 mobile anti-aircraft gun with twin 37mm autocannons positioned in the front plaza of Dragon House where it would have a clear shot at any incoming aircraft and could also be used to defend against any enemy armored cars or ground troops assaulting the citadel. The steel treads of the thirteen-ton weapon cracked the tiles covering the plaza floor and made the groundskeepers unhappy. The commander in charge of Dragon House security would have preferred more anti-aircraft installations but didn't want to attract too much attention from the enemy reconnaissance planes that flew with impunity at 70,000 feet, out of reach of any North Vietnamese weapons. Only the new Soviet missiles could reach the spy planes and the Soviets weren't in the mood to share their latest technology with Hanoi… not yet at least.

Granier knew that the armored vehicle's weapons could demolish the tower he was in within seconds if he was discovered. It was a sobering thought and kept him vigilant on restricting any movements that might attract attention.

After several hours, Le Duan appeared with his entourage of guards and walked up the steps to Dragon House. He was greeted by the other ministers outside and took a few moments to visit before going inside. Although introverted and reclusive, Le Duan was a good politician and spent time chatting with those that mattered most when it came to his current agenda.

Granier had no way of communicating with Coyle or

Bruno, but they knew it would take time and patience to track down Le Duan. Granier knew it would be a long day waiting for Le Duan to reappear and settled into his hidden cubby. His stomach grumbled from lack of food. He could feel his energy level dropping as the heat of the day rose with the sun. He knew what he needed to do to stay alert. He considered different scenarios of what might happen and came up with strategies to deal with them. He mentally disassembled, cleaned, and reassembled the different types of weapons he had used during his service in the US military and when he was growing up in France. His grandfather's Napoleon-era dueling pistols were a particular challenge. He thought about the long hunts his grandfather would take him on to teach him the skills of a woodsman. He replayed his grandfather's instructions and advice when they rested by the evening campfire and when they traveled through the forests and mountains. He thought about studying the ground six feet in front looking for booby traps when he was a marine in the Pacific War, then looking up into the shafts of sunlight piercing the jungle canopy in search of Japanese snipers in the trees. He thought of the adrenaline rushing through his veins as he climbed a steep hill covered with long grass where he and his buddies knew the hidden enemy was waiting somewhere near the top to kill them. Granier never let himself dwell on any one event too long. He changed his memories to prevent falling into a dream — one of meticulous detail with another of adrenaline-pumping action. As the sun grew close to the horizon, he squared away his memories and focused on the mission at hand.

It was almost dark when Le Duan reappeared flanked by his guards. There were multiple exits through the citadel perimeter walls. Granier was sure Le Duan would take the one closest to his home. He would need to move quickly to catch up with the first secretary and his guards once they left the citadel. He kept his scope on Le Duan looking for clues on where he might exit. To his surprise, Le Duan did not turn left or right or even go straight. He went down a narrow flight of stairs that disappeared below ground along with his armed escorts.

In less than two minutes, Granier had lost sight of his target. He exited the watchtower and climbed down the side of the tower, then slid down the drainpipe to land on the ground. He crouched down and duck-crawled along a masonry wall out of sight of the guards. He stopped at the end of the wall and waited until two guards on patrol walked past his position. Sticking to the shadows and using the trees as cover, he moved across the ground until he came to within a few yards of the stairs leading underground. There was a guard at the top and was a sign in Vietnamese that he couldn't read. He stayed hidden and waited patiently. The guard moved off to bum a cigarette from one of his comrades on patrol as he passed. Granier moved to the stairwell and slipped down the stairs.

As he approached the bottom, he saw a metal door. He climbed down the rest of the stairs and reached for the doorknob. It occurred to him that if he opened the door and found someone on the other side that he would be discovered if there was a struggle. He glanced back up the stairs and saw the guard return to his post at the top of the stairs. Granier decided to risk it. He opened the door, stepped through the doorway, and closed the door behind him.

It was pitch dark. There was no light seeping in from around the doorframe. It was a tight seal. He lifted his hand to see if there was any light whatsoever. There was none. He couldn't see his fingers just two inches from his face. He didn't know where he was or where Le Duan and his guards were. He heard a drip of water and its echo. It must be a big room with a concrete floor he thought. He felt along the wall by the door and found what he thought was a light switch. He flipped the switch, and the overhead lights flickered on. He was right. He was standing at the entrance of a large room with a floor and walls of concrete. There was no furniture. Just emptiness. A water pipe attached to the ceiling was dripping a slow leak from one of the joints. It struck him that he was in an air raid shelter probably build for the politburo members and their administrative staff. Still unarmed and feeling a little stupid, he went in search of Le Duan and his guards. He searched several hallways that lead to numerous dorm rooms and a common bathroom with showers. There were other rooms including a kitchen filled with boxes of rations, a medical bay which included an operating table and boxes of medical supplies and medicine, and a room with a gas-powered generator with a large electrical panel and air pipe leading up through the ceiling. The pipe fed into an air processor then divided into multiple pipes that disappeared through the ceiling. He imagined they led to air vents throughout the bunker.

After searching the entire underground bunker, Granier moved back into the main hall and saw a small hallway covered with a heavy drape that he had somehow missed. He opened the drape and saw a heavy steel door with a locking wheel like something from a submarine or warship. He went back and turned off the lights, then felt his way back to the hallway. He moved inside and closed the drape. He felt his way to the submarine-type door, turned the wheel, and opened the door. There was another dark hallway. He couldn't see the end of it. He found a light switch on the wall, but he decided not to turn the lights on until he knew what was at the opposite end of the corridor.

He moved down the corridor occasionally scraping against the wall and correcting his course. He came to another door that matched the submarine door on the opposite end of the corridor. He knew the odds were high that someone would be on the opposite side of the door. He attempted to turn the wheel. It didn't budge. It was locked. He was unsure what to do, then reached into his pocket and pulled out the bicycle wrench he had used to make the slingshot bow. He tapped on the heavy door three times and pulled out his bayonet as he waited...

After a few moments, the wheel on the door turned and the door opened. There was a guard armed with a submachine gun. Before the surprised guard could react, Granier reached through the doorway, grabbed the guard by the shirt, and pulled him into the corridor. He plunged his bayonet into the guard's chest killing him. He helped him fall to the ground to avoid excess noise. Granier took the guard's submachine and a satchel of ammo clips. He moved into the room on the opposite side of the door and found himself in what looked like a basement. Leaving the guard's corpse in the corridor, he closed the steel door locking it.

Granier climbed a wooden staircase leading to another door. At the top of the stairs, he opened the door a sliver and peeked through the tiny gap. What he saw almost made him fall back down the stairs. It was Suong walking down a hallway past the door. It took him a moment to recover from the shock. He knew Suong was Le Duan's bodyguard, and it made sense that she would be in his house protecting him, but he hadn't put the two together until that moment. *Of course, she would be there, you idiot,* thought Granier. The problem was now there were two people that knew what he looked like and if either saw him, they would know it was an American operation not French as Coyle had planned.

He considered going back through the corridor and out through the citadel. But he still didn't know where Le Duan's villa was in relation to the city and Coyle and Bruno's location. He needed to go out through the house to the street and read the street signs. It was such a simple thing, but the mission depended on it. He also needed to recon the house and the location of the guards for Bruno and Coyle when they returned.

He listened for voices and footsteps through the gap in the door. Nothing that was nearby. He opened the door a bit more and took a quick peek around the opposite end of the hallway. Nothing. He surveyed the layout and decided on his next move into an open doorway fifteen feet away. He moved quietly but quickly. The open doorway was an empty washroom with a couple of stacks of folded clothes and bedding. There was a wooden tub with a paddle to wash the clothes, a washboard for stubborn stains, and another tub with a mangle to wring the water out of the laundry before hanging it to dry outside. In a country with low-cost labor, it was cheaper to have a laundrywoman than a new electric washing and drying machine.

Granier could see the end of the hallway was connected to the kitchen. He checked both ends of the hallway and made his next move. As he entered the kitchen, he saw a guard standing outside the kitchen door leading to the side of the house. The guard was facing away from the kitchen and did not see Granier.

Granier opened a swinging door and peered into a large vacant dining room. The furniture was a fusion of Vietnamese and French. The painting on the wall was a depiction of the Battle of San Domingo – an 18th century naval battle between French and British ships of the line that the French won. On the wood-inlaid French sideboard below was a Vietnamese-made porcelain vase and a bronze water dragon. An electric wooden fan hung from the vaulted ceiling over the dining table and chairs. It was ultra-luxurious by Vietnamese standards which Granier found strangely decadent for a communist leader's home.

The next room was the villa's entrance hall with a curved stairway leading to the second floor. Through the front door's side windows Granier could see two soldiers armed with submachine guns standing guard with the backs to the doorway. Granier considered going upstairs but decided it was too risky. The odds of their being guards on the second floor were slim. The guards would most likely be deployed at the entry and exit points on the exterior of the house with two or three guarding the interior. He had already eliminated one of those guards. He moved through the entryway and into the living room. He heard a door opening and closing back in the entryway. He moved to have a look. There was now a guard at the bottom of the stairs leading to the second story. He figured there could still be a third guard inside the house, and he still hadn't found a way out of the house without being seen.

The living room was connected to a large study. Granier made a swift search of the desk hoping to find valuable intelligence. He found nothing of use and moved on. On the opposite side of the study were two doors, both closed. With his path blocked back to the two exits he had encountered, Granier had little choice but to press on. He moved to the first door and cracked it open. The room was dark. He saw a dark figure move across from him and froze. A moment later, he realized he was seeing his reflection in a mirror. He opened the door further and glanced inside to find a large bathroom with a claw-foot bathtub, toilet, and vanity with a mirror. He backed out and closed the door.

He cracked open the next door and saw a parlor more oriented toward the family with a child's rocking horse in the corner and what looked like a wooden toy chest. There was a large open area with two wing-backed chairs and lots of room for the children to play inside on rainy days. There was no rug on the floor like the other more formal rooms which made it easier to roll toys with wheels and clean up the spills that always come with children. There were windows on two sides of the room and an electric ceiling fan to keep the children cool during the hot season. He could see a pool in the backyard surrounded by brick walkways and a patio with lounge chairs. More decadence. There was also another door that Granier imagined led to a mudroom and the backdoor to the villa. There would also be a door on the opposite side of the mudroom leading to the hallway he originally entered. Knowing that the third guard could be posted inside the mudroom, Granier was cautious when opening the door. It could all go bust at that point if he was discovered. He had no doubt that he could overpower a surprised guard, but the scuffle would alert the other guards inside and outside the house. He would have to make a run for it through the back door and the mission would need to be abandoned as reinforcements were brought in or the first secretary and his family were moved to another location. He opened the door and saw a guard standing outside of the backdoor with his back away from Granier. He also found the open doorway leading to the hallway. Now familiar with the villa's layout, he had seen enough. It was time to get away unseen if possible.

He decided to exit through one of the family parlor windows on the side of the villa with no exterior doors. He knew that area of the exterior would be patrolled by one or two guards. It didn't matter. It was the only way out that made sense. He moved to the window and cracked it open a bit to make sure it would open, then he waited in the darkness. He heard two guards approaching and talking quietly. He could smell the cigarettes they were smoking through the crack in the windowsill. They moved past without noticing anything amiss. Granier wasted no time once they moved around the corner of the villa. He carefully opened the window, removed the metal screen, and slipped out. He closed the window and replaced the screen. He climbed over the fence into a neighbor's yard. He climbed two more fences and crossed two more yards before moving back out to the street.

He could see that the guards in front of Le Duan's villa were undisturbed. He moved to the closest street and made note of the street sign which were primarily in French with Vietnamese printed below. He moved off in the darkness to find Coyle and Bruno.

Once back with Coyle and Bruno, Granier reassembled the scope on his sniper rifle as he explained the layout and location of the villa. There wasn't much time before sunrise. "Only eight guards for the leader of the country? It seems light," said Bruno.

"I agree, but by the looks of it, they're trying to keep a low profile. That's why they built the tunnel," said Granier.

"It makes sense but still feels odd."

"Well, if it makes you feel any better, they have an entire battalion of crack troops plus armor two blocks away."

"That's not very reassuring," said Coyle.

"One more thing… there was a woman in the village that I recognized from the days when the Deer Team fought alongside Ho Chi Minh and the Viet Minh. She was a scout," said Granier.

"Why is she in Le Duan's villa?" said Bruno.

"I'm not sure. But if she sees me, she'll know it's an American operation."

"So, we kill her," said Bruno.

"No. I think we should take her hostage after we exchange Le Duan and his family for the prisoners. She must mean something to Le Duan if she is in his home."

"I think his wife or one of his children would be a better choice," said Bruno.

"Wait a minute. We can't take children hostage," said Coyle.

"Coyle's right. The woman will be enough," said Granier.

"You hope," said Bruno.

"Trust me. She'll be enough. Her name is Suong."

"Well, we don't have time to argue. I figure the sun will rise in fifteen minutes. We need to get moving," said Bruno. "Alright, but just to be safe. I'll remain out of sight and take an overwatch position with his sniper rifle. I'll eliminate the guards in the front, the two-man patrol, and the guard at the kitchen door. You two will need to take out the guard at the back door and those inside the house."

"No problem," said Bruno getting antsy to fight.

"When they hear my shots from outside, the guard inside will most likely take Le Duan and his family down the basement and attempt to exit through the underground corridor. That will be your best position to ambush them," said Granier. "We go now."

They checked their weapons and headed for the villa.

When they arrived at the villa, it seemed to be calm. The soldiers were patrolling and standing guard in their usual places. That was a good sign. Granier pointed to the place he would take up his overwatch – a tall tree with thick branches on the opposite side of the street and down the block. It was far enough away to give him a good angle on his targets and had a wide trunk that he would use as cover as he climbed. They decided to execute their move into the hallway and basement on Granier's shot taking out the first guard. They split up.

Granier moved to the tree and climbed up until he was twenty-five feet off the ground then positioned himself inside the trunk's fork into two main branches. It was a good position that allowed him to use a large notch from a long-gone branch to steady his weapon. Through his scope, he could see the guards standing at the front door. He knew he had to give Bruno and Coyle enough time to get into position. The sky was starting to lighten, and his position would soon be exposed.

Bruno and Coyle climbed over several walls and through backyards as Granier had done to escape but in reverse. When they came to the wall surrounding Le Duan's villa, Bruno climbed part of the way up to have a look. The two guards were patrolling that side of the house. Bruno ducked back down and waited. After a minute, he pulled himself back up and took another look. It was clear. They climbed over the wall and moved to the side of the villa. Bruno set his submachine gun down and pulled out his bayonet. He threw a rock into some bushes to get the guard at the backdoor's attention. The guard complied walking over to investigate. Bruno waited until he passed the corner of the villa and moved up behind him. He plunged the knife into the guard's temple and helped him fall to the ground. He was dead.

Bruno lifted the body over his shoulder as Coyle carried his submachine gun and opened the backdoor. They moved inside. Bruno set the guard's body down in the mudroom.

Coyle headed down the hallway and into the basement closing the door behind him while Bruno waited out of sight in the mudroom.

It was time. Granier lined up his first shot – one of the two guards patrolling around the side of the villa. He aimed for a headshot. His rifle cracked as it fired and the guard went down. The other guards looked around to find where the shot came from. Granier fired again, killing the second patrolling guard.

Inside the villa, Bruno listened to a guard's boots climbing the stairs and shouting in Vietnamese. He waited for the family to gather and climb down the stairs.

Outside, the remaining guards had seen the muzzle flash from Granier's second shot and opened fire at his position in the tree. Without flinching, Granier took his third shot and killed the guard outside the kitchen door.

Bruno listened as the family moved down the stairs and entered the hallway. He waited until the door to the basement opened before turning into the hallway and moving toward the guard standing at the doorway. He was turned away and didn't see Bruno.

As the children, Le Thi, Le Duan, and Suong armed with an automatic pistol climbed down the stairs while the guard held the door open and kept watch toward the kitchen. Bruno moved swiftly with his bayonet and killed the guard by plunging the blade through his ribs and into his heart. The guard fell to the floor.

At the bottom of the basement stairs, Coyle stepped out with his submachine gun. Suong raised her pistol. Coyle shook his head like that was a bad move. Suong knew that Le Duan and his family could easily be killed in the crossfire. She lowered her weapon. Coyle took it from her.

The gunfire around the tree was getting heavy. Chunks of wood from bullet hits pelted Granier in the face making it hard to aim. A bullet nicked his shirt but didn't touch him. He fired and took out one of the guards by the front door. The remaining guard was brave and kept his ground firing back. But Granier was a far better aim and killed him with the next shot. Granier could hear the troops and armor assembling in the Citadel. It wouldn't take long. There was nothing more he could do from the tree. There would be too many of them for a sniper to handle. He climbed down and moved off into the long shadows of the morning as the sun broke the horizon.

Bruno moved on to the basement stairs and closed the door behind him. They ushered Le Duan and his family deeper into the basement away from the stairs and doorway into the hallway. "I know you," said Le Duan in French. "You are the French paratrooper Bigeard."

"Good guess," said Bruno.

"Why is France doing this?"

"France isn't doing this. I am. You captured several of my officers at Dien Bien Phu and failed to release them when the truce was called. I want them back."

"In exchange for me?"

"… and your family."

"You will not touch my children."

"No. Not as long as you cooperate."

"What do you want me to do?"

Bruno pulled a list from his pocket and handed it to Le Duan. "Those men in a truck," said Bruno.

"And we go free?"

"Yes."

"What if they are already dead?"

"Then you have a big problem."

"How do I know you will keep your word?"

"You have a battalion marching to the rescue. It should be me that is worried."

"You must have a plan to escape."

"Of course. I am French. We always have a plan."

They heard the front door breached and troops stomping into the villa and down the hallway. The door at the top of the stairs was kicked open. "You're on," said Bruno.

Le Duan called out telling his men to keep back and not to enter the basement. "Tell them that if they attempt a rescue I will kill you without hesitation. You say you know me, so you know I will keep my word," said Bruno.

Le Duan relayed the message and read the names off the list instructing the commander to fetch the prisoners and bring them in a truck. The commander acknowledged Le Duan's instructions. "Now what?" said Le Duan.

"Now we wait," said Bruno.

"You'll never live through this."

"I think you'd be surprised at what I can live through."

Granier watched from another concealed position that gave him a good view of the street in front of the house. The villa was surrounded by NVA troops and armored vehicles. Nobody could get in or out without being seen. It took six hours before a truck holding Captain Hoang and five other prisoners pulled up in front of Le Duan's home.

Inside the basement, the commander shouted from the doorway informing Le Duan that the prisoners had arrived. "They are here as you asked," said Le Duan.

"You will remain here. If I do not return in five minutes, my man will shoot you and your family. Do we understand each other?" said Bruno.

"We do."

"I would suggest you inform your officers not to interfere with my inspection of the prisoners. This will all be over soon if you cooperate."

"So, you say."

Le Duan called up to the commander and gave him orders not to interfere with the French man inspecting the prisoners. "You will do what is required, yes?" said Bruno to Coyle.

Coyle nodded. Bruno walked up the stairs holding his submachine gun. The commander accompanied him to ensure his men complied with Le Duan's orders. The villa was filled with NVA soldiers who all wanted to kill the

Frenchman that had taken their leader and his family captive. Bruno moved past them. A lieutenant stepped in front of Bruno as he approached the front door preventing him from exiting the villa. He shouted at Bruno and pointed his pistol at his head. The commander ordered the officer to stand down. The lieutenant was obstinate and stood his ground. The commander ordered his soldiers to shoot the lieutenant if he did not reholster his weapon and move out of the way in the next ten seconds. The lieutenant begrudgingly complied and stepped aside. Bruno and the commander stepped through the doorway.

Outside the villa, Bruno was faced with an overwhelming show of force. He didn't flinch and walked to the back of the truck. He opened the flap to reveal the six prisoners, all surprised to see him. "Hello, my friends. Your comrades have not forgotten you. You will soon be free once again," said Bruno.

The prisoners stood and saluted Bruno as their eyes filled with tears. Bruno turned to Captain Hoang and said, "Are you alright, Captain?"

"Yes, Major," said Hoang.

"Actually, it is colonel now."

"Yes, Colonel. I never gave up hope. I knew you would come."

"I'm sorry it took so long. I didn't know you were alive until recently. You will all stay here. We will be joining you shortly."

Bruno nodded his approval of the prisoners to the commander, and they returned to the villa.

When Bruno returned to the basement, he said, "Alright. You've kept your part of the bargain. We will release you and your children, but your wife will be coming with us to ensure we are not followed."

Coyle looked surprised at the change in plans now taking the wife hostage, but he said nothing. Bruno was clearly in charge of the situation and Coyle would follow his lead.

"That's unacceptable," said Le Duan.

"It's not like you have a choice but try to see it from our point of view," said Bruno. "We have little doubt you will attempt to prevent us from leaving the country with our comrades. We have no reason to cause harm to your wife unless something goes wrong and you're not going to let that happen as long as we have her. Once we clear the border, we will free your wife and she will be free to return to you."

Le Duan considered for a moment, then said, "Which wife?"

Coyle and Bruno exchanged a look and Bruno said, "You have more than one?"

"Yes."

"The one named Suong," said Coyle jumping in.

Le Duan turned to Suong as if asking permission. "Of course, I'll go," said Suong. "You've made up your mind. Le Thi is the mother of your children."

Le Duan turned back to Bruno and said, "If you harm her in any way, I will use all my power to hunt you down and see that you suffer."

"I would expect no less," said Bruno.

Le Duan hugged Suong and kissed her on the cheek. She let him but did not reciprocate his affection and said, "You take care of yourself, Le Duan. And don't forget to duck when they're shooting at you."

Le Duan gave the commander orders not to hinder the truck in any way. The French and the prisoners would be allowed to leave the country without molestation. The commander confirmed the order and escorted Bruno, Coyle, and Suong out of the house.

Outside the commander stood aside as they climbed into the truck. Suong road upfront with Bruno driving. "We will not harm you," said Bruno trying to reassure her.

"I'm not worried," said Suong. "You just gave me my freedom."

Bruno didn't press for an explanation. He started the

engine and drove down the street. Le Duan walked out of the villa and watched the truck drive away. The commander stepped up next to him. "I want no harm to come to Suong unless she approaches the border. Under no circumstances is she to be allowed to leave the North. She knows far too much about the politburo and our plans," said Le Duan.

"And if she dies?" said the commander.

"Then she will be a martyr of the revolution."

As the truck rounded the corner, Granier appeared from behind a tree and jumped on the truck's runner board. Suong was stunned to see him but couldn't help smiling a bit. "Howdy," said Granier as he opened the door. "Do you mind scooting over?"

Suong slid over and Granier climbed in and shut the door. "What are you doing here, Rene?" said Suong.

"I saw you passing by and decided to jump on."

"Seriously?"

"I'm here to save you."

"Save me? From whom?"

"Yourself."

"I don't need saving."

"I beg to differ."

"Are you with the French now?"

"For the moment. You need to come with me. We could be together again."

"Together again?" said Bruno surprised.

"Shut up, Bruno. I'll explain later."

"That's impossible. You need to let me go," said Suong. "Le Duan will never let me leave the country."

"You know she is his wife, yes?" said Bruno.

"What?" said Granier stunned. "You married him?"

"Yes. But it is over. We are getting a divorce," said Suong. "It's better this way. I'm not a babysitter."

"No, you're not. You're a hunter like me. So, I am saving you after all?"

"You are doing no such thing. I am saving myself."

"Where will you go?" said Bruno.

"Back to my family and tribe in the Western hills. I've had enough of politics."

"They'll find you there," said Granier.

"They will try. But I am not so easy to find as you well know."

"Yeah, I do. But maybe we can help you with that."

"What do you mean?"

"You'll see."

"They're following us," said Bruno looking in the side mirror.

Granier looked at his mirror and saw a convoy of military vehicles following a half-mile back. "We'll need to lose them before we arrive," said Granier. "We need a bottleneck of some sort."

"I agree."

"We still have six grenades?"

"Yes."

"Alright. We'll find something between now and the plane."

"What plane?" said Suong. "That's how you are getting out... by plane?"

"Yeah... sort of."

"The North Vietnamese Air Force has a T-28 Trojan that they seized when a Laotian pilot defected earlier this year. They have been training their pilots with it. I'm sure they will use it to hunt you down before you cross the border."

"It's a big country. They've got to find us first," said Bruno.

"We'd better tell Coyle just in case," said Granier.

On the outskirts of Hanoi approaching the hidden DHC-4, the truck approached a village surrounded by rice fields. The convoy of NVA vehicles was still keeping its distance. As the truck passed a small bridge over a canal, Bruno saw another truck overloaded with bags of rice stopped by the side of the road. The driver was paying a farmer for his rice still stacked on his water buffalo cart. Bruno hit the brakes and pulled over. "I've got an idea. Wait here and leave the engine running," said Bruno opening the door and jumping out.

Bruno ran across the street and jumped in the rice truck's cab. The keys were in the ignition. He started the engine. The driver ran to the cab and opened the door. Bruno leveled the barrel of his submachine gun at the driver and said, "Sorry. I need to borrow your truck."

The drive backed away. Bruno threw the truck in gear and gunned the engine heading towards the bridge at the edge of the village. He floored the accelerator, but it didn't do much to increase his speed. The truck was weighed down by the load of rice. As he crossed the bridge, he cranked the wheel hard to one side. The truck skidded to a halt sideways on the bridge and several bags of rice flew off the top of the load. The momentum of the load of rice tipped the truck on two wheels and then over on its side. It crashed down spilling dozens of bags of rice onto the road.

Hearing the crash, the villagers came out to investigate and saw the rice bags strewn across the road. Several bags had broken open and were leaking rice. The villagers grabbed whatever they had that could carry rice and ran toward the truck. It was a feeding frenzy with villagers scooping up rice with their hands and filling their containers. Unhurt and pleased with himself, Bruno crawled out of the cab and headed back to the waiting truck.

He hopped in the cab, threw the truck in gear, and sped off in the opposite direction. "That should buy us a few minutes," said Bruno.

"You sure do enjoy destroying things," said Granier.

"It's a talent."

As the truck was leaving the other end of the village, the military convoy pulled up to the wrecked truck as the villagers scrounged for loose rice. There was nowhere in sight to cross the canal except the bridge. The commander shouted at the villagers to get out of the way. They ignored him and kept filling their containers. The commander grabbed a submachine gun from one of his soldiers and shot it up into the air until the villagers ran off. He ordered his men to clear the wreckage. They tied ropes to the truck and tried to pull it with their vehicles, but the rice bag prevented it from moving off the bridge. Exasperated, the commander ordered an armored car with a 37 mm cannon to blow the truck off the bridge. It fired three high explosive rounds which blew the truck to pieces and set its remains on fire but didn't do much for clearing the bridge. He finally ordered the armored car to push the truck into the canal. The armored vehicle pushed the burning metal hulk into the water causing the canal to overflow and flood the village. His soldiers removed the remaining truck wreckage and the torn rice bags. In all, it took eight minutes to clear the debris enough for the convoy to pass. The convoy raced through the village to make up time. The commander radioed an airfield and asked for air support to shadow the escaping truck.

## Hanoi Airfield

Loaded with two .50 Cal machine gun pods and four rocket pods on six hardpoints, the captured T-28 Trojan took off. Once in the air, the pilot banked hard and headed south to rendezvous with the convoy. It would be his first mission against the enemy and he was anxious to prove himself. The sun was low on the horizon and he knew his time in the air would be short. He had not learned to fly at night and would need to set his plane down before dark.

## Hanoi Countryside

The truck sped across the countryside. Bruno was pushing the engine to the limit and keeping a close eye on the temperature gauge. "Any sign of them?" said Bruno glancing in his door's side mirror.

"No. But I doubt we lost them," said Granier looking in his door's mirror.

"No, no. That would be too easy. We should be coming up on the plane shortly. You'd better let the others know."

"Right," said Granier opening his door and stepping back out on the running board.

"Where are you going?" said Suong alarmed.

"I'll be back in a minute."

Granier climbed along the side of the truck and swung himself inside the back to join Coyle and the six prisoners. "Everything okay?" said Coyle.

"Yeah. Fine. Bruno's driving stunt slowed them down and we're approaching the plane's hiding place. There is a good chance that there are NVA soldiers at the plane, so everyone should keep their heads down until Bruno checks it out."

"Got it."

"How long to prep the plane before takeoff?"

"Five or six minutes once we clear off the camouflage, I think."

"You just get the engines going. Let these guys clear the camouflage. We don't know how far back the NVA convoy is, but we're guessing it ain't far. I can hold them off for a bit but once they get into position, they will easily flank us."

"I'll do my best."

"I'd better get back," said Granier climbing out the back of the truck and heading to the cab.

He opened the cab door and climbed in. "Are we ready?" said Bruno.

"They know what to do," said Granier. "How close are we?"

"It's around that next bend."

"Okay. Let me off before the turn. I'll make sure Coyle has enough time to take off."

"Don't be late," said Bruno slowing the truck.

"I won't," said Granier preparing his sniper rifle.

"I'll go with you," said Suong.

"Not this time," said Granier opening the door and stepping onto the running boards.

As the truck slowed to a roll, Granier stepped off and moved into the trees along the road.

Suong felt strange watching him go like she was losing something. All the years with Le Duan, she had suppressed her feelings for Granier. Watching him move into the jungle reminded her of the times they had together fighting the Japanese. It was like a competition. Both hunters. Both killers. Kindred spirits. At that moment she was reminded how much she missed those times. Survival, hunting, and passion. Without it, she had forgotten who she was. What she was meant to be. It was too much. As the truck once again picked up speed, she opened the door. "Wait!" said Bruno.

It was too late she was gone, running into the jungle, searching for Granier. "Shit!" said Bruno. "That can't be good."

Around the bend, Bruno saw the DHC-4 sitting at the edge of the jungle. The camouflage had already been pulled off. The villagers had found it. There would be guards. He was sure of it. He pulled the truck over and told everyone to stay in the truck. He advanced toward the plane.

As he suspected, there were three guards armed with old rifles. They were militia. As he approached, they shouted at him. One of them fired a warning shot in the air to drive him away. Bruno didn't flinch and kept advancing. He lowered the barrel of his submachine gun. The guards were between him and the plane. He couldn't shoot them without hitting the aircraft. As all three guards took aim, Bruno fired a burst into the ground near their feet. Their eyes went wide and they retreated into the jungle. Bruno let them go. Men that would not hold their ground weren't much of a threat. Bruno called out to Coyle and the others.

Carrying the satchel charge, Coyle ran to the plane and gave it a quick visual inspection to make sure nothing was amiss. It was as he had left it several days before.

He climbed in, dropped the satchel charge, and moved into the cockpit. He dropped into the pilot's seat and began his start-up routine just as he had done a thousand times before, checking every control he would need to fly the aircraft.

Granier was already in position overlooking the road. Still no sign of the NVA. He heard someone approaching from behind. He whipped his rifle around and pointed it toward the intruder – Suong. "What are you doing here?" said Granier.

"I don't know," said Suong. "Remembering, I think."

Granier understood and couldn't help but smile a bit. In a way, he was proud of her. "Alright. You know the routine. Keep down. You can spot for me," he said.

"You're not going to kill them, are you?"

"Only if I need to. Why? Are you getting squeamish?"

"No. It's not that. They're my countrymen."

"Not anymore."

"I suppose you are right. Soon they will be hunting me."

"Maybe."

"What do you mean "maybe?""

They heard the cranking of the DHC-4's propellers and the rough growl of its engines starting. An armored car appeared on the horizon followed by a convoy of trucks. "Here they come," said Granier repositioning his rifle and peering through the scope.

The armored car was a Chinese-built, Soviet-designed BTR-40 with twin 7.62 SGMB medium machine guns.

Granier aimed at the left front tire and fired. He hit the tire but with little effect. He fired again.

With two bullet punctures, the front tire flattened and folded under jamming itself in the wheel well. The driver was unable to steer, and the vehicle drove itself into a roadside ditch. The convoy stopped. The gunner on the damaged armored car opened fire with his twin machine guns strafing the surrounding jungle.

It had little effect on Granier and Suong. They could hear the aircraft's engines revving as if to propel the plane forward. "Coyle will be taking off soon," said Granier. "We need to buy him a few more minutes and keep the road clear."

Troops poured out of the trucks and took up defensive positions. They fired blindly at the unseen enemy in hopes of creating suppressing fire. Another armored car back in the pack pulled forward and advanced on the road.

Granier aimed and fired.

A bullet ricocheted off the armor in front of the driver's portal. Startled by the accuracy of the shot, he closed the armored windshield limiting his visibility to a small slit. He slowed the vehicle to prevent it from crashing.

Granier took out the front tire as he had done with the first vehicle, but the armored car had moved up almost a hundred yards in front of the convoy. The gunner laid down suppressing fire allowing the troops to advance. Granier fired several more rounds taking out several soldiers but revealing his position with his muzzle flashes.

The troops had closed the distance between themselves and the enemy sniper. The gunfire concentrated on his position. He was forced to duck as it became more intense.

"On your left, 160 yards. A squad moving into the jungle," said Suong.

Popping up, Granier swung the barrel around and aimed the scope. He fired.

The commander leading the squad fell into a ball with a leg wound. Two of his men grabbed him by the arms and pulled him into the jungle where the rest of the squad waited.

"They'll flank us for sure," said Suong.

"It's time to go," said Granier shouldering his rifle.

Keeping low and just inside the jungle, Suong and Granier moved back in the direction of the plane. They heard the plane's engines revving to full throttle. They ran to the edge of the jungle and looked out.

The DHC-4 sped down the road toward the convoy and took off. "They've left us," said Suong.

"We'll be alright," said Granier watching the plane gain altitude. "We need to keep moving."

The convoy commander was surprised to see the plane, especially when it turned east rather than south. *Why east?* he thought. *Why not south to the border and safety?* The answer didn't matter now. It was out of his control. He radioed the airbase and instructed them on the direction of the enemy plane. They would send their pilot to intercept and destroy the plane if crossed the border.

Bruno and the freed prisoners watched from the jungle. Granier and Suong joined them. The plan was always for Coyle to fly alone. When the NVA saw the plane taking off, they would assume that everyone was on board, and Coyle would lead them away allowing the team to escape. Granier would take the team to a safe house near the border and let the freed prisoners rest and build up their strength for the crossing. At the border, they would need to move quickly to avoid being caught.

It was a half-hour to the coastline and out to sea. Coyle hoped to catch the anti-aircraft guns below off guard. They would expect him to cross the border to the south. He had no intention of doing what they expected. He knew they were watching and reporting his movements to their commanders. That's what he wanted. That's what Bian needed.

He was only a few miles from the coast of North Vietnam when an enemy fighter flew past his aircraft, then took a sharp turn in front of him. Coyle had to make a quick turn to avoid hitting the Trojan. He hadn't expected to see any North Vietnamese aircraft, but the sight of a fully armed

T-28 made his blood run cold. Coyle was no coward, but he knew when he was outgunned. Hell, he didn't even have a gun.

The Trojan made a wide turn and pulled in behind the Caribou. The novice pilot was almost ashamed that his first kill would be a transport plane and not an enemy fighter. It was embarrassing but he had his orders. If he felt the enemy plane was exiting North Vietnamese territory, he was to shoot it down. Territorial waters extended twelve nautical miles offshore. If the DHC-4 flew past the shoreline, it would only take the plane four minutes to reach the edge of North Vietnamese territory over the sea. Even for the T-28 with its powerful engine, he would only have a couple of strafing passes at the transport plane. Failing at such a simple task would cost him his career as an aviator. The thought of never flying in real combat was too painful. He would take no chances. To avoid the accusation of being trigger-happy in the death of the first secretary's wife, he decided to fire a warning shot at one mile out when he was clear of any ship close to shore. If the plane didn't change course and head back to land, he would destroy it.

Coyle knew he was in big trouble and the plan he had helped conceive was falling to pieces. He had flown a T-28 and knew its performance and abilities. It had a powerful Wright R-1820-86 Cyclone nine-cylinder air-cooled radial engine with 1,425 hp. Even fully loaded with armament, the Trojan was three times lighter than the DHC-4 and almost fifty percent faster. It won't be much of a dogfight even if the Caribou had weapons, which it didn't. Coyle's mind raced to come up with a solution. He had originally planned to belly-land the aircraft in the ocean and then use the satchel charge to blow it to smithereens but that required no witnesses. That plan was out the window. He needed something that the enemy pilot could witness.

Coyle could see that the pilot chasing him did not have much time in the cockpit. His moves were jerky, and he tended to overcorrect. Even in the slower plane, Coyle felt all was not lost. He just had to be clever and outfly his pursuer. He too knew that time and distance to the edge of North Vietnamese territory was limited. He needed his plane to be shot down before he reached the sea border but not in the way the enemy pilot was hoping.

The Trojan moved in behind the transport plane. The enemy pilot selected his weapon – two MATRA Type 122 6 x 68mm rocket pods. Even though the rockets were unguided, the pilot felt the transport plane was moving so slowly that it would be an easy target. The high explosive rockets would obliterate the enemy aircraft.

Coyle banked his aircraft so far to one side, he felt sure its wings would rip off.

The enemy pilot was surprised by how quickly the plane in his sights had moved. He countered by turning in the same direction. As usual, he had overturned his fighter and ended up on the inside track of the two aircrafts' turning radius. He quickly realized that it was not a mistake at all but a brilliant maneuver. If he slowed his plane, the enemy plane would fly right into his kill zone. But the enemy rarely did what was expected, especially one as experienced as Coyle. As he slowed his plane, the transport plane suddenly turned out of the radius in the opposite direction. The enemy pilot had lost his prey for the moment. His heart leapt as he realized how close the transport plane was to international waters.

In the cockpit of the DHC-4, Coyle was battling the beast. It felt like the transport plane was fighting his every move trying to wrestle the controls out of his hands. The airframe groaned. He wondered when the engines would stall leaving him helpless against the enemy fighter. Flying was his only hope. His maneuver away from the Trojan was a slice turn that decreased his altitude. His new plan required that he fly as low as possible. To carry out the plan successfully, he would need to once again lose his pursuer for thirty to forty-five seconds. He watched the enemy pilot increase his airspeed as he entered a turn to get behind

Coyle's plane. Coyle responded from a fighter's instinct and maneuvered the DHC-4 into a series of displacement rolls that would eventually bring his aircraft in behind the Trojan. The maneuver was performed at such a low altitude, the inexperienced enemy pilot didn't recognize it and had no idea what was going on until it was too late. To his complete embarrassment, Coyle's plane pulled in behind his fighter. If the transport plane had weapons, he would have been a deadman. The enemy pilot had a knee-jerk reaction and pulled up hoping to once again get behind the transport plane that was only a mile away from the territorial limit.

Coyle put his final plan into action. He turned his aircraft back to the west in the direction of the shore and directly into the setting sun. He lowered his altitude to just  forty feet off the ocean's surface and decreased the power to the engines to just above stall speed. He set the autopilot to go straight making the aircraft an easy target and released his pilot's seat harness. He moved into the cargo hold and opened the rear door. He looked down at the ocean. Whitecaps crowned the tops of the waves. That was a good thing. They would hide his splash.

The enemy pilot pulled in behind the Caribou heading straight into the sun. The golden light was blinding. He decided it was time not to be fancy and changed his weapons to machine guns. He would just shoot the son-of-a-bitch out of the sky. He aimed and fired a burst. It was hard to follow the tracers that disappeared into the sun, but he could see that they were close to the Caribou's left engine. He fired again.

Coyle turned to see tracer round shred the left engine. It caught fire sending a trail of smoke behind the plane. *More camouflage* thought Coyle. He picked up a pair of diving fins and tied them to his belt. He kept his boots on. He figured they might soften the impact. He grabbed the satchel charge. He steeled himself. He pulled the fuse ignition wire and the satchel began to smoke. It was a very short fuse — only seven seconds. He set the charge down next to the half-empty fuel bladder and moved to the door counting down as he went. He waited until there were only two seconds left. He didn't bother taking a deep breath. Even at the stall speed of sixty-seven miles per hour, the water would feel like concrete and knock the wind out of him. He jumped.

With the sun still blinding him, the enemy pilot fired again at the smoking plane and this time it blew up. The explosion was much bigger than he expected and startled him as he pulled up. The transport plane has been obliterated before his eyes. Complete destruction. He figured the fiery secondary explosion must have been the wing tanks. What confused him was that his tracer rounds never hit the plane as far as he could tell. He wrote it off to the sunlight and smoke trail blinding him. A win was a win and would be the first kill sign on his aircraft.

Curled up in a tight ball with his arms protecting his head, Coyle hit the ocean at the same moment the aircraft exploded. As expected, he bounced… three times like a flat stone across a pond. Whack. Whack. Whack. It felt like a baseball bat hitting him wherever he landed on the water. A wave stopped him from bouncing a fourth time. It was like hitting a wall. The wind was completely knocked out of him. He struggled to tread water and stay on the surface until he could breathe in a gasp of air. The first one wasn't much, but it kept him alive. The second was a little easier. He watched the flaming pieces of his aircraft fall from the sky and land in the ocean. Some floated for a few minutes, most went straight down never to be seen again. He watched the enemy aircraft head for shore.

Coyle looked at the distant shoreline. It was difficult to tell how far he would need to swim before reaching land. He figured it was at least five miles. He knew there were sharks in the area. That had been part of the original plan to explain the lack of corpses. Now, he was wondering if he would survive. He swapped his boots for his fins and tied the shoelaces to his belt. His first strokes toward land were excruciatingly painful and he wondered if he had broken some of his ribs. But after the first mile, it got easier, and he felt better. He just hoped the scheme was convincing and Bian's father would be accepted as dead.

After traveling for seven nights through the countryside on stolen bicycles and bribing a truck driver heading south on backroads, the team and the newly-released prisoners finally reached the safe house. They waited two extra nights for Coyle to rendezvous with them. He never showed. They could only suspect the worse. Bruno and Granier had promised Coyle that if he didn't make it back, they would make sure Captain Huong was reunited with his daughter. Granier would attempt to make a deal with Brother Nhu to save Bian by turning her into a double-agent that Nhu controlled. The entire plan was full of risks and the only way to know if it would work was to see it to the end.

Just as they were getting ready to leave, Coyle walked through the doorway. "You're alive," said Bruno.

"Don't sound so surprised," said Coyle.

"I thought the sharks would get you for sure."

"They almost did. I had to kick more than one in their noses as they came in for a bite."

"Feisty. I like it. And did your plan work?"

"I think so. I sure blew the hell out of that aircraft."

"It's good to see you, Coyle. You look like shit," said Granier.

"I feel like shit. I was a long swim."

"What do you need?"

"I could use some hot food and a good night's sleep."

"We can do that."

Coyle ate a chicken rice soup that Suong had made, then slept for eighteen hours straight. Suong was washing Coyle's dishes outside the house using the rainwater from a clay container. Returning from guard duty, Granier saw her alone and approached. "I think he liked your soup," said Granier.

"Yeah, he ate enough for two men," said Suong.

"You know that I don't care about what you did to survive?"

Suong considered for a moment, then said, "It was more than survival, Rene. I loved him once."

"Once?"

"He changed. I changed. The world changed."

"But you don't love him now?"

"I don't think love is that easy to just turn off. It takes time. It certainly did with you."

"It never stopped for me, Suong. Never."

"It's because you are a man. You want what you can't have."

"That's not it. At least not all of it."

"Ah, we're being honest now."

"I know we can't have what we once had. Like you said… things have changed. But we could have something new. Come with me to Saigon."

"I can't, Rene."

"Yes, you can. I'll take care of everything. A defector with your past access to the leadership in the North would be invaluable to the CIA. Hell, we could even go to America if you wanted."

"And that's the problem…"

"What is? Going to America?"

"No. Going anywhere. The north is my home. It's all I have known and all that I want to know. And as far as giving up information to the CIA… that's not going to happen. I may not believe in Le Duan or the Politburo, but I still believe in the revolution."

"The revolution is nothing more than Marxist propaganda."

"To you, maybe. But to me, it's the embodiment of Ho and all he believes. And when he's gone, it will be the only thing we can hang onto in our grief."

"Well, he ain't dead yet."

"Thank the heavens."

"Be reasonable. You could have a real-life in the South... with me."

"I'm not leaving, Rene. When you leave for the border tomorrow, I'm staying in the North. I've made up my mind and I won't change it. I am not abandoning my country and its people. Not for you, not for anyone."

When Coyle woke, he washed the salt residue off his clothes using rainwater from the large clay container just outside the front door. The inside of his thighs was chapped and bleeding from the long walk once he had reached the shore. He didn't care. He wanted to get back to Saigon as soon as possible. He was unsure of what had happened to Bian while he was away.

True to her word, Suong watched as Granier and the others headed toward the border. Before disappearing over a small hill, Granier looked back and met Suong's eyes one last time with sorrow for what was lost and longing for what might have been. But most of all there was love and the respect that only warriors share. And then he was gone. She turned and headed east to the homeland of her ancestors.

The team and prisoners crossed the border where Granier had crossed many times previously. While the enemy patrols often changed their routines and routes, Granier knew how to evade them. It was just a matter of patience and skill. The others followed his lead.

Once across the border, Granier hired a truck and driver to take them to a military airbase in Danang. From there, they caught a ride on a C-47 carrying a load of weapons and communication gear in need of repair back to Saigon. Before leaving, Coyle sent Bian a telegraph telling her that he was alive and carrying a package for her. He estimated their time of arrival at Ben Hoa Airbase outside of Saigon. The plane took off and they had begun the last leg of their journey, or so they thought...

# AP BAC

Helicopters made a substantial change in the way the ARVN fought the Viet Cong. Before the use of American helicopters and pilots, the Viet Cong could attack and even occupy villages throughout the country with relative impunity. Once notified of the incursion, the ARVN troops would mobilize using trucks and other vehicles. Because the roads were bad, especially during the rainy season, it could take the government troops a full day to reach the contested area. By then, the Viet Cong would be well informed of the enemy troop movements. They would either set up an ambush for the ARVN or simply retreat into the nearby mountains or jungles before they arrived.

When the ARVN started using helicopters, warfare changed. The American advisors knew how to take advantage of military technology and used it to great effect against their naive enemy. With the development of forward operating bases, the ARVN troops could fly to almost anywhere in the entire country within a matter of minutes. Plus, they could deploy troops in multiple landing zones at the same time flanking enemy positions. They surrounded occupied villages so quickly, they often caught the Viet Cong off guard. They were forced to fight rather than flee. The number of battles increased dramatically with the ARVN winning the vast majority.

For almost a year, the Viet Cong were completely baffled as to how to fight the airborne enemy effectively. Having fought against American helicopters in Korea, the Chinese advisors came up with strategies, but many were impractical because of the terrain and weather. Unlike Vietnam, Korea did not have dense jungles or vast flooded areas like the Mekong Delta which hampered on-foot mobility. What was once a great advantage for the Viet Cong was now a hindrance that could easily trap them or expose them to enemy artillery and aerial assaults as they tried to flee. The fear of helicopters was so great that the Viet Cong would often flee the battlefield upon hearing the deep thrum of approaching rotor blades.

With the addition of hundreds of American-supplied armored personnel carriers, the ARVN gained a second big advantage – they became invincible. The lightly armed Viet Cong had nothing that could penetrate the thick steel plate that enclosed the APCs. Armed only with a heavy machinegun, the APCs were often used as bulldozers plowing down trees and piercing impenetrable jungles. They could blow through the dirt dikes surrounding rice paddies that the Viet Cong liked to use as cover against an advancing force. The wooden huts that made up the villages could easily be plowed under by the armored vehicles giving the enemy few places to hide. The Viet Cong became demoralized, and many abandoned the revolution and went home.

The South Vietnamese 7th Division under the command of Colonel Bui Dinh Dạm and the advisement of Lieutenant Colonel Vann was the tip of the spear and had more success at fighting the VC than any other military unit. In 1962 alone, the 7th Division killed and captured over 2,000 Viet Cong and cut the supply line of thousands more.

Starting in November of 1962, the leaders of the Viet Cong had enough of constantly retreating from their enemy and decided to take the offensive once again. They would learn to fight the American helicopters or die trying. It was a bold move that many in Hanoi questioned. It was after all against Mao Zedong's doctrine of "choosing to fight the enemy only when victory was assured." The VC commanders of the 261st Battalion and the 514th Battalion were ordered to destroy the strategic hamlets in their region and engage the enemy if they responded with sweeping operations. The VC commanders selected Ap Tan Thoi in Dinh Tuong Province as their headquarters for the operation and set up a radio transmitter to communicate with their units in the field.

Between 28 and 30 December 1962, an American counterintelligence aircraft intercepted enemy radio signals and located the VC radio transmitter. After studying the intercepted messages, the South Vietnamese and American intelligence personnel believed the VC had deployed a reinforced company to protect the transmitter. Certain that the VC unit was no larger than 120 soldiers, the ARVN 7th Infantry Division was instructed to assault Ap Tan Thoi and capture the transmitter.

Ap Bac was the settlement to the east of Ap Tan Thoi. Planned by American advisor Captain Richard Ziegler, the mission was codenamed "Operation Duc Thang I." The plan called for three rifle companies from the 11th Infantry Regiment, 7th Infantry Division, to attack the village from the north; the Dinh Tuong Civil Guards Regiment to assault from the south; and a company of thirteen M113 armored personnel carriers with an infantry company on board attacking the village from the southwest. The M113 carriers and the infantry company could act as both a mobile reserve and a reaction force, so it was positioned where it could be shifted to the contact area if the VC began to retreat. In addition, the ARVN would also deploy two rifle companies from Tan Hiep airfield, which would be brought to the battlefield by helicopters from the US Army 93rd Transportation Company.

If the ARVN troops could capture the radio transmitter and the majority of the VC company guarding it, it would be a successful mission. Vann who supported the mission and Colonel Dam who would command the troops were hopeful and suspected that the element of surprise and quick reactions to a changing battlefield would be the keys to success.

January 2, 1963 - Tan Son Nhut Air Base, South
Vietnam

The night before the mission, Scott could hardly sleep. He

wasn't afraid, he was excited. Being the squadron commander's copilot had paid off. A week earlier, he had been transferred to the 93rd and was given his own Shawnee to command. This was his first opportunity to fly as a pilot in battle. He was confident but still ran over all the key points of the operation in his head as the night stretched on.

It was still dark when he rendezvoused with his aircrew at the mess hall. He sat down to a breakfast that included French toast and bananas smothered in butter and maple syrup, four strips of bacon that he would dip in the syrup, a scoop of scrambled eggs, coffee, and orange juice. It was going to be a long day and he wanted to make sure he had enough energy.

There was a short mission briefing where the commander went over the plan one more time and informed his aircrews of any last-minute changes. Ten helicopters would take off from Tan Son Nhut Air Base with the initial assault force, an ARVN company in the 1st Battalion, 11th Regiment, then land at a forward operating airfield at Tan Hiep to pick up two more rifles companies from the 1st Battalion before heading to the hamlets. When the briefing ended and everyone headed for the choppers, Scott's previous commander, who had been waiting in the back, waved him over and said, "Did you have your first mission vomit as commander?"

"No, sir. I feel fine. Excited, but fine," said Scott.

"Well, you are a better man than me. I threw up for ten minutes in the privy, then walked out the tarmac and threw up on my co-pilot's boots."

"Really? I must be missing something."

"No. You're just more ready than I was. You're already a good pilot and you're gonna make a great commander, Scott."

"Thank you, sir. I hope I don't let you down."

"You won't. You'd better go before they take off without you."

Leaving the briefing room, Scott saw that his crew chief

was already loading up the ARVN troops standing on the apron. His crew chief, Staff Sergeant Tomer, was a veteran of the Korean War and knew his job inside and out. Scott was grateful to have such a soldier as part of his crew. He found his co-pilot, Lieutenant Terry Daniels, already seated in the cockpit.

## Tan Thoi and Ap Bac, South Vietnam

The American and South Vietnamese intelligence had been wrong. Viet Cong Colonel Hai Hoang was the field commander of a composite battalion made up of the 261st and 514th Battalions stationed in Ap Tan Thoi and Ap Bac. In all the Viet Cong had 320 soldiers, most of which were veteran fighters. There were an additional thirty locals that carried ammunition and acted as stretcher-bearers for the wounded. When Hoang first received reports of ARVN forces approaching, he didn't panic. He knew they would be coming. He had been waiting for them since the VC intelligence agents in Dinh Tuong had reported the arrival of seventy-one truckloads of ammunition and other supplies from Saigon, about forty miles to the northeast. The fact that he was facing an entire division plus armor and air support didn't rattle him. He had been in battles with worse odds and had won.

His troops were in deep trenches with overhead trees helping them stay hidden and giving them extra protection against artillery and aerial attacks. To the south and west of Ap Bac, the VC took up positions in a series of one-man foxholes in front of an irrigation dike, which afforded them an unobstructed field of fire in the rice fields in front of the village. The irrigation dike stretched between the two villages connecting the two VC positions. Behind the foxhole line, the irrigation dike enabled the VC to reinforce their defensive positions and resupply ammunition without exposure to enemy small arms fire. It was a big advantage.

Hoang's light machinegun emplacements were fortified

with sandbags and earthen berms. His artillery consisted of one 60mm mortar that had been captured along with its ammunition from the South Vietnamese. Each VC squad had been given at least one BAR automatic rifle with a large amount of ammunition.

Vastly outnumbered and outgunned, Hoang held few illusions of winning the battle. That was not his mission. He and his men were to try new strategies to combat the American helicopters that transported the ARVN to the battlefield. The two villages and the radio transmitter were the bait. The Viet Cong were ready and waiting. At 4 a.m., VC scouts around the two settlements heard the distant sound of engines. Hoang ordered his troops to their positions. The villagers from both settlements fled to nearby swamps where they would wait out the battle they knew was coming.

Along with the other nine H-21helicopters in the operation, Scott set his Shawnee down north of Tan Thoi. Escorting the Shawnees and armed with rocket pods and machine guns, five Bell UH-1 Iroquois gunships, commonly known as "Hueys," hovered nearby. The ARVN company carried by the Shawnees disembarked and took up defensive positions. There was no enemy fire. The ARVN company commander had instructions to wait until the two other rifle companies in his battalion had landed before advancing. The Shawnees took off and were followed by the Hueys. Although no shots had yet been fired, the battle had begun.

While the ARVN company waited for their entire task force, two South Vietnamese Civil Guard battalions arriving on foot approached Ap Bac from the south. Hoang ordered his VC soldiers to wait and stay hidden until one of the enemy battalions had closed to within one hundred feet of their defensive positions before opening fire. VC radio operators using captured US handsets listened to the Civil Guard unit commanders as they approached. At that moment, the VC knew the exact positions of all the enemy forces attacking them and were able to concentrate their defenses.

When one of the battalions, Task Force A, approached the southern end of Ap Bac, the VC opened fire. The first volley killed several Civil Guard troops, including the lead company commander, and wounded the task force commander. Seeing so many of their comrades killed, the Civil Guard troops took up covered positions behind a dike and returned fire. They had no interest in advancing. Within the first few minutes of battle, the South Vietnamese troops had lost their momentum and were fighting for their lives under a barrage of enemy fire coming from multiple directions. The wounded Task Force A commander ordered artillery strikes on the VC positions, but the Civil Guard forward observers were too frightened by all the gunfire to stand up and watch where the rounds fell. As a result, the majority of the artillery shells fell behind the VC foxholes and landed in the hamlet of Ap Bac.

The battalion commander of Task Force B which had not yet engaged the enemy waited for instructions of the overall Civil Guard commander Major Lam Quang Tho, the Dinh Tuong provincial chief. None came. They held their position a half-mile to the west of Task Force A.

North of Tan Thoi, the rest of the 11th Infantry Regiment had arrived by helicopter and advanced on the village hoping to flank the VC in foxholes in front of Ap Bac firing on the Civil Guard Task Force.

Just as with the ambush of the Civil Guards, the hidden VC of the 514th Battalion waited until ARVN troops were within twenty yards of their position before opening fire. The better trained ARVN soldiers immediately hit the dirt and returned fire reducing their causalities.

When word came by radio of the Civil Guards' situation and the ambush on the 11th Infantry Regiment, Vann boarded his L-19 reconnaissance aircraft and his pilot took off for the battlefield. The plane was followed by the ten Shawnee helicopters now loaded with the two reserve rifle companies and the five Huey gunships.

Vann's aircraft sped ahead of the helicopters allowing him to quickly survey the battlefield. He saw the placement of the VC light machine guns to the west of Ap Bac. He radioed the commander of the incoming choppers and requested that they land 300 yards to the west of the southern Ap Bac tree line where they could avoid the VC machine guns. The helicopter flotilla commander chose to ignore Vann's advice and ordered his pilots to pass over Ap Bac and land on the southern end of Ap Tan Thoi in between the two VC forces. Because of the twin-rotor blades, each Shawnee helicopter needed a large land area. Instead of landing in a neat group, the ten helicopters were forced to spread out. Some landed in the rice fields just 200 yards from the VC's foxholes in front of Ap Bac. The VC's small arms and machine gun fire easily pierced the plexiglass windshields and sheet metal skin of the aircraft wounding aircrew and passengers. Bullets punched through the cockpit controls and engine shrouds making one of the aircraft inoperable. The South Vietnamese troops poured out of the helicopters that were drawing most of the fire from the VC. The ARVN took up positions behind the dikes' earthen berms and returned fire. The operable helicopters took off leaving behind the heavily damaged Shawnee and its wounded crew.

Using their 7.62mm machine guns and 2.75-inch rockets, the five Huey gunships opened fire on the VC positions in hopes of suppressing enemy fire enough to let the American aircrew time to escape. It was to no avail. Enemy bullets continued to rip into the downed aircraft.

The VC hated the helicopters and their aircrews. Once they got them in their sights, the VC were like a dog with a bone. Their mission was to find a way to destroy the American helicopters and that was exactly what they were going to do. The battle raged between the two enemies, both wanting to get at the other.

As the Shawnee headed back to their airbase, Scott listened to the radio. He could hear that the Huey gunships were not having the needed effect and that the crew of the damaged H-21 was still in danger. He did not know the stranded aircrew well. He had only been part of the group for a week and had spent much of that time preparing for this mission and studying maps. He hadn't known anyone outside of his aircrew long enough to call them a "friend." But it didn't seem to matter. There was an unwritten code between warriors – No Man Left Behind. If the situation were reversed, he would hope that someone would have the guts enough to come back for him and his crew. He flipped his headset switch to intercom, "I'm going back. If anyone doesn't want to go back I understand and I'll land to let you off. Speak now or forever hold your peace."

Nobody responded. Not a word. Scott wondered if the intercom was working, so he said, "Hooah!"

Everyone onboard responded with "Hooah!" and Scott knew his crew was with him. Overwhelmed with pride in his men, his eyes teared up as he turned his aircraft around and headed back to Ap Bac.

As the Shawnee approached the battlefield, Scott came up with the idea of using the damaged helicopter as cover. The closer he came to the downed helicopter the more VC shifted to his aircraft. Bullets punched through the windshield and smashed into the cockpit's electronics sending a shower of sparks down on Scott and Daniels. Just as they touched down, an enemy bullet severed a hydraulic line and red fluid squirted everywhere. The aircraft's controls lost power. They too were now stranded. "Shit!" said Scott. Another bullet penetrated the canopy plexiglass directly in front of him. He looked down at his uniform covered in hydraulic fluid and saw the color changing on his left leg. He felt a twinge of pain and saw the hole in his pants three inches above his knee. "Oh, crap. I'm hit," said Scott.

Daniels looked over with a panicked face and said, "What do I do?"

"A bandage from the first aid kit," said Scott calmly.

Daniels opened the cockpit's first aid kit and patched Scott's wound. There was a lot of blood and the gauze filled turning red. "Another," said Scott feeling faint.

Daniels swapped out the gauze and applied pressure. Scott groaned. "I'm sorry, but we gotta stop the bleeding," said Daniels.

"Yeah, yeah. You're doing the right thing. Just keep doing it," said Scott searching the first aid kit for a bandage with gauze straps. Another bullet popped a hole in the windshield. "It's like being in a fishbowl," said Daniels.

Scott put the new bandage on top of the one already over the wound and said, "Wrap these tight and tie them off. We gotta get outta here."

Daniels finished wrapping the wound and helped Scott out of the chair. As Scott rose, his eyes rolled back into their sockets, and he fainted. Daniels dragged Scott out of the cockpit and into the cargo area. He leaned him against the bulkhead. The crew chief and gunner were busy firing back at the VC through the doorway. "He all right?" said the crew chief.

"He fainted. He's got a pretty bad leg wound. I think he's lost a lot of blood," said Daniels. "Do you have a plan, Chief?"

"Yeah, not dying."

There was a deep whooping sound. The sergeant moved to the windows on the opposite side of the aircraft and looked out. A Huey gunship was swooping into land. "Gentlemen, the cavalry has arrived," said the crew chief with a grin.

It didn't last long. As the Huey approached a bullet hit its rotor. The aircraft wobbled for a moment, then flipped on to its side and its rotor blade dug into the mud and snapped. It crashed into the field on its side.

"God dammit," said the crew chief. "Gunship's down."

"That's three. What the hell is happening?" said Daniels.

"I have no fucking idea, but it sure is pissing me off," said the chief.

Sergeant Arnold Bowers, the crew chief from the 1st damaged helicopter appeared in the doorway and said, "Everyone okay?"

"Bowers, what in the hell are you doing here?" said the crew chief.

"Someone's gotta check on that downed Huey. I thought I'd give it go."

"Our pilot got hit in the leg. He fainted," said Daniels.

Bower lowered Scott to the deck of the helicopter so he was lying down. He raised his legs slightly using a backpack. He pulled off Scott's belt and wrapped it around his leg above the bullet hole. He cinched it tightly with the buckle and said, "If his leg starts to turn blue loosen the belt a bit to let the blood flow, but not too much or he'll bleed out. We need to get him outta here ASAP or he's gonna lose that leg, maybe die," said Bowers. "I'm gonna check on the Huey, then move my crew into here. You guys got more cover. We're getting chewed up pretty good. Everyone but me has at least one bullet hole and we're running low on ammo."

"See what they got in the Huey," said the crew chief. "We'll give you covering fire until you reach the downed gunship."

Bowers nodded, moved toward the back of the helicopter, then took off running toward the Huey. Enemy bullets zinged past his head while others kicked up clumps of mud. Bower heard rotor blades. He turned to see yet another Shawnee approaching from the distance.

As Bower approached the Huey, he could see the co-pilot and pilot struggling to free themselves from their harnesses. Bower heard a soldier screaming in pain toward the passenger area of the Huey. He climbed up and dropped into the open doorway. The door gunner was flat on his back holding his dislocated arm. Bower reached down, grabbed the dangling arm, and said, "Let me help you with that."

Without further consent, Bower put his boot on side of the gunner's chest and gave the arm a good pull, then released it so it popped back into its socket. The gunner yelped, then said, "That's a lot better. Thanks."

"Don't mention it. Gather whatever ammo you can. We're getting out of here."

"Where are we going?"

"Back to base, I hope."

Bower moved into the cockpit and used his knife to cut the harnesses from the pilot and co-pilot. Both men were banged up with cuts and bruises but no bullet wounds or broken bones. Bowers climbed up through the doorway and helped each of the aircrew out of the aircraft. He turned to see the third Shawnee swooping into land by the two downed Shawnees and it immediately came under heavy fire from the VC in the hamlets. Smoke rose from the Shawnee's front engine compartment and Bowers knew that it was disabled. It landed hard in the rice field. Like the first damaged Shawnee, it was alone without cover. The VC were taking full advantage and filling it with bullet holes. "All right. Change of plans. You guys head for the second downed chopper. It has the best cover. I'm checking on the crew of the Shawnee that just landed. They're getting hit pretty hard by the VC," said Bower.

"You're gonna get your ass shot off if you keep this up," said the gunner.

"Probably."

Bower took off running through the rice field toward the third downed Shawnee. The Huey crew headed for the second Shawnee drawing enemy fire. Seeing their brethren aircrew make a run for it, the four remaining Hueys unleashed hell on the VC positions driving them to cover and reducing the barrage. The downed-Huey aircrew made it to the relative safety of the second downed Shawnee unscathed.

## Ben Hoa Airbase, South Vietnam

The C-47 carrying the team and freed prisoners landed at Ben Hoa Airbase and taxied to the apron. Coyle opened the backdoor as the plane was rolling to a stop and saw Bian standing in the distance. She didn't see him. He called out to her and waved. She waved back and ran toward him. Coyle helped Captain Hoang and the other prisoners step from the plane. As she approached and saw her father for the first time in nine years, Bian couldn't contain her composure and burst into tears. Her father cried too as they hugged each other like they would never let go. Coyle grinned. It seemed all worth it just to see the father and daughter reunited. "Don't move," said Bian to her father as she released him and turned to Coyle. "I can't believe you did it."

"Yeah. I have a little trouble believing it myself. Of course, I did have help," said Coyle as they embraced.

"I owe you everything."

"We're still not out of the woods. You know that, right?"

"Yes. Of course. But my father is free."

"Yeah. I guess they can't take that back."

"Did your plan work? Do the NVA think he is dead?"

"Yeah. It worked. But to be safe, we should keep your father hidden. At least until I can negotiate with Brother Nhu."

"Yes. I have already arranged it. My father will stay with my uncle."

"Good."

The pilot of the C-47 stepped out of the aircraft and said, "Coyle, didn't you say your son was a Shawnee helicopter pilot?"

"Yeah. Why?"

"You need to listen to the radio… now. There's a strong signal on the radio in that communication hut with the antennae," said the pilot pointing.

Coyle turned to Bian, "Something's wrong. I gotta go."

"Yes, go," said Bian. "We'll be okay."

Seeing the concern in his eyes, Bruno and Granier moved up beside Coyle as he headed for the communication hut.

Inside the hut, the American radio operator and several advisors were already listening. "What's going on?" said Coyle.

"The VC have shot down three Shawnee and a Huey," said the operator.

"Where?"

"Someplace called "Ap Bac." It's only forty miles from Saigon."

"Are there survivors?"

"I don't know but there is one hell of battle going on. It's like nothing I have ever heard of."

"It's probably nothing. He's probably not even there," said Granier.

"No. He's there. I can feel it," said Coyle anxious. "I need to be there. I need a plane."

"We'll find a plane. You figure out the location," said Bruno.

"Okay," said Coyle.

"Meet us outside once you have the location," said Granier.

"Right."

Bruno and Granier left. "A map. I need a map," said Coyle.

"On the wall," said the operator as he pointed to the map on the wall.

Coyle combed over the map until he found the hamlet of Ap Bac. "I'm borrowing this," said Coyle ripping the map down and folding it up.

"You know someone there?"

"Yeah. My son. What channel is that?"

The operator told him the channel and Coyle left.

## Ap Bac, South Vietnam

In the sky above the battlefield, The Huey gunships were doing their best to suppress enemy fire, but the VC were no longer afraid and fired back whenever the gunships drew near. It was a different experience for the American pilots who were used to seeing the enemy run for their lives when the gunships approached. The VC were staying in their foxholes, and it was working. The gunships were burning through their ammunition and were forced to break off their attacks and return to their airbases to reload and refuel. They coordinated their rearming missions as best they could so at least a couple of gunships remained in the fight at all times.

The VC were well dug in their foxholes, and it was hard to see them from the air because of the trees over their defensive positions. Vann's reconnaissance plane flew low over the VC positions to draw enemy fire and pinpoint the line of foxholes. The VC didn't take the bait. They withheld fire until the plane passed over their positions. Using the limited visual information they had gathered, they pieced together the enemy's positions. Vann and his pilot used the radio to call in artillery and airstrikes. Vann felt like everything was moving in slow motion as he watched the ARVN get torn to shreds by enemy fire.

Vann was relieved when he saw two AD-6 Skyraiders appear on the horizon. He radioed the pilots and guided them in. The "Spads" as they were nicknamed, lined up their bombing runs with the forward edge of hamlets. Hearing the approaching planes, the VC ducked down into their foxholes and pulled over their camouflaged covers. The warplanes swooped in one at a time and released their napalm canisters over the enemy positions. The tree line turned into a wall of flame that reached fifty feet in the air. The huts and buildings in the two hamlets caught fire. Everything was burning. Each of the Skyraiders made a strafing run on where they thought the foxholes were located, but they were well-camouflaged.

In the rice fields, the ARVN troops cheered at the sight of the aircrafts' napalm explosions and strafing runs. Many stood up to see where the VC would run. But they didn't run. They stayed in the foxholes, then popped up and fired on the ARVN standing in the fields. More ARVN were wounded, and several were killed. Seeing that airpower no longer scared off the VC was demoralizing for the ARVN troops pinned down in the fields.

As the Skyraiders finished their strafing run they returned to their airbases to reload. It was at that moment ARVN 2nd Armored Cavalry Regiment arrived at the edge of the battlefield with 13 M113 armored personnel carriers.

Seeing their arrival from his aircraft, Vann was convinced that the armor could easily turn the tide of the battle to favor the ARVN as it had done many times previously. Vann radioed Captain James Scanlon. Scanlon was the senior adviser to the commander of 2nd Armored. Vann told Scanlon the situation on the ground – that four US helicopters had either been destroyed or immobilized about 1,500 yards southeast of the armored regiment's current position. Scanlon was told by Vann to get Scanlon's South Vietnamese counterpart, Captain Ly Tong Ba, commander of the 4th Mechanized Rifle Squadron, to rescue the trapped South Vietnamese troops and the American aircrews from the downed helicopters.

What Vann and Scanlon didn't know was that Captain Ba had received standing orders not to engage the enemy with his armor unless he was sure he could win the conflict with few casualties and no armor losses. Diem and his family saw the ARVN armor as their best defense against any coup attempts and they did not want to lose it no matter the cost. To ensure its survival and availability, only the most loyal commanders were placed in command of armored units.

Ba told Scanlon that he would not take orders from

American advisors. He would survey the battlefield himself and determine the correct course of action. Scanlon reminded Ba that Vann was in a reconnaissance aircraft and could see the battlefield far better than they could on the ground. Ba was unmoved by the argument and ordered his scouts forward.

Hearing the report from Scanlon, Vann was furious. He demanded to speak to Ba directly. With Ba on the radio, Vann unleashed his frustration demanding that his unit advance on the enemy and save the American aircrews that were fighting on behalf of the South Vietnamese. Without a word, Ba handed the radio handset back to Scanlon and said, "Please tell your commander to fuck off."

Hearing Ba's reply from Scanlon, Vann was unhinged. He calmed for a moment to think, then radioed Captain Ziegler at the Tan Hiep command post and told him to ask the 7th Division commander, Colonel Cao, to order Ba to advance toward Ap Bac immediately. Cao had received instructions from his superiors and had given the original order to Ba not engage the enemy if it meant putting his armor and troops at risk. But Cao knew that the Americans would be angered if the ARVN did not save their aircrews. Vann was a hothead, but Cao knew that the American generals listened to their advisors in the field, especially Vann. He also knew that Diem and his family did not want to lose American support which was essential to keeping them in power. As the most successful commander in the South Vietnamese military, Cao decided to use some of that fame and disregard his superiors' orders. He radioed Ba and told him to advance on Ap Bac.

Hoang watched through his binoculars as the ARVN armored entered the muddy rice paddies and advanced on his position. It was not only the helicopters that had plagued the Viet Cong. Armor was also their Achilles' heel. They had no weapons that could penetrate the thick steel plating on the APCs. Hoang was not going to give up even if it meant that many of his men would be sacrificed. The VC had to find a way to defeat the American technology if the revolution was to be won. Hoang ordered the troops of the 261st and 514th Battalions to use every technique they had practiced to stop the South Vietnamese armor. He reminded them that retreating through the muddy rice fields would result in certain death from American aircraft and artillery. The VC braced themselves for the next phase of the battle.

As the APCs entered the rice paddies, a fourth H-21 helicopter attempted to save the downed American aircrews. Coming in for a landing, the Shawnee was hit by multiple streams of gunfire from different directions. Smoke filled the air as one of the engines caught fire. The pilot was able to control the crash into the muddy field and landed fifty yards away from the third-wrecked helicopter. Like their brothers before, the rescuers were pinned down by VC gunfire and unable to escape.

The APCs had little problem crossing the shallow streams and climbing the dikes that divided the fields. Their steel treads chewed through the mud and plants. As the APCs approached the hamlets, the gunfire slowed to the occasional crack of a rifle from an arbitrary location. The silence of the Viet Cong indicated that they had left their positions in the foxholes and were seeking to escape before the APCs arrived. The battle seemed to be over.

Two of the lead APCs lowered their ramps and released two ARVN squads into the rice field. The troops were slowed by the knee-deep mud and a shallow layer of water. Before they could get to assigned positions, the Viet Cong opened fire with machine guns, small arms, and mortar rounds. Multiple ARVN troops were killed or wounded by the initial barrage. Raked by machine guns, the ARVN survivors dove face-first into the muddy water and sought refuge behind the dikes. The VC shifted their fire to eight of the APCs moving across the field toward the hamlets. Within the first three minutes, six APC gunners were killed when each was shot in the head. Their machine guns went silent. None of the other APC crew members wanted to take the place of the dead gunners. In most cases, the machine gunner was also the vehicle commander which meant many of the vehicles were leaderless.

When more APCs advanced through the field and roared toward the village, the VC climbed from their foxholes and threw grenades at the steel machines. The grenades did little to no damage to the armor vehicles, but the crews inside were demoralized. The APCs stopped their advance, turned, and took up new defensive positions behind the downed helicopters.

Watching from above, Vann could hardly believe his eyes. The VC had blunted the armor attack with nothing other than a few hand grenades. He was stunned and even embarrassed. Nothing made sense. The ARVN had clear advantages in firepower, airpower, artillery, and armor and yet they failed to drive off the VC as they had done so many times before.

A French-built twin-engine SNCAC Martinet flew toward the battlefield. A WWII relic, the well-worn Martinet was more than ready for retirement and was only used to deliver mail to nearby military bases. It was the only aircraft Bruno and Granier could find with a full tank of fuel. Already at maximum RPMs, the engine whined.

Inside the cockpit, Bruno acted as a navigator with the map as Coyle pushed the plane as hard as he dared. Sitting in the passenger area Granier checked his sniper rifle and his sidearm.

The battlefield was not hard to find. Black columns of smoke rose from the wrecked aircraft and napalm strikes marked the area well. Coyle did a flyover to get a layout of the situation. His heart leapt as he looked down at the four downed Shawnee and the nearby Huey. "Do you know his tail number?" said Bruno.

"No. But I'm sure it's an H-21," said Coyle feeling stupid

that he didn't know the details of his son's aircraft.

"It's alright, Coyle. We'll find him. There's an airfield at Tan Hiep. We can probably hitch a ride from there."

"Yeah. We're not doing that."

Coyle banked the plane hard as it descended toward a road on the edge of the battlefield. "Oh, no, Coyle. That's not a good idea. We're no good to your son if we are dead," said Bruno.

"We're landing. I'd buckle up."

Everyone strapped in as Coyle lined up the plane to land on the road. "You see those trees, right? I mean, you see the trees along the edge of the road. Those are big trees," said Bruno.

"We're not going to hit them. We've got plenty of room."

Coyle set the aircraft down on the dirt road full of ruts and puddles from recent rain. The Martinet fishtailed as Coyle struggled to keep it on the road and away from the tree trunks. There was a loud crack. Bruno looked out the side window to see a piece of the right-wing tip flaying in the wind like a broken kite. Bruno had faced many a battle, but few were as terrifying as Coyle's landing. The aircraft came to stop. Coyle cut the engines, unbuckled, and bolted from the cockpit. He didn't waste any time climbing out of the aircraft and running to the trees at the edge of the rice fields. He ran thirty feet into the muddy field before he started to draw enemy fire from the village of Ap Bac. Bruno and Granier called him back to the safety of the tree line. As bullets kicked up bits of mud and zinged past his head, Coyle climbed up the embankment. Granier and Bruno reached down and pulled him up into the trees. "Coyle, you need to calm down or you're gonna get yourself killed. We will find your son. Just give us a few minutes to survey the battlefield," said Granier.

"He may not have a few minutes, Granier," said Coyle angry.

"You're right, Coyle. But you going off half-cocked isn't

going to help him. We need a plan. I'm going up into a tree and have a look."

"Okay. Good."

Granier slung his sniper rifle and climbed up the tallest tree he could find. Once he got himself situated in the crotch between two branches, he unslung his rifle and peered through the scope. He had a good view of all the damaged helicopters and the enemy position at the edge of the two villages. He spotted several enemy machine gun positions that were laying down much of the fire on the helicopters and the ARVN troops trying to protect them.

Granier repositioned his scope on each one of the downed aircraft to look for survivors. He had no idea what Coyle's son looked like, but he knew he was a pilot of one of the Shawnee helicopters. He saw a large cluster of crewmen hiding within and behind the second downed helicopter where they had gathered. It made sense. The first downed helicopter was between them and the enemy line and offered some additional cover. The odds were good that if Coyle's son was a pilot of one of the downed choppers, he would be in that group. Granier climbed down and explained the situation to Coyle and Bruno. "Loan me your rifle," said Coyle.

"Why?" said Granier suspicious.

"I need the scope to find my son."

"Right," said Granier handing Coyle his rifle.

Coyle climbed up the tree and peered through the scope scanning the downed aircraft. "He's gonna get himself killed if he doesn't calm down," said Bruno. "I've seen me like this before when Brigitte was in danger."

"It's his son. It's hard to blame him," said Granier. "Do you have any children?"

"Not that I know of," said Bruno, then reconsidered after remembering all the women he had been with over the years. "Probably."

Coyle spotted Scott in the second-downed Shawnee and said, "I've got him. He's in the second Shawnee like you said."

Coyle climbed down, handed the rifle back to Granier and said, "So, what's the plan?"

Tan Hiep Airfield, South Vietnam

Refusing to give up, Vann landed at the Tan Hiep airfield to talk directly with General Cao. He asked Cao to deploy the airborne battalion held in reserve to the east side of Ap Bac which was the most likely escape route the Viet Cong would use. If the ARVN paratroopers could trap the VC in the hamlet, Vann believed the elite battalion could annihilate the enemy and win the battle. Cao refused. He did not want to waste his paratroopers against a dug-in enemy force. If the VC escaped, Cao would destroy them with artillery and airstrikes as they crossed the rice paddies. Vann accused Cao of being a coward because he did not want to risk more ARVN casualties. Cao accused Vann of wanting to waste the lives of South Vietnamese troops to save a handful of Americans.

When Vann realized that it was useless arguing with Cao, he climbed by into his L-19 reconnaissance aircraft and took off.

With Vann gone, Cao considered the American advisor's words and past deeds. There was little question that much of Cao's success as a commander was due to Vann's guidance and operational plans. Cao ordered the 8th Airborne Battalion to drop behind the M113s in the rice paddies to help save the trapped Americans. He also ordered the second Civil Guard battalion to attack the southwest flank of Ap Bac in hopes of drawing away enemy forces from the front line of foxholes.

Ap Bac Battlefield, South Vietnam

As Granier was going over the plan to save Scott and the American aircrews, the sound of approaching aircraft engines caught the team's attention.

In the distance, five American-crewed C-123 providers carried 300 ARVN paratroopers to the battlefield. As they closed on their drop zone, VC fire from the hamlet hit the lead aircraft. While that damage was minimal, the commander ordered all the pilots to change course but failed to notify the ARVN jumpmasters in the cargo holds. The paratroopers jumped on schedule.

Instead of landing behind the M113 armored carriers, the battalion of paratroopers landed just two hundred yards in front of the VC foxholes. The Viet Cong had their choice of targets and killed a dozen paratroopers in the first few minutes after the drop. The paratroopers grabbed their dead and wounded and pulled back as best they could while the Civil Guard battalion and M113s gave them covering fire.

Hopeful that their rescue plan would not be necessary, Granier, Coyle, and Bruno watched as the ARVN troops once again failed to dislodge the Viet Cong from the village and save the American airmen, many of which were badly wounded and could not be moved quickly. The slaughter of the paratroopers made Bruno sick. As a French paratrooper commander, he knew only too well what the elite soldiers were facing. A part of him wanted to go out into the field and join them, but he knew he needed to stay on mission if he was going to help Coyle rescue his son.

With the VC concentrating their fire on the paratroopers, Ba saw his chance. He ordered four of his APCs, including his command vehicle, to advance to the wrecked helicopters and rescue the Americans while the machine gunners in the other vehicles gave them covering fire.

Unsure of how long the VC fire would remain focused on the paratroopers, the APC drivers drove through the muddy rice fields like bats out of hell. Ba's APC approached the second downed H-21 where the majority of the aircrews had gathered. He lowered the ramp and waved them inside the vehicle. The gunner provided covering fire with the machine gun as the Americans rushed forward and climbed into the safety of the APC's armor. Daniels prepared to move Scott, who was once again conscious. He wrapped Scott's arm around his shoulder and headed toward the open door of the APC just a few yards away.

A mortar round landed behind the APC. Shrapnel flew through the open end of the vehicle's turret and killed the gunner. Seeing his comrade killed by a mortar blast, the APC's driver panicked and closed the ramp. The passengers were jostled as the driver reversed and the APC pulled back. Ba lost his footing and his head hit on the vehicle's bulkhead. He fell to the floor unconscious.

Standing in the field unprotected, Scott and Daniels watched with dismay as the APC turned and left without them. Bullets kicked up mud as some of the VC refocused their fire on the escaping Americans. Daniels lifted Scott back through the doorway of the helicopter and said, "Do you think they'll come back for us?"

"I sure as hell hope so," said Scott wincing in pain as Daniels set him back down on the deck. "In the meantime, we keep as low as possible."

"What if the VC come for us?"

"Don't worry about that. We just need to focus on staying alive."

Granier was once again up in the tree watching through his scope. "Did they get them all out?" said Coyle standing below.

"Almost. There are a couple of crewmen that were left behind," said Granier. "It looks like the VC are focusing their fire on those crewmen. They're tearing the shit out of those helicopters."

Coyle climbed the tree until he was next to Granier. Granier handed him his rifle and Coyle peered through the scope and said, "Fuck. It's Scott."

"They will probably send another APC to rescue them," said Granier.

"It doesn't matter. Until I know my son is safe, I'm not going to stop," said Coyle handing the rifle back to Granier.

Reaching the ground he turned to Bruno and said, "I going out there."

"Alright. I will go with you. But if I die, you will need to explain to Brigitte. Deal?"

"Deal."

"Granier, we're going to the downed choppers."

"Yeah. I figured. Give me three minutes then go. I'll do my best to give you cover."

"Okay."

Granier swung his rifle around and spotted the enemy machine gun closest to the downed chopper. He closed his eyes for a moment and took a deep breath to calm himself. When he opened his eyes, he put the scope's crosshairs on the gunner's head and squeezed the trigger.

The bullet pierced the side of the gunner's head and exited the other side. He slumped over the machine gun dead. Angrier than a hornet as seeing his friend killed, the loader pushed his comrade out of the way and manned the machine gun. A moment later, his head exploded in a red mist. The machine gun fell silent.

Granier moved to the next closest machine gun position and repeated his movements as if it was a training exercise. Two more Viet Cong fell dead. The machine gun crews were easy targets. Focused on their mission of killing the American aircrews, the gunner and loader didn't move except to reload. With all the gunfire on the battlefield, there was very little warning that a sniper was targeting them until one of them dropped dead. The loader was predictable in his actions and quickly joined his comrade. In all, Granier killed five machine gun crews in the three minutes he had allotted himself. The rate of gunfire across the battlefield dropped considerably. Granier gave Coyle and Bruno the signal to go.

It was too far to belly crawl to the downed aircraft. Coyle and Bruno kept as low as possible as they headed out into the muddy rice field. Coyle took the lead as Bruno kept focused on possible threats and sprayed the closest VC positions with his submachine gun. He didn't hit anything. It was too far for an unaimed shot. But his bullets were close enough to drive some of the VC in the foxholes to duck behind cover.

Granier continued searching for targets. When he found one, he aimed and fired. He rarely missed his first shot, but never his second. More VC dead, less gunfire directed toward the American aircrews, Coyle, and Bruno. But even with his help, there were still hundreds of VC firing their rifles from their foxholes. Only their heads and arms were exposed as they popped up, fired, then hunkered back down into the safety of their holes. It was like shooting varmints in the desert. Up and down, up and down. They were not easy targets like the machine gun crews.

Bruno and Coyle's boots were covered in mud slowing them down. Each step was a major effort as they sunk knee-deep in the soft clay. The brown water prevented them from seeing where they were stepping and caused suction when they pulled their boots out of their muddy foot-hole.

As they approached the second downed aircraft, Daniels saw them and didn't recognize their uniforms. He fired his pistol barely missing Coyle. Bruno reacted by swinging his submachine gun around. Coyle pushed Bruno's barrel down and said to Daniels, "Hold your fire. I'm an American."

"Sorry. I didn't recognize your uniform," said Daniels.

"Where is Scott Dickson?"

"He's right here. He's been wounded pretty bad."

Coyle's eyes went wide, and he ran toward the helicopter's doorway. "How do you know Lieutenant Dickson?" said Daniels confused.

"I'm his father," said Coyle climbing into the helicopter and checking Scott's wound. The large amount of blood and Scott's pale skin panicked Coyle.

"Coyle, what are doing here?" said Scott.

"Saving your ass."

"Why?"

"Because I'm your father. Apparently, that's what we do."

Bruno moved up and looked inside. "Bruno, I'd like you to meet my son, Scott Dickson," said Coyle.

Bruno shook Scott's hand and said, "Nice to meet you."

"You're French?"

"Oui," said Bruno looking around the heavily-damaged aircraft. "I see you like destroying aircraft like your father."

Ignoring Bruno's comment, Coyle turned back to Scott and said, "Do you think you can walk?"

"Maybe. I get kind of light-headed when I sit up."

"Alright. Do your best not to faint and hold on," said Coyle slinging his submachine gun and turning back to Daniels. "Will you help me carry him?"

"You bet," said Daniels.

"Bruno, we're gonna have to carry him. We'll need covering fire."

"Yes, yes. Of course," said Bruno moving off to the edge of the aircraft.

"Your friend's kind of an asshole," said Scott.

"Yeah. Well, in his defense, he thinks his criticism is helping," said Coyle putting Scott's arm around his shoulder and grabbing his belt on the opposite side.

Daniels put Scott's other arm over his shoulder and grabbed his belt. "Bruno, we're ready when you are," said Coyle.

Bruno popped out behind the aircraft and laid down a barrage of covering fire on the closest enemy positions and said, "Go, go."

They set off across the muddy field. It was even worse than before as Daniels's and Coyle's boots sank deeper in the mud. Bruno followed changing his submachine gun's magazine and firing short bursts toward the enemy positions as he ran.

In the distance, Granier saw them and increased his rate of fire hoping to drive the enemy's heads down.

The VC in the foxholes saw the American's trying to escape across the field and refocused their fire.

A bullet hit Daniels in the leg. He fell into the rice paddy. "Bruno!" shouted Coyle as he struggled to handle Scott on his own.

Bruno continued to lay down covering fire until his gun was empty. He slung the weapon as he clomped over to Daniels screaming his head off. "It's just a leg. Stop your whining," said Bruno lifting Scott up and over Coyle's shoulder, then picking up Daniels and lifting him over his shoulder in a fireman's carry.

They once again, set off across the field as bullets zinged by them and pelted the muddy water.

Seeing the soldiers trying to rescue the aircrew, the paratroopers and ARVN troops increased their rate of fire on the enemy positions.

In response, many of the VC switched their targeting back to the ARVN and paratroopers.

In the tree, Granier fired again and again. His rifle clicked empty. He reached for another clip. There was none. He was defenseless, unable to cover the rescue team. He watched, helpless, as they struggled across the field. As they approached the embankment, Granier jumped out of the tree and ran out to help them. Between carrying the wounded and plodding through the mud both Bruno and Coyle were exhausted. Granier pulled Scott from Coyle's shoulder and sped ahead with him to the safety of the trees. Coyle went back and helped Bruno by carrying Daniels between them. Granier set Scott down and went back into the field. He lifted Daniels over his shoulder and ran through the mud and up the embankment. Bruno and Coyle followed. Finally, they were safe behind the line of trees. Everyone collapsed, exhausted.

An APC sped down the road toward them, kicking up mud with its treads. It slowed then stopped. The ramp went down. An ARVN sergeant stepped out and said, "Compliments of Captain Ba."

They loaded Scott and Daniels into the APC where a medic attended to their wounds. Coyle climbed in and stayed by Scott. Coyle turned back to Bruno and Granier. There were no words for what they had done to save his son. Coyle just nodded his gratitude and they nodded back. The ramp closed. Bruno and Granier watched as the APC wheeled around and sped off toward the hospital at Tan Hiep airfield. Granier turned to the damaged Martinet aircraft and said, "We can't leave that thing for the VC."

Bruno pulled the two grenades from his pocket. Granier smiled and pulled his own two grenades and said, "Bit overkill, don't you think?"

Bruno shook his head, no, and pulled the grenades' safety rings. Granier followed suit pulling his own grenade's rings. They tossed the grenades through the plane's open doorway and ran to a nearby tree hiding behind its massive trunk. The plane exploded and burned quickly. "Problem solved," said Granier.

"Yes, yes. I am a problem-solver extraordinaire," said Bruno.

"Good, Mr. Problem-solver. You can figure out how were are going to get back to Saigon."

"We shall walk."

"It's forty miles."

"Don't be a pussy, Granier. It's a nice evening for a stroll."

The two warriors set off down the road with their favorite weapons slung over their shoulders.

In an aircraft over the battlefield, Vann got on the radio and called Cao once again. He pleaded with him to regroup his forces already in the field and order them to make one final push all at the same time. Vann was sure the VC would fold under the onslaught of the superior number of troops and armor. Cao refused. He had lost enough men. They would hold their positions until nightfall and hopefully, the VC would retreat leaving the ARVN the battlefield so they could claim victory.

Vann was crestfallen. The plan he had approved failed. Strangely, he felt that the ARVN and the American aircrews had paid for those two hamlets. They owned them and had a right to collect what was due. But it wasn't to be.

As night fell, neither side had given up their positions, but the ARVN and the VC ceased fire from lack of clear targets.

The ARVN tended to their wounded and carried them off the battlefield. Their losses were massive – eighty-three killed and over 100 wounded. It was the single worse day of battle since the war had begun. The ARVN troops and commanders were demoralized.

The Americans had three crewmen and advisors killed and eight wounded. In addition, they had lost five helicopters. The advisors in command were stunned by the losses.

Hoang knew that when the morning came, the ARVN troops would close on his positions from three different directions. They would once again bring up their armor and launch new artillery and airstrikes. To make matters worse, the Viet Cong were low on ammunition, and they had suffered heavy casualties. After having held off a South Vietnamese force five times their size, Hoang's troops had only suffered eighteen killed and thirty-nine wounded. Light compared the ARVN and American losses. But if Hoang did not pull his troops from the battlefield while there was still time, a conflict that the Viet Cong had clearly won, could easily become a resounding defeat.

He sent scouts out and when they returned, they reported that the eastern flank through the rice fields remained open. There was an opportunity for his soldiers to escape and Hoang took it.

Under the cloak of darkness, the Viet Cong

disassembled their radio transmitter and carried it away. The transmitter had not been captured. It was their talisman. They quietly climbed from the foxholes that had protected them, collected their dead and wounded, and leapfrogged back through the smoldering villages. They crossed the rice fields in near silence careful not to slosh the muddy water. When they came to the canal, they transferred their wounded to sampans. The local forces that had fought beside the Viet Cong melted away in different directions. They would once again become part of the local population and wait for another opportunity to help their comrades. Hoang's two companies marched on to their base in the Plain of Reeds without being detected. The Battle of Ap Bac was over.

The next morning, dozens of journalists arrived by whatever means of transport they could find. Halberstam, Sheehan, Browne, and Peter Arnette – a New Zealand journalist working for the Associated Press, called in all their favors and arrived by military helicopter. Even though they were all experienced war correspondents they were shocked by what they saw. There were still dozens of bodies of dead ARVN soldiers strewn across the rice paddies. And then there were the damaged American Shawnee helicopters all stuck in the mud and the Huey gunship completely destroyed laying on its side. Smoke rose from the two hamlets both severely burned. The thirteen APCs with new gunners in their turrets stood like sentinels to ensure that the VC didn't return while the ARVN collected their dead. It was a first. It was news. Cameras clicked away from every angle. There was plenty of carnage to fill the pages of their newspapers and magazines. Several film crews panned across the battlefield as on-camera reporters narrated what was visible. The world would see the battle of Ap Bac just a day after it happened.

Halberstam and Sheehan found Vann sitting in the doorway of one of the downed Shawnees. They could see that he was distraught. "Are you alright, Colonel?" said Sheehan.

"Yeah. Just tired," said Vann.

"Do you mind telling us what happened?"

"What happened? The VC kicked our asses that's what happened. It was a fucking disaster."

"How was that possible, Colonel?" said Halberstam.

"It wasn't. That's the crazy part. There is no way we should have lost. The ARVN had every advantage. It was a miserable damned performance, just like it always is. These people won't listen. They make the same mistake over and over again in the same way. Their commanders were too worried about pissing off Diem and saving their jobs. The VC held their ground when common sense dictated they should have fled. Brave sons of bitches."

"So, you think this all goes back to Diem?"

"I don't think. I know. Diem and his family are gonna lose this war and we are gonna lose it with him unless something radically changes before it's too late."

"So, there's still hope?" said Sheehan.

"Have you been listening to me? How do you keep faith with your men after something like this?"

"But you said—"

"I know what I fucking said, Sheehan."

"You're tired, Colonel."

"That's for damned sure. We're all tired. Fucking exhausted."

Vann laid down on the helicopter's deck and closed his eyes. He was asleep within a few seconds. "We should go and let him sleep," said Halberstam.

"I'm going to stay for a while," said Sheehan his eyes moist. "Until he wakes up."

"You do that, Neil. You're a good friend and that's what he needs right now. Give me your camera and I'll take some shots for you," said Halberstam.

Sheehan gave Halberstam his camera and watched him walk toward Ap Bac.

## Saigon, South Vietnam

As expected, General Harkins declared that the operation was a major success. The enemy had been driven from the battlefield and the two hamlets of Ap Bac and Ap Tan Thoi were once again under the control of the South. Without criticism of their shortcomings in tactics, battle readiness, and the relationship between ARVN commanders and their government leaders, the South Vietnamese military failed to learn useful lessons from the battle. History would repeat itself again and again in the South costing the lives of its soldiers and civilians. More American aircrews and advisors would die.

## Hanoi, North Vietnam

While the battle of Ap Bac was small compared to the many battles that would come in the Vietnam War, it was an important moral victory for the Viet Cong and the North. For the first time, they had stood and fought a large South Vietnamese force. Against overwhelming odds, the Viet Cong had won their first de facto victory. Hoang and his men had successfully held off well-equipped ARVN forces supported by artillery, armored units, and American airpower. Their positions had been hit by more than 600 artillery shells, dozens of napalm canisters, hundreds of rockets, and tens of thousands of heavy machine gun rounds and autocannon shells released by thirteen warplanes and five UH-1 gunships. Always willing to exploit to help their revolution, the North Vietnamese created postage stamps to commemorate their military's great victory at Ap Bac.

# AUTHOR'S LETTER TO READER

Dear Reader,

I hope you enjoyed *The Uncivil War*. While researching the book, I learned so much about how the Cold War effected the Vietnam War. Had Kennedy lost the showdown with Khrushchev during the Cuban Missile Crisis I question what would have happened in Vietnam. Would he have pulled back withdrawing the American advisors, SOG teams, and aircrews already in-country?

Sign-up for my never-annoying newsletter and receive a bonus epilogue of The Uncivil War. I will also send you new release updates, special offers, and my thoughts on just about everything. Sign-up for my newsletter here: https://dl.bookfunnel.com/hjcboqld1f

The next book in The Airmen Series is *Cry Havoc*. Testing the will of his people, President Diem attacks the foundations of South Vietnamese culture and society. Unable to control Diem and his family, JFK must revaluate America's mission in Southeast Asia and find a new path. Should the US military to take more control of the war? Is it time to put boots on the ground and fight the Viet Cong directly? Here's the link for *Cry Havoc*: https://www.amazon.com/dp/B09Q5XB791

If you enjoyed reading my books, please tell your friends, neighbors, and any household animals that read. Every sale helps pay for my coffee addiction.

Thank you,

David Lee Corley – Author

## LIST OF TITLES & READING ORDER

The Airmen Series
1. A War Too Far
2. The War Before The War
3. We Stand Alone
4. Café Wars
5. Sèvres Protocol
6. Operation Musketeer
7. Battle of The Casbah
8. Momentum of War
9. The Willful Slaughter of Hope
10. Kennedy's War
11. The Uncivil War
12. Cry Havoc

The Nomad Series
1. Monsoon Rising
2. Prophecies of Chaos
3. Stealing Thunder

Facebook Page:
https://www.facebook.com/historicalwarnovels

Shopify Store: https://david-lee-corley.myshopify.com/

Amazon Author's Page:
https://www.amazon.com/David-Lee-Corley/e/B073S1ZMWQ

Amazon Airmen Series Page:
https://www.amazon.com/dp/B07JVRXRGG

Amazon Nomad Series Page:
https://www.amazon.com/dp/B07CKFGQ95

Author's Website: http://davidleecorley.com/